A GLORY ALL HER OWN

AN EMPIRE OF ESTALLIUM NOVEL

REBECCA SIMKIN

<u>DEDICATION</u>

*In memory of my beloved husband, François Gauvin,
who always believed in me, even when I didn't.*

*Additional thanks to: Members of the Bloor West
Writers Group for their feedback and encouragement
over the years; my mother, Leah Simkin, for final
reading comments; Rodney V. Smith for assisting
me with formatting and launching my first novel; my
partner Michael Korba for logo and map designs;
and my best writing friend Maaja Wentz for all of
her encouragement, advice and friendship.*

A Glory All Her Own

Rebecca Simkin

GWARDAHAR
ESTALLIUM
(proper)
CITY OF
ESTALLIUM
(Seat of the Empire)
MONUMENT ROC
STELLA
D'ALBA
VESPARIA
River Estallene
EMPIRE OF ESTALL
(Trillas)
ASTRUM AUREUS
CELESTIA
N
W
E
S

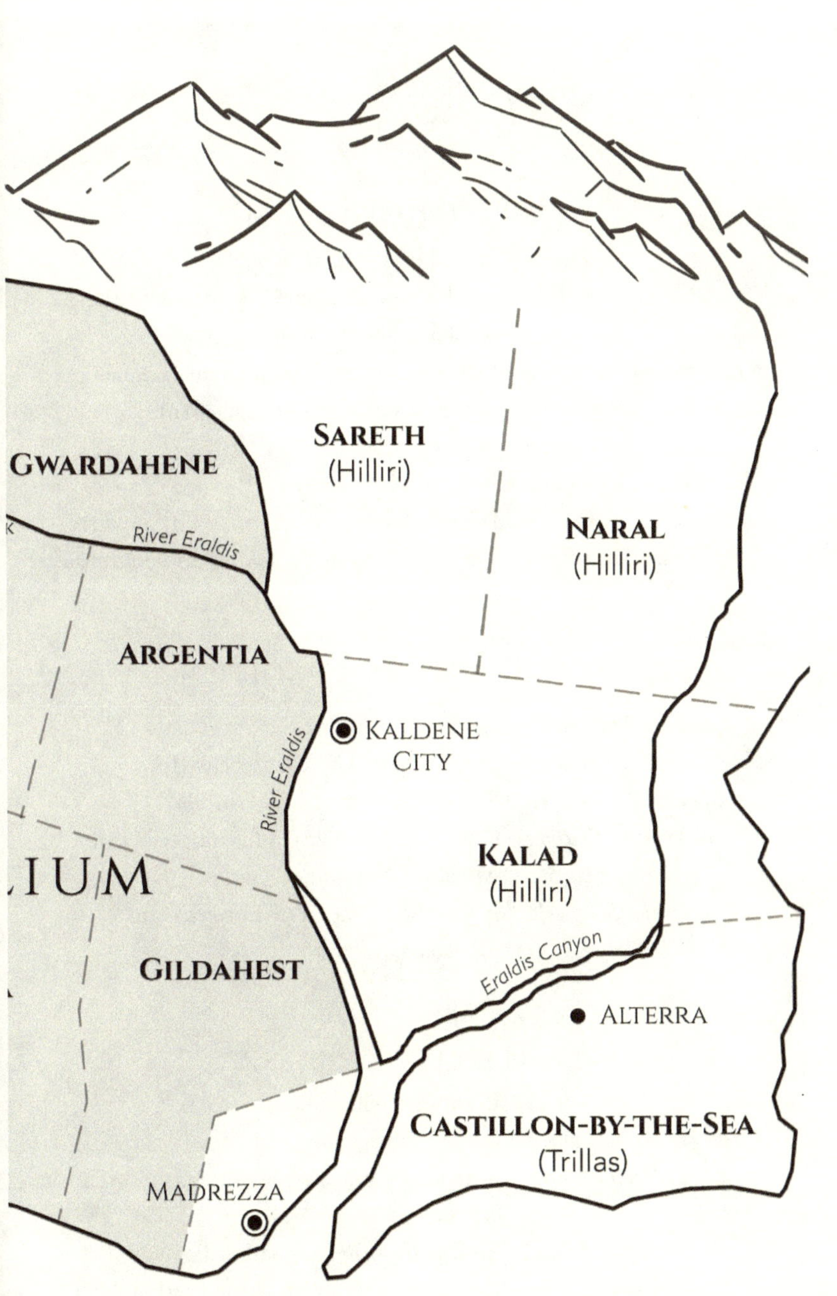

GWARDAHENE
SARETH
(Hilliri)
NARAL
(Hilliri)
River Eraldis
ARGENTIA
River Eraldis
KALDENE CITY
LIUM
KALAD
(Hilliri)
Eraldis Canyon
GILDAHEST
ALTERRA
CASTILLON-BY-THE-SEA
(Trillas)
MADREZZA

GLOSSARY

HILLIRI FROM KALAD:

Daria	Friend of Lirienne, a healer
Dor	Healer and infirmary supervisor of the border military camp
Lirienne Godehera	Daughter of the King of Kalad, a healer
Selana Godehera	Lirienne's older sister, a silversmith
Talora	Valran's wife, a soldier
Tarkhan Godehera	King of Kalad
Tarlen	Friend of Lirienne's, a palace gardener
Valran Godehera	Lirienne's brother, a soldier and commander

TRILLAS FROM CASTILLON:

Carlosi Calimero	Lord of Castillon
Leonardo Calimero	Eldest son of Carlosi (deceased)
Lorenzo Calimero	Son of Carlosi (aka the Slasher)
Marcusi Trieste	Cousin to Lorenzo on his mother's side
Pagolo	An elderly servant of Carlosi
Renata Jocanda	A childhood friend of Lorenzo and Marcusi's, a scout

HILLIRI FROM ALTERRA:

Adina	Ergamin's wife, a healer
Bethna	Goatherding young girl
Ergamin Lotreah	Mayor of Alterra a town in Castillon (Ergin for short)
Kinal	Bethna's brother, a goatherd
Nia	Lirienne's alternative name used in Alterra

PLACES

Alterra	Town of Ergin and Adina in Castillon near the border of Kalad
Argentia	A province of the Empire located on the banks of the river Eraldis opposite Kalad.
Castillon-by-the-Sea	A small independent land occupied by both races, originally only Trillas, located at the mouth of the river Eraldis
College of Marukar	The headquarters of the healers
Eraldis	A river dividing the lands of the Hilliri from the Trillas
Estallium	(the Empire) the united lands of the Trillas people. (does not include Castillon)
Gerlamaine	A lake in Kaldene City
Gildahest	A province of the Empire south of Argentia located on the banks of the river Eraldis
Kalad	A kingdom of the Hilliri people located on the banks of the river Eraldis
Kaldene City	The capital of Kalad where the palace is located
Madrezza	The main town in Castillon on the sea shore
Naral	Hilliri land north of Kalad east of Sareth
Sareth	Hilliri land west of Naral, north of Kalad

SPECIAL WORDS

Guardians	The all-powerful beings the Hilliri and Trillas both believe control their world.
Maru	The power of the Hilliri
Mundatar	Weakling (Hillirian name for Trillas)
Sibyl	A priestess of the Trillas, interpreter of the wishes of the Guardians
Starbright	A time, once a month, when the night sky is so full of stars that it is easy to see

CHAPTER ONE

Cornea, pupil, retina, iris, vitreous chamber... Lirienne marveled at the complexity of the eye. She studied her patient, a silversmith from the Miners Guild. The man massaged the back of his neck and looked up at her. She read panic in his gaze.

"Please, can you fix it? If I can't work, my family will starve."

He wrung his hands as he spoke. Judging by the many patches on his clothing, Lirienne figured that even working, the man wasn't earning much. A speck of solder had lodged in his cornea, burning a small area. She could remove the material, but if she couldn't repair the lens perfectly, his guild would dismiss him. She squeezed his arm.

"Don't worry. I'll make it as good as new." The man's shoulders relaxed.

She caught the infirmary supervisor's scowl as she looked up from examining her patient. As a Prestige member of the Healers Guild, she wasn't required to treat commoners, but she hated watching people suffer when she could help. She couldn't wait idly by for members of the nobility to arrive for her to treat.

At first, patients had fawned over her, awestruck to meet a genuine princess, until she started wearing the traditional veil to work. While it affected her vision somewhat, most of her work was done with her eyes closed, using only her mind.

Blocking out the infirmary with its drab green-gray walls and its rows of examining beds and healers in silver robes tending to their patients, she stepped up onto the box the College had provided to help her reach her patients. Its necessity embarrassed her. Her people, the Hilliri were typically shorter than the Trillas, the race of people who lived in lands to the west and south, but even by her people's standards, Lirienne was small.

She opened the man's shirt enough to lay his chest bare. She tugged off her protective gloves and placed both hands on his skin. For a moment, she had the sense of looking up at herself as she linked her awareness with his body. She thought of the stillness of the lake by the city at sunrise. Her patient could see this image too.

He sighed and stilled.

She cut off the connection with his mind and kept focus only on his body. As she probed, she felt her awareness drawn down through the veins and arteries into his blood. Following along, she found her way into the afflicted eye. Her mental view was now directly behind it. With her power, she nudged the offending particle until it lifted to the surface of the cornea. It was difficult work, but Lirienne had trained for this since the age of ten.

Tears welled in the eye at her mental encouragement, and the little bit of metal was borne away to the corner and out onto the cheek.

Her hands remained on his chest, sustaining the link between her mind and his body. To repair the cornea, she needed to coax the endothelial cells to reproduce more rapidly than usual. Lirienne grew warm with the effort. The delicate application of her power, maru, required intense concentration and a deep knowledge of the workings of the body.

At last, the lens was smooth and whole. Lirienne checked its integrity and smiled. He would be able to work again without difficulty.

Shouts and sounds of a scuffle in the hall intruded on her focus. She broke contact with her patient. As the sounds grew louder, she recognized a voice among them. It was her brother, Valran, stress creeping into his clipped commands. As he staggered through the infirmary doorway, Lirienne froze. Five soldiers, their bodies lacerated and bruised, their clothing drenched in gore, surrounded him as he clutched the limp form of his wife, Talora. Lirienne stepped back at the sight. As a healer, she was accustomed to blood, but this was the result of violence.

Troubled by the disturbance, her patient rose from his bed, bowed three times, and thanked her half a dozen more as he exited the infirmary. Lirienne focused on her brother and his wife.

Valran, a short, whipcord lean man, trembled as he waited. "I need help here now."

Snapping out of their bewilderment, infirmary workers rushed to his side. They took his wife with care and laid her on Lirienne's work bed. There were scratches and purple bruises on her face but Lirienne could see these were not the cause of her failing strength. She inspected Talora's body. Three arrows intruded deep into her torso and hip. Talora's clothing, the steel gray of the Warriors Guild, was soaked to a deep crimson, and the room filled with the coppery tang of blood. She needed attention fast, but Lirienne hesitated. The College frowned on its healers treating family members, but Lirienne was the only Prestige member available. She had to do what she could to help and worry about the consequences later.

Lirienne turned to her assistant. "Get me a wash basin."

The white-haired boy of about twelve scrambled to the washing station and returned a moment later with a bowl of steaming water, soap, and a towel. He withdrew. The other workers in the infirmary also pulled away to give her space.

Lirienne cleansed her hands and dried them with quick and efficient movements. She stared at her brother's stricken face as she tore open Talora's jacket at the neck. "What happened? I thought you were just going to the border to check our defenses."

Val looked at the floor. The infirmary was silent.

Lirienne examined her new charge. She could feel her brother's eyes following her movements as she stepped up onto her box for a better view. She placed her hands on her patient's upper chest. Her mind connected with the body. Intense pain flooded her senses, as if she was the one who was hurt, but with determination her connection held. She erected a shield between her mind and her patient's mind to avoid further leakage. She hoped it would stick. She didn't want to receive any unwanted emotions or images from her sister-in-law's mind. It happened sometimes, and more often with Lirienne than she liked.

Her awareness went down through the layers of skin, muscle, and bone, following the blood through the arteries. She worked as fast as she could, but she could sense Talora's failing strength. A cut inflicted by a sword still bled profusely, and she had lost a great deal of blood. Nothing Lirienne had learned in all her years of study would help reverse this. The damage had happened hours ago.

Lirienne focused—applying maru to knit up the muscle until the edges of the cut closed together. She felt her maru dip as she worked. She was tired. Using maru cost a healer much, but it would be a while before she reached her limit. Lirienne sensed a flutter in Talora's heartbeat. She bit her lower lip as she redoubled her concentration. Talora was family. She couldn't afford to fail.

The arrows were next. One of the three had nicked the liver. Another had punctured a lung. A third had sunk deep into the muscle of Talora's hip.

She wrapped a cloth around the fletchings of the arrow piercing the lung and reached over the body to grip it as hard as she could with her delicate hands. She twisted it gently, ever so slightly. It moved. As it shifted, she eased the arrow out. While she did this, she sensed the gap where the arrow had been. To repair it, she mentally pushed the edges of the hole closed. Talora's breathing rasped. Lirienne chewed her lip as she worked. At least the wound was clean; there was no smell of taint.

She focused her mind on the lung next, enticing Talora's body with her maru to make repairs at a much greater rate than normal. She observed that the lungs obeyed and the tear closed up. Talora's heart beat unevenly. Lirienne scowled. Talora should be recovering.

She repeated this procedure again with the arrow that had pierced the liver, checking for damage. With time, a puncture would heal naturally, but being weak already, Talora didn't have the resources to spare, so Lirienne elected to looked after it. As she succeeded in repairing the liver, Talora coughed and sputtered. Lirienne eased her pain by attacking the swelling that had built up in the area around the injury.

The third arrow was lodged in a fleshy spot on the side of her hip where there were no organs. Though deeply embedded, it wasn't nearly as dangerous as the others were. She called her assistant to help, for she simply didn't have the strength to extract it on her own.

After she finished with the arrows, she checked for more damage, mentally reaching deep into the body to every limb and back again. She noticed a tiny aneurysm, a bulging blood vessel close to the heart. Beads of sweat formed on Lirienne's forehead as she attempted to shore up the artery walls by increasing the number of cells in the area. The blood flowed thickly through the region, causing pressure to build. As soon as she repaired the spot, a new bulge formed a little further along.

The veil rubbed against her eyelashes and nose. She pulled it back over her head to fall behind her. Sweat trickled into Lirienne's eyes. She shut them and concentrated harder, but as soon as she repaired the new bulge, another two popped out. Talora began to tremble, though she wasn't conscious.

Lirienne's breath came in short puffs as she redoubled her focus. Talora wheezed too, in spite of the repair to her lung. A flutter of panic caught hold of Lirienne. There was a chance that she might fail—that her kinswoman might die. She looked up at the people waiting around her. Everyone's face expressed concern.

Valran inched closer and clasped his wife's hand.

"Lirienne, will she be all right?" He sounded small and frightened.

A wave of cold passed through her. She sensed Talora's pulse leap and sputter. She steeled herself as she looked up at her brother, trying to make her expression bland and unworried, but it was futile. Dread filled her as Val's face became a mask of pain. He crumpled to the ground, shuddering as he sobbed. A lump caught in her throat in sympathy. His companions pulled him to his feet again and he leaned on them and wept.

Lirienne engaged her healing focus once more, desperate to find some way to help. Talora's heartbeat became increasingly difficult to discern. Her breath was so shallow that her chest barely rose. Lirienne's thoughts darted about as she struggled to determine what to do. All her training failed her. Even with such a formidable a gift as maru it wasn't always possible to save a life. There was only one hope left.

She turned to her assistant. "Get a Master." She admonished herself for not having done this sooner.

He stared at her, but didn't move. Talora's breathing was shallow. He was young, but he read the situation right. She had refused to see it. There was no point in fetching a Master.

Tears welled up in Lirienne's eyes. She caressed Valran's hair as he leaned over his wife. "I'm sorry, Val. I tried. She's lost too much blood." Her voice sounded mechanical. The lump in her throat made it hard to swallow.

She kept a link with Talora to monitor her heart rate. As her pulse faded, her breathing became shallow until, finally, she gave a cough and one last shuddering breath. The heartbeat ceased.

Lirienne withdrew her mind and her touch. Her assistant, anticipating her need, brought her another washbowl, and she dipped her hands in the warm water to cleanse the blood from her fingers.

Lirienne tidied up her workspace, her concentration far from her task. Valran's weeping echoed throughout the infirmary. His cries increased in pitch as he wailed for his love. He would not marry again. He couldn't. The Hilliri never did.

After a long while, Valran's cries ceased. He shook a little as he lifted himself from his wife's body and straightened out his rumpled uniform.

Lirienne touched him tenderly on the shoulder. "There wasn't enough time."

Val's expression became harsh. Lirienne stepped back. He pushed her away and she stumbled. She would have fallen if not for the quick wits of her assistant, who propped her up. She straightened her silver robe and brought herself back up to her full height.

Valran sneered. "You mean there wasn't enough maru, sister. You wasted yours on that pathetic silversmith so that you were too weak to save Talora."

Lirienne shook her head. She had no words.

Valran spun around and left, leaving Lirienne with her mouth open wide and tears streaming down her cheeks.

CHAPTER TWO

Lirienne was the first to arrive for the family meeting her father had called the following day. The king, a lean, almost gaunt man with platinum hair and ice blue eyes, sat at his large wooden desk piled high with the tools of his trade: documents, ledgers, and maps.

At this moment, the idea of sitting in his place seemed entirely distasteful to her. She was a candidate to be heir to the throne of Kalad, as were her other siblings, but she had never coveted the role as the others did. Watching her father only made her happier with her current duties.

She bowed low, hoping the extra respect might calm the king's wrath, or at least, not fuel it any further. She took a seat in a chair opposite the desk.

Her sister, Selana, arrived next, wrapped in a shawl covered with tiny multicolored jewels. A spectacular confection—all of her sibling's costumes were—but the festive outfit didn't suit the somber occasion. They were supposed to be mourning. Selana gave an impressively deep bow to their father and smiled at Lirienne upon rising. Was there a small challenge in her expression? Lirienne allowed herself the tiniest eye roll in response. Selana could be like that.

"Greetings, father."

Selana sat beside Lirienne and smiled. "I see Valran is going to keep us waiting again."

Lirienne chafed at this. "He had to look after some funeral details. He won't be long."

Selana looked briefly at the ceiling.

The king stood up and leaned against his desk. "That's enough, girls."

A breeze buoyed the drapes. The king glanced over their shoulders at the door behind them. He scowled for a moment and then schooled himself into the bland expression Lirienne hated: the one that showed no hint of emotion. Lirienne swiveled as Valran entered the room.

"Good of you to join us, son."

Valran looked down at his feet. His pale complexion made starker by the dark circles under his red-rimmed eyes. "I apologize for keeping you waiting, father. The Sibyl came to ask for some details in preparation for the memorial." The last few words came out choked and tight.

Lirienne wanted to squeeze his hand and tell him life would get better, but she couldn't—not here, not yet. Val had barely spoken to her since his wife died. Now he kept his gaze firmly on the king. He bowed toward their father and took a seat on Lirienne's other side.

The king kept his expression flat. "I'm sure it will be a splendid tribute to a remarkable woman." The words were kind enough, but in that particular tone, they sounded false.

Lirienne gave in and reached out to touch Val's hand. "Indeed, she was remarkable."

Val pulled back at her touch. He swallowed hard and said nothing as he kept his eyes looking forward.

The king rubbed his hands together. "Very well then, let's get down to the business at hand: the selection of the Primary Heir."

Lirienne couldn't believe her ears. This wasn't the time for another discussion on succession. Selana brightened at the words, though. Val hunched over a little and continued to observe his feet.

The king persisted. "But first I want a full explanation of why there was an incursion into Castillonian territory. Valran?"

Valran's pale skin blanched even further. He took one deep breath and set his shoulders back where they belonged. Lirienne was proud of his strength. He moistened his lips. "I was riding along the escarpment on our southern border with my unit. We were checking the security of a stretch of the border there. About an hour east of the river, we came to a spot where the bridge over the gorge is double-wide—enough to admit a wagon rather than only single riders. We spotted a group of Trillas in mid operation, attempting to dismantle their side of the bridge."

The king snapped upright. "We have a treaty that allows for the building of crossings to facilitate trade. They were violating the treaty?"

Valran nodded. "I believed so. I saw them. There were about eight of those bloody Mundatar." He wrinkled his nose. There was no love lost between the Hilliri and the Trillas and the use of this rude name instead of their proper one showed this. Ever since the Trillas people had settled in Castillon, less than a hundred years ago, the Hilliri despised them and their proximity. They were just too different—too strange. "They were knocking out boards and taking down the landing area at their end of the bridge. I felt we had to do something, and we had enough soldiers present to deal with the issue right there and then, so I gave the order."

The Trillas were different from her people. Their darker complexions and unseemly habits—especially toward their women—repelled the Hilliri.

"You were correct to deal with the dismantling of the bridge," her father agreed, "but why did you continue on into their territory? The report says your unit attacked a nearby village."

"After we subdued the workers at the bridge, I realized we were very near to Alterra," Valran said, keeping his eyes trained on the floor.

The king's eyes narrowed. "You attacked Alterra?"

Valran's eyes snapped back up to his father's face. "I knew how much you wanted to resolve that issue. You're always telling me to seize opportunity and take initiative."

The king rubbed his chin. "I have said this. I think you'll agree, though, that the cost was very high. Was it worth it for Talora's life?"

Val's eyes widened. Even if it was true, the statement shocked Lirienne too. Her brother stared sharply at her, but he said nothing.

Selana cleared her throat and sat upright. "Talora would have lived if Lirienne hadn't used up her maru on a commoner."

The king's unyielding stare landed on Lirienne. She shrank back in her seat. "Is this true?"

Lirienne shook her head. Healers could only manage a few patients in a session, but the damaged eye had hardly cost her anything. "I did heal a commoner of a minor ailment, but it would not have mattered. Talora had been bleeding for hours before they brought her in. She was weak. I gave her everything I had, but a healer can only do so much."

She watched her father's face as she spoke, but his expression never changed. She knew he didn't like healers. Valran too, was quiet.

At last, her brother broke the silence. "We did achieve what you wanted, even though the cost was great. We have taken back that village of defectors. I set a complement to guard our position and returned with our wounded."

The king balled up his fists until they shook. "I couldn't let those renegades simply leave our borders and thumb their noses in my direction as they did it. Others would have followed their lead and emptied our great kingdom of Kalad of all of its talented craftspeople and the lucrative tax revenues they bring us. You have done me a great service in this. I realize the personal cost you have borne as a result is very unfortunate. You have also angered our neighbors. We now hold territory across the gorge, inside their borders. We must prepare for retaliation. Whatever happens, we mustn't cede that village, at least, not until it's empty and all of the citizens of Alterra are returned to Kalad and to my rule."

Valran saluted, accepting his orders. "I've sent a second unit out to hold the village, but we're certain to see some reprisal from Castillon. The Alterrans apparently had an agreement with them. They had permission to settle there. It is possible that the Lord of Castillon will consider it his duty to protect the place."

The king scowled. "That old fox Carlosi is always happy to skirmish at the first opportunity, whether he has reason or not."

Lirienne had heard that about the man as well. She tried to understand what was at play. "I thought they didn't have an army of their own."

Her father bobbed his head in ascent. "You are correct, but that doesn't mean they can't do some serious damage. They have weapons and fighters who know how to use them. They aren't a numerous people, but they hold fast to the land they occupy. I want to keep that portion of land now that we hold it. By taking over the village with a show of strength, we can prevent the Alterrans from spreading their aberrant beliefs to the rest of my kingdom. It doesn't hurt Kalad to increase our borders a little either. Castillon will hardly miss that small part."

Valran rubbed the armrest on his chair. "Knowing their lord, I'm afraid we're up for a fight, though."

The king waved his hand. "Kalad has enough resources to deal with whatever irritations Lord Carlosi sends our way. But enough of that, I think we must turn our thoughts back to the original reason for this meeting: what to do about the succession of this kingdom."

Selana cleared her throat and raised her hand. The king glanced her way, raising his eyebrows to signal that she could speak.

"We have had many discussions about this, father, and none have led to any conclusions. You seem to want to delay your selection indefinitely. I, for one, would be glad if you would finally make a choice so that we can proceed with our lives knowing what to expect."

"I haven't made my choice yet, Selana, because you are all still young and your characters are not fully formed. I expect to live a long, healthy life, so there is no rush on that account."

Lirienne thought otherwise. Her father found it convenient to delay his decision so that he could keep all of his children in line. While he might very well live a long life, by not choosing he risked tumbling Kalad into a state of turmoil should something unexpected happen to him. He might well live another thousand years, but there were dangers to being a ruler, and dangers just in living. "Father, Valran seems most suited to my mind. He has shown leadership qualities and good decision-making skills."

Her father leaned toward her. "Are you saying you don't want to be considered, Lirienne?"

She shook her head. She never wanted to see her older sister on the throne, or she would have withdrawn herself long ago. For the sake of everyone, she would keep herself in consideration.

Her father signaled his approval. "Good. While I agree with you, Lirienne, I think we have to consider the problem resulting from recent events. With Valran's loss, we must take into account that even if he is chosen, he won't have an heir of his own."

He was correct. Lirienne hadn't been thinking about this, but Valran couldn't remarry. The Hilliri married only once, even though they lived long lives. There was a deep taboo regarding the very idea of remarriage. The intense mind-to-mind connections they made with their partners meant that a subsequent lover would sense the lingering thoughts about the first one. It was a distasteful idea in the extreme.

The king shifted to look at Lirienne. "Whether I choose Valran or one of my daughters, we need there to be an heir for the next generation."

Selana looked unhappy. Lirienne sympathized. Neither sister wanted to marry just yet. They hadn't found anyone to their liking, though Selana, being much older, had been searching for longer.

Selana swallowed hard and stood. "Father, if it is your wish, I will accept Lord Farnor's proposal. But, for this, I would ask to be the chosen heir."

Lirienne balled her hands into fists. She had no proposal at hand to counter her sister with, but she knew that Selana despised the man. Was she so desperate to be queen that she would marry a man she disliked in order to receive the honor?

The king smiled that flat smile again. "Sit down, Selana, I won't have that man anywhere near my throne."

Selana's relief blended with her disappointment. Lirienne

relaxed her hands. The king focused on her.

"I believe Lirienne might have better luck finding a suitable man to marry. She is younger and more biddable. If she produces a child, that child could be Valran's heir. I doubt Lirienne would mind all that much. She seems to prefer her duties as a healer to the obligations of a ruler."

Lirienne bowed her head, though her thoughts continued to spin. As the youngest daughter, she was used to being overlooked. "As you wish, father."

It sounded so compliant. He had said so himself. She wanted to scream. Was there any end to the burden and obligations of being born to the royal line?

She thought of all the men she had been introduced to already, each one more ambitious than the last, all hopeful that they might have the chance to rule through her. Lirienne might seem docile, but she wouldn't have it. She would have to try to find someone, though, or Selana would end up the mother of the next king or queen. Her husband would have to be compliant and not ambitious to be suitable, or he would have trouble. She thought of the endless days of introductions to come. She would do it, of course, for Kalad and for Valran and for her father, like a good daughter. Like a good princess. Her father was right; she was biddable.

CHAPTER THREE

Lirienne walked through the many pathways of the palace toward her chambers as she began to think and plan. She needed to review every noble family in the three Hilliri kingdoms. She mustn't rule out a marriage to a noble house in another Hilliri land, although it might mean moving away for a while. A trip to the archives would therefore be in order. She could consult the palace matchmakers, but she'd found them wholly unhelpful in the past. They seemed occupied with the physical attributes of a candidate, leaving his personality unconsidered. For Lirienne, that simply wouldn't do.

Thoughts of the impending conflict with Castillon plagued her, as well as Valran's reaction to her affection, and also her grief at the loss of a family member. Her stomach churned. Too much had changed too fast. She longed for her garden refuge. Hopefully, it would be unoccupied.

Her guard took up a position outside the door to her chambers as she swung it open and went inside. The scent of fresh cut flowers greeted her. Someone had been thoughtful. She went straight to the garden door, ignoring the comfortable living room with its carpets and overstuffed chairs. It was open, and a light breeze blew in cool air. Late winter in Kalad still held on to its chill.

She stepped out into the tiled courtyard. The garden was walled in on all sides, so that the only way in or out was through her chambers, save for the one padlocked gate that the gardeners used. A young man was there, his back to her as he pruned one of the droopy boughs of an ornamental tree. Had it been any other worker here in her sanctuary, she would have been disappointed not to be alone, but this man always made her smile.

"Tarlen!"

The young man placed his shears on the ground. He bowed slightly and grinned, looking her in the eye. He was beautiful, with a golden tone to his pale skin and light green eyes. His golden hair, cropped short, curled around his sweet, boyish face. Lirienne shook her head and approached him. He took her hand and kissed it in mock chivalry.

Lirienne rolled her eyes. "Just what I need, another suitor." She was glad he was here.

The young man cocked an eyebrow and looked at her questioningly. "My lady, what grieves you?" After a moment of awkward silence, he looked pained. He shook his head. "Forgive me, lady, for the unfortunate choice of words."

Lirienne waved him off. "Well... first of all... I need to get married as soon as possible."

She sat down on a stone bench. The garden was already looking overgrown in spite of the earliness of the season. The rain sometimes did this in the city.

Tarlen dusted off his hands on his sage green work robe and sat beside her. They had known each other for many years, otherwise he would never have been so presumptuous.

"Tell me," he said.

Tarlen's father was the Master Gardener of the palace. Ever since Tarlen was a boy, his father had brought his son along when he worked, showing him how to use maru to make plants grow and bloom. Lirienne, a child herself then, had grown attached to the boy. They played in the palace gardens while his father worked. She had no older friend.

"Since my sister-in-law died, there is a concern that no heirs for the next generation are forthcoming, so my father wants me to wed and produce some. Selana is expected to do the same, but if she happens to be first, her child is likely to be chosen." She couldn't really say more.

Her friend's eyes widened. "You don't want your sister to be first, I guess."

Lirienne shook her head. "She would manipulate the child. What kind of ruler would that make?"

It wasn't really a question. They both knew about her grandfather. His wife had effectively ruled in his stead for the whole of his reign.

"But?" His eyebrows lifted in inquiry.

"I don't like to trouble you with my problems."

"But of course, you will..." His green eyes sparkled. He really was beautiful.

"You're so good to me, Tarlen."

"I am, aren't I?"

Lirienne laughed a little at this. It had always been easy between them. She straightened her features. This was no joking matter. "I just don't see how this is going to work. It's not like I haven't tried already."

Tarlen schooled his own features into seriousness and Lirienne suppressed a grin. "You know, my lady, we get along well enough, you and I."

Lirienne's mouth opened. She wracked her brain for something to say. "Are you suggesting something?"

Tarlen shrugged and pursed his lips. "I'm just saying that if you need a husband that you are fond of and you get along well with, I'm here for you."

Lirienne placed a hand on her friend's hand and looked him in the eye. Could he be serious? He held up a twig. After a moment, it began to glow and grow, until it was a full nosegay of purple blooms. He offered it to her and she took it. The scent was strong and bright.

"Thank you. That was nice, as was your offer." Of course, he wasn't an appropriate husband for a princess. While he was a good companion, he wouldn't have made a good partner, and the Hilliri lived too long to be bound to the wrong person. "I think you're sweet to ask, Tarlen, but even if it were possible, it wouldn't be wise."

Tarlen dug his fists into his waist. "Don't you think I would make a great husband?" Lirienne held his gaze and tried not to grin. She didn't want to hurt his feelings. "Tarlen, I've seen how you look at healer Jasor, and I've noticed that he looks back at you the same way. I wouldn't want to be an obstacle to your happiness."

They had never spoken of it before, but Lirienne wanted him to know she was aware, and that she wasn't the sort to judge.

Tarlen looked away. It wasn't easy to admit to one's secret desire. Especially if it was one which others would disapprove of. Slowly he shifted his gaze back to her. "Now why did you go and do that? We were having such a nice talk."

His eyes filled with tears, which he erased with a quick wipe of his sleeve. Lirienne squeezed his arm and stood. Tarlen stood as well. He fetched his shears and returned to pruning. It pained Lirienne that she might have hurt her friend, but anything less than honesty would have hurt him as well. Perhaps she should speak to healer Jasor and help push things forward between them.

She wrinkled her nose at the thought. It was too much like something Selana would do. Lirienne would rather be more like her mother had been. All she had known of the woman who had died giving birth to her and her brother was her kindness to others, as related by the many that she had touched.

Once, when she was a small child playing in her father's lap, she had touched his face with her bare hands. Thoughts had seeped from her father's anguished mind into her childish one. Her shields had never been very good, even then. Lirienne hadn't understood the complicated emotions back then, but as an adult, she reviewed what she had learned until it began to make some sense. The king had never really gotten over his wife's untimely death.

Her father felt an enormous guilt over the loss of her mother. It didn't fit, but later Lirienne learned one key piece of information that pulled all of the pieces together: he had never called for a healer to assist in the birth.

There was a knock at the door. Lirienne heard it through the opening into the garden.

"Come in." She turned and entered her living space. The door swung open and Selana swept in, still wrapped in her bejeweled shawl.

Lirienne stiffened. "Greetings, sister. We just spoke. Do you have more to say?"

Selana settled on one of the wide divans and crossed her legs. "I wanted to hear your plan, Lirienne. You always have a plan."

Lirienne scowled. "What kind of plan?"

"Why, a plan to find a husband, of course."

Lirienne smoothed her dress as she attempted to clear away her annoyance. "It's hardly worth mentioning. Of course, I'll have to review the royal families of the three kingdoms to make sure I haven't missed someone. I'll have to widen my search by considering much older men as well. I think I won't bother with the palace matchmakers. I haven't found them to be all that useful in the past."

Selana snorted at this. "I have to agree with you there." She picked some lint from the upholstery.

"But?" Lirienne knew there was always a 'but' with Selana.

Selana sprang up again. There was a restless energy in her—a secret she had to tell, no doubt. "I've been over the lists already. We've been introduced to the best of the possible lot, I'm afraid. There's no point in going over it again."

Was she trying to distract Lirienne from the task?

"I will, though. Just to be certain. I'm sure you understand how important this task is now that Valran has no wife to give him children."

Stepping over to look down at Lirienne from her greater height, Selana tilted her head as if considering. "Interesting how things have taken a turn. I'm wondering if Valran would even be willing to accept a child of yours as his heir. He's still angry at you for not being fully charged when he brought Talora to you." Selana shook her head.

Lirienne flushed. It was cruel of Selana to bring up the strife with her brother. She was correct though. Lirienne would have to find a way to make amends.

Selana swirled around once, making the gems on her shawl wink in the light. "You won't be seeing him for a while. He's gone back to the border with his unit to push further into Castillon."

Hearing this disappointed Lirienne. She didn't want this issue between them to continue any longer. Now she would have to wait until he returned.

Selana shrugged. "I wouldn't worry about it, sister. Valran will eventually come around. In any case, I'll beat you in this race, so don't waste too much time on it."

Selana wrapped the shawl tighter around her slim form and marched for the door. Having delivered her message, she exited without further comment, leaving Lirienne trembling with anger she couldn't express. Whatever secret her sister had, Lirienne couldn't do any more than she had planned.

She headed back out to her garden, preferring even the tension with Tarlen to the rage her sister always seemed to bring forth in her.

A fist thundered on her door. She spun back around to find a messenger panting in the opening.

"Yes?" The terse reply shamed Lirienne, who was usually demure with servants.

The messenger hesitated for a moment and then composed himself.

"The College of the Marukar requests your immediate attendance in the infirmary, my lady. There are wounded soldiers expected shortly."

"There's been another confrontation with Castillon?"

The man gave an expression of distaste. The Trillas were universally disliked in Kalad and in the other Hilliri kingdoms.

"Yes, my lady. The supervisor asked if you could come early for your next shift."

He bowed and left, leaving Lirienne with her stomach churning. It was her duty to provide healing for her class. The military officers would be noblemen and in need of her ministrations. She grabbed a wrap for extra warmth as the day was already cooling and headed out the door.

CHAPTER FOUR

The tea was sharp and sour tasting, like last year's cherries: dried out and reconstituted. For all she knew, that might have been exactly what it was. Lord Pirvan had presented her with the tea in an intricately carved wooden box the afternoon before, when the palace matchmakers had first introduced them. He was the eighth suitor she had entertained this month. While the war raged on to the south, the finest suitors the three Hilliri kingdoms had to offer came to court Lirienne and her sister. She had sniffed the tea and smiled, pretending out of politeness that she appreciated the vile-smelling gift.

This afternoon she ordered a pot of the tea and prepared for their next encounter, though she felt the urge to throw the nasty stuff away. Her suitor watched as she sipped.

"It is a bit of an acquired taste, I'll admit, but once you get used to it, it's very refreshing. It's what we drink in Naral almost exclusively."

Lirienne tried not to make a face. She hiked up her eyebrows. "Is that so?"

She hoped he didn't see her struggling. Her suitor, the eldest son of Duke Kestrine, brother to the King of Naral, was somewhat older than Lirienne thought suitable, but she wanted to be sure that she didn't overlook someone. He wore a wide collar of shaggy fur that covered his shoulders, probably for warmth. It was much colder in the north. He was ordinary looking, but she was more concerned that he should have some personality. So far, it didn't appear that he did.

He leaned forward toward her. "Have you ever been to Naral, my lady Lirienne?"

She smiled. "Many times. Of course, as you know, I'm related to your king."

He brightened at this.

Lirienne continued. "I believe my mother was his first cousin once removed."

Lord Pirvan grinned. "That makes you his first cousin twice

removed! I love genealogy."

Lirienne coughed. The tannic quality of this particular drink dried out her mouth. She licked her lips. "I guess that means you and I are related as well."

Of course, they were, as were all of the noble families, often in more than one way.

He nodded emphatically. "Indeed, that makes you my..."

Lirienne stood up and gathered her robes. She couldn't handle another genealogy lesson. He had already recited the family tree of his own noble lineage in detail. "A cousin of some sort, I'm sure. Who isn't my cousin? That is an interesting question."

The man dipped his head a little, though his gaze turned inward, still calculating their familial connection. Lirienne walked over to the window and looked out. It was a beautiful day. Perhaps they should go for a walk through the garden. The formality of a tea was too much for her.

She regarded her suitor. "I fancy a walk in the garden, sir. Would you kindly accompany me?"

She held out a hand for him to slip an arm over. He sat where he was and blinked. At last, he looked focused again and rose from his chair.

"Of course, my lady." He presented his elbow for her to slip her hand through.

She tugged him a little to get him moving in the right direction. "This way. We shall visit the Rose Garden. I particularly like roses."

Lord Pirvan stared at Lirienne as if she was a new sort of animal he had never seen before. Lirienne released a breath slowly, so it wouldn't seem like the sigh of exasperation it really was. All she wanted was a little personality in her suitors.

They walked without speaking for a while. Lirienne enjoyed the warmth of the sunshine in the open spaces. She guided him through a maze-like walkway into a section filled with early spring roses. Normally roses didn't bloom in the first days of spring, but the Gardeners Guild sent their best members to work at the palace. They had figured out how to make certain kinds of flowers bloom out of season using their maru talents.

It delighted Lirienne to see the riot of color and to smell the powerful aromas that emanated from the special blooms. Her suitor might be dull, but at least she could take some time to enjoy the beautiful day and the sunshine.

Lord Pirvan rambled on about his family for a while longer.

Lirienne listened politely, asking the occasional question to appear interested. This day was going to be very long.

They wandered for a while. The palace was a tangle of buildings and courtyards constructed at various times, with conflicting styles of architecture representing various eras. No one had tried to make it into one unified thing. The palace was what it was. Much of it was crumbling from rot.

At length, they crossed paths with Selana, dressed outlandishly in a bright green robe covered with tiny rubies. Lirienne set about introducing her to Lord Pirvan. Selana curtsied and kept eye contact with him as he again mentioned their shared lineage. It didn't take long to notice that Selana found him more interesting than she did. She could have him if it suited her. For now, though, she was obliged to keep him company.

"So, you think that we're second cousins twice removed then?"

He bobbed his head eagerly, delighted in Selana's interest. "Yes, and if you look from my maternal grandmother's side, we're also fourth cousins thrice removed."

Selana batted her eyelashes. Surely, she wasn't any more impressed than Lirienne was with these details, but she hid her boredom more skillfully than her sister.

They found a bench that could accommodate the three of them and sat. Lirienne continued to nod politely as the genealogy lesson played out over the next half hour.

A young page walked along the path, looking around as he went. He had an envelope tucked into his belt and his dusty violet gloves continued to reach for it every few steps. When his gaze fell upon Lirienne, his eyes opened wider and he changed course for her position.

In his haste, he nearly neglected to bow as he delivered the envelope to her.

"Thank you." She immediately tore the seal and read it while the others waited. She looked up at them when she had finished. "It's from the College of the Marukar. A battle has gone badly. I've been summoned to work." She leaned toward Selana. "Sister, I hope you will keep our guest company while I go to the infirmary. Lord Pirvan, my apologies for abandoning you, I hope that you understand that my duties must come first. It's been a pleasure."

"Indeed, it has. I would be delighted to continue on after your work is done, my lady." He bowed.

"If I can still hold a conversation after my shift, I will gladly continue with you then." It was unlikely this would happen.

As she left the area, she gave one last glance back. Selana was laughing and Lord Pirvan was smiling too. She doubted that Selana would consider the man, he didn't have an interesting enough personality, but if she were in a hurry, it was hard to say what lengths her sister would go to in order to secure a place of power for herself.

CHAPTER FIVE

The infirmary was full of patients, additional healers, and comrades accompanying many of the wounded. A buzz of activity and chatter filled the room. Lirienne went to her post with the little box on the floor. A patient was already lying on her work bed. Several officers gathered there and stared at her as she looked over the list of injured awaiting attention from a Prestige healer. She looked back at them and placed the list to the side.

"Gentlemen, I'm going to have to ask you to leave so that I can work." Her comment caught the eye of the day supervisor, a short, round woman. The officers just stared at her as if they didn't understand. She observed their faces. Slight signs of trauma were apparent to the skilled observer; they all had just come from battle.

Lirienne cleared her throat. "I will attend to your commander now, gentlemen, but I need silence to work. Please wait in the room across the hall. I will come to you with news when I'm done."

This time it appeared the words had sunk in, for the officers slowly filed out of the room. Lirienne looked down at this first patient.

The commander appeared to be a man of middle years, though it was difficult to tell since the Hilliri lived so long and aged so slowly. He lay on her healing bed, his face almost white.

Shock or blood loss, Lirienne thought with detachment. She slipped off her silver gloves and set to work assessing and healing his wounds.

When she had finished, she released her mental connection to her patient. He would live, although it had cost her considerable resources. He slept now and looked relaxed, if not healthy. She picked up the soiled bandages scattered around his bed. When she leaned down to collect a few that had fallen on the floor, a hand grasped her upper arm.

Her patient was awake.

"How do you feel, my lord?"

He squeezed his eyes shut. "You'll be better soon. I've taken care of all the important injuries. You should rest now."

He licked his dry lips. "Tell him I almost had the bastard."

Lirienne furrowed her brow. "Who?"

"The Slasher. Lord Valran wanted us to report if we had seen him."

She shook her head. She didn't understand.

"The man who killed Lady Talora. We call him the Slasher—on account of his techniques."

He was likely delirious, but he said they had named Talora's killer the Slasher, an ominous label. It occurred to Lirienne that it might be unwise to name an opponent for his abilities. It gave him more power. Not the real kind, but naming him fixed him as someone who was hard to beat.

She wiped the perspiration off her brow and called the porters over to take him to a private room where he could convalesce. She rinsed her hands and was about to go out to speak with his subordinates when the infirmary supervisor trundled over.

"Where are you going? There are four more sub-commanders waiting. You must work on two of them."

Lirienne blinked. She hadn't really absorbed the list because of all the people around her. On top of everything, the constant sight of the wounded and the sharp coppery tang of blood made it hard to think.

"I was just going to speak with the officers I had sent outside to wait."

The supervisor pursed her lips. "That's what your assistant is for." She waved at the porters. They brought another patient over to her bed and Lirienne sent her assistant to speak with the officers in the other room.

She checked the list again. There were indeed four more patients waiting as the supervisor had said, but she was the only Prestige healer in the infirmary at this moment.

She regarded the supervisor. "Has another Prestige healer been called for the other two on this list?"

The woman shook her head. "We haven't one to spare. Lady Daria worked the last shift. She's gone to rest. You'll work on the next two patients and the other two will just have to wait until the next shift starts."

This response shocked Lirienne. She leaned toward the woman, speaking in a low voice. "That's hours away. Those soldiers might not be able to wait that long. Isn't there a Master available?"

The woman shrugged. She looked tired. "I have orders not to

call them unless someone in the Royal Family is ill."

Lirienne raised her brows at this. They meant her, her siblings and her father. Her cheeks grew warm as she realized the level of privilege bestowed on her. Yet, the recent conflict with Castillon was changing the demands of her work, and every minute of time that passed made mending more difficult as patients deteriorated. There were so many injured and no extra help; surely the Masters hadn't anticipated such great need when they created their rules.

Before the fighting began, she had typically seen one or two patients per shift. She puzzled on this. She should only be working on three at the most, unless the supervisor was willing to check her levels and approve her for more. After all, some injuries took less maru to heal than others. Unfortunately, her supervisors were reluctant to do a check on her since she had a reputation for sloppy mental barriers. No one wanted to listen in on her private thoughts. She didn't blame them, but these officers were going to die without care. Wasn't that more important?

She returned to examining the soldier lying on her bed; her gloves off and her mind making contact with the patient's damaged body. As she worked, she stewed about the wrongness of the order of things. They triaged the injured according to severity, with those of higher rank taking precedent. It looked as if the two unfortunate soldiers waiting were not well-born enough to merit quick attention from a healer. She hoped they would rally and repair on their own.

When she finished the two patients allotted to her, Lirienne turned her concentration inward, her awareness delving down into her own body, checking her maru levels. She had used less than expected. The thought of those other soldiers going without medical care kept nagging at her, so she had tried to be efficient. She promised herself that she would attempt another treatment if she felt up to it. She waved the porters over and they picked up the officer she had just finished healing.

"When you're done with him, please bring the next one to me."

The porters bowed and carried their charge away. She washed her hands and sat down for a few moments. She would likely have to tangle with the supervisor over this.

A new man was brought over to her a few minutes later. She studied him, his skin paste-white with more red than gray in the color of his uniform. She made mental contact with his body but sensed no pulse. No heartbeat either.

A rage swelled within her. She covered the man's face and

waved for another patient. The porters took the body away in silence. If another healer had been called for at the beginning of triage, this man might not have died.

The next wounded soldier, a young woman, was brought in and placed before her. As she stepped back onto her little box, a coppery scent filled her space, which set off Lirienne's memory of another recent treatment. Talora, similarly soaked in gore, had been laid out just like this.

As she began her work, she sensed a presence beside her. The supervisor approached, ready to spar with a Prestige healer. That took some pluck.

"This patient must wait for the next shift, Lady Lirienne. If you continue, you will be in breach of the College rules on patient limits."

"I will take full responsibility, madam. I checked myself and I'm strong enough to do this."

The supervisor looked cross and dug her fists into her waist. "If you insist on breaking College rules, I will have to write up a report and send it to the Masters for review. Is that what you really want?"

Lirienne shook her head. "I don't, but I also don't want to see this woman die because of an inflexible set of rules. We weren't at war when the Masters first decided they shouldn't be troubled with healing minor nobles. The rules must change, or we're going to lose too many soldiers. I'm healing this woman. If you're concerned about the rules, I suggest you measure my levels. You will see that I have enough maru for this task."

The supervisor opened her mouth to respond, but a disturbance broke out on the other side of the room, which distracted them both. Lirienne looked over to see several soldiers weeping over one of their comrades as a healer covered his face.

Saddened, Lirienne could only stare at the supervisor, who struggled to school her own features during the commotion. This scene would replay itself repeatedly if College procedures didn't change.

CHAPTER SIX

Lirienne stared at the coffered ceiling. The sculpted squares, carved with ornate floral motifs, were overlaid with gold leaf. The work was faded with age and corroded by the breath of thousands passing by, as if her country, Kalad, rested on the decaying glory of a bygone era.

The war was growing, and with it came more and more injured.

Her stomach grumbled. They hadn't let her eat before calling her in. By the time someone came to fetch her, she felt slightly dizzy. A small breach in protocol. An attempt perhaps to school her.

She inhaled deeply before entering the small room where the seven silver-robed Masters sat at their long, heavy oak table. The left-most Master held his hand up, stopping her mid-step. Their eyes bored into her with silent reproach. It was hardly the first time the panel of College Masters had called her in to discuss her behavior, but after weeks of conflict, they might have reached their limit.

Over the past month she had tried repeatedly to heal more soldiers than the basic rules allowed, leading to daily confrontations with the infirmary supervisors. Sometimes she was allowed to proceed, a tacit agreement that she was on the right side of things, but every now and then, she would encounter a stickler of an infirmary supervisor, someone who loved enforcing the rules more than saving lives, and then she would end up in trouble with the College Masters.

Her feet ached from working for hours in the infirmary, but they made her wait without a place to sit. Her stomach growled and she swayed a little.

Finally, the smallest among them, a woman sitting just right of center, exhaled and began. "We're unhappy to have to meet with you again."

Indeed. Lirienne was unhappy too. Here she was once again, her face hot with anger at having to defend her actions.

"We have taught you how to monitor your maru levels, and to withdraw from your work before you exhaust yourself. You may only work on three patients with serious injuries per session; that is the rule. We shouldn't have to keep telling you this. Did we make a mistake in granting you the full honors of Healer?"

At least Lirienne had learned to keep calm and listen to the lectures. Before, she used to argue in her defense, but that never helped. She shook her head. "No, mistress, I'm sorry. I will try harder to comply." Lirienne learned from experience that this was the only thing they wanted her to say.

She had done what she always did. She healed injured soldiers. It wasn't pleasant work. They were damaged, bleeding, and dying. There were always too many of them and too few healers. And healers could die if they completely drained their power. But Lirienne would never let herself get so dangerously low, and the infirmary supervisors always kept careful watch over their staff.

Three patients was only an estimate. An easy rule of thumb for a supervisor, but every wound needed a different amount of healing. This time, the supervisor had not been willing to verify precisely how much maru Lirienne had to spare, nor would she accept her assurances. The supervisor simply went by how many patients Lirienne had treated, avoiding the uncomfortable, but more accurate, direct testing method.

The seven Masters scowled even though they could hear her contrition. She sensed that something was different this time. There was a shortage of healers already, and very few were members of the nobility that they called "Prestige Class." Would they expel her after all, despite needing her skills and her birthright? That would be foolhardy. She was fighting to make sure people didn't die.

She plucked up her strength and resolve. If her usual response was no longer enough, she would have to try something else. These Masters had to start thinking differently in order for more people to be healed.

"I do monitor my levels, it's just that the supervisors don't actually test me to verify. I'm happy to submit to testing after the first three patients, then every time thereafter. You know, more people would be able to receive treatment if all the healers did this all the time."

She knew the problem. Testing required contact with the healer's mind and body, and she had earned a reputation for sloppy barriers. Thinking of it made her cheeks hot.

Well, one couldn't be good at everything.

The Masters looked to each other, gauging reactions to her offer. They rarely spoke, but somehow managed to read one another's expressions well enough.

The central Master was their chairman. He stood—a good sign that things were wrapping up. Lirienne began to relax.

"My lady," the Master began. His controlled tone was harsher than she expected. Lirienne braced herself for the worst. She closed her eyes for a moment and made a silent prayer to remain a healer. If she wasn't a healer, what use was she in this world? "I must ask you to obey your infirmary supervisor and cease working when instructed, no matter what method is used to determine your levels. We would hate to have to strip you of your designation. The rules are there for your protection and as guidance for the supervisors. We know that the services of all healers are desperately needed in this time of war, but this kind of disciplinary problem is unacceptable and will be dealt with regardless of our needs."

Unacceptable, Lirienne recognized, because if she came to harm, they would be in trouble. Her father, who distrusted healers to begin with, would be furious. They must want to avoid his wrath at all costs. At least in this she understood and sympathized with the Masters. No one wanted to provoke the king's anger.

The Master was still standing and appeared ready to finish his pronouncement.

"If we have to call you here again, it will be to collect your robes and send you back to your father."

Lirienne's cheeks burned even hotter. She must avoid dismissal from the guild.

The Master looked at his colleagues. He wasn't done yet.

"You're used to a life of privilege, my lady, as a royal princess, and may not have had too many restrictions placed upon you during your youth, but the College of the Marukar is a special place, and if you wish to remain in service with us, you will abide by our rules, no matter what you think of them." He sat and folded up the ledger book in front of him. "You are dismissed."

So—the truth was finally out. They claimed that healers were in great demand, yet they would rather send her away than have her take any risks.

She couldn't accept that.

"Test me, please." She blurted out the words before realizing how inappropriate it was for her to make the challenge. It was too late to take it back, so she breathed in and repeated her request. "Test me. I have healed three patients, two of whom were seriously damaged and near dying, and I wasn't allowed to eat anything yet."

The woman on the right of the chairperson bolted up and scowled at her colleagues. "You should have been allowed to eat before coming here. Who ordered this?"

The others remained silent, averting their eyes from the woman's sharp stare.

She addressed Lirienne. "I will test you. Approach and take off your gloves."

Lirienne tugged on each finger of the fine-spun silver cloth until the gloves slipped from her hands. "If I'm completely drained, then I will agree to your terms and give you no more trouble, but I think you'll be surprised. My abilities are not that remarkable. If you tested every healer fully, we would be able to heal many more soldiers."

Lirienne believed she wasn't the only healer who was being limited. If she could prove it, perhaps more soldiers would live.

She held out her hands. The Master grasped them. At once, a familiar disorientation took hold as she saw her own face through the woman's eyes. Lirienne kept her mind carefully walled away from the Master's curious thoughts and, after a moment, her orientation righted. The woman released her hand and slipped her gloves back on. She gave one more fleeting look at her colleagues and stepped away from the oak table.

"You may leave, Lirienne. It seems I have some business to discuss with the others here."

Lirienne still wanted to know what the Master had found out about her. "But what about my maru levels? Can you tell me?"

The Master looked at the floor for a moment, then at the other six. "Your levels are fine for another two patients with significant injuries."

CHAPTER SEVEN

Lirienne returned to the infirmary to finish her work after a quick snack. Now, at the noon hour, the place overflowed with even more patients. Soldiers, bloodied and wrapped up in bandages, sat on benches or stretchers around the edges of the infirmary, their companions leaning where they could as they waited. Healers worked in the center of the room, each stationed at a single bed. She scanned their faces and saw their fatigue and disheartenment. She understood their shared burden. So much work to do and so many harmed. Her personal guard stationed himself just outside the door.

Two more patients, the master had said. It pleased her to know she was right. Healers could do more. They just needed permission to go ahead and checking to be sure they were okay.

The Hilliri always avoided mental contact when they could. The gloves which they usually wore permitted them to close themselves off, creating a barrier against raw mental leakage—all those messy personal emotions and thoughts. She understood the desire for healers to remain professional and clinically detached when dealing with patients, but now that they were at war, the cost of not measuring healer levels was much too high. They must consider the needs of their people to be greater than their need for privacy. Why didn't the College Masters see that?

As she edged along the narrow space between beds, Lirienne caught her friend Daria's eye.

The woman grinned, clearly pleased. "I see they sent you back."

Lirienne shrugged. "Back to Patch or Pitch. Not much of a reward."

It was her friend's term—a lighthearted way to talk about a difficult subject: the decision whether to heal or to skip a patient whose severe injuries weren't worth the extreme effort and expenditure of maru.

Her friend huffed. "Well, at least you can fix up a few more soldiers now." Both Daria and Lirienne agreed that healers could do more.

"I was hoping they would consider doing regular direct

assessments so we could work on more patients during every shift, but this is only for me and only today."

Daria grinned. She always managed to be cheerful even though the work was grim. "By the way, I hear your brother has returned with a captive."

Lirienne turned in interest. "Someone of note?"

Daria chewed her lower lip. "The one they're calling the Slasher."

A chill ran through Lirienne at the mention of the name. At last, they'd captured the man who had killed Talora. If her brother had his way, the killer wouldn't live long.

She signaled to the waiting porters to bring in a new patient for her. Two soldiers carried in a man on a stretcher. Lirienne consulted her patient list: a senior commander. His leg was piled high with blood-soaked bandages. A coppery scent filled the air around her. Lirienne lifted the bandages to inspect the damage. Shards of broken bones protruded through a ragged hole in the man's flesh. She grimaced as she noted the filth encrusting the outer edges of the wound. The senior commander mumbled quietly in his delirium.

The College had sent a few healers to work on the front lines, preparing patients, healing them just enough to stop the bleeding, leaving the deeper and more complex work to the College healers to handle when they brought the patients back to the city. This man looked untouched, save for the bandage, which was useless. Lirienne concluded that there must be more injured at the front than they could cope with.

She shook her head and began, pulling off her silver gloves once more. Like all Hilliri, her palms were covered with a layer of slightly shiny skin where they were particularly sensitive. She need only touch her patient to mentally access the inside of his body.

She prepared herself, building a smooth porcelain-like wall between her innermost thoughts and the work she was about to do. Once ready, she placed her hands lightly on his skin. Lirienne felt the world spin as her awareness slipped into his body. She saw through his eyes as he looked up at her. It always began like this, but then she mastered her control, and her vision righted itself. She searched through the corridors of his body, muscles, blood vessels, and organs, checking each as she went.

While she labored, the patient murmured to himself. "Sweetness and light... a kiss for your love?" He pursed his lips.

An image flashed into Lirienne's mind of a pretty woman

reaching for the soldier and coming in close for a kiss. She blushed. When her attention focused on healing, her barriers would slip. The patient's memories of an intimate interlude with his wife were leaking through. She tried to ignore what she saw.

"What are you doing?" A male voice spoke, shocking Lirienne out of her healing trance. She looked up to see the infirmary supervisor hovering over her patient.

"This man is too injured. Move on to the next."

Lirienne blinked. "But sir, I can do this. It's a simple bone regrowth. I've already done the assessment."

The supervisor frowned. "So, they sent you back. Don't you lead a charmed life?" He was referring to her disciplinary hearing. The man had a sarcastic streak Lirienne didn't appreciate. He was the one who had reported her.

"They tested me and deemed me able to heal two more patients."

The man exhaled. "Fine, but don't expect special treatment when you're completely exhausted." He turned and moved on.

Refocusing on her task, Lirienne completed repairs on the leg and then dealt with a cracked rib, in spite of the College's policy to let the minor injuries heal on their own in order to save healer energies. The College Masters preached endlessly about conserving maru, but it seemed disingenuous when few supervisors bothered to check levels the most accurate way. The senior commander would be in pain and weak for a long time, and she didn't want to make it any worse for him.

A fine sheen of sweat built up on her face. She used her sleeve to mop it. She was definitely tiring, but she was determined to heal one last injured soldier.

She hailed the soldiers to bring the next patient while her assistant came and changed the soiled sheets. They laid the injured man very gently on her healing bed. One of the men who carried him in looked pleadingly into her eyes. The haunted look gave her a chill. She'd seen that gaze many times since the war had started.

She lifted the bandage on the man's arm to see the damage, but lowered it instantly when she caught a glimpse of the gaping hole in the middle of his upper arm. The smell of putrefaction plucked at her gag reflex. She breathed through her mouth to avoid the harshest scent. The man was unconscious. Regrettably, the arm might have to go.

She calmed herself in order to do her work. As before, she built up her barriers and mentally delved down into the body of her patient, searching for damaged places. She did her best, but the seepage of thoughts from the last patient had worn her nerves down.

The arm was the worst, but there were other hurts. As her awareness traveled along his body, she visualized the muscles, blood vessels, and bones. She had a lot of work to do. The muscle and bone of the arm required regeneration, a difficult task, and then she must wrap everything in newly grown skin, which she would stretch and expand from a nearby area, and then reconnect. As she submerged her thoughts in the healing trance, focusing on the wounds, she also sensed the man's troubled conscience writhing in turmoil.

Her barriers notwithstanding, flashes of battle imagery assailed her as she worked, throwing off her concentration and making the task more difficult. Twice she had to pause to focus on rebuilding her shields. Sweat broke out on her brow. She continued her work, sensing her energy wane. She checked herself. There should be enough.

The thoughts of her charge writhed in confusion as she worked. She redoubled her focus. An intense vision of swords cutting through limbs and blood streaming out from the wounds assailed her. So much blood! He broke through her weakened barriers. An image flared at her — a comrade dropping to the ground. An arrow came out of nowhere to pierce his chest. Lirienne could feel his despair as he watched his friend die in his arms, just as if she had experienced it herself. More arrows rained down on them as he tried to shelter the dead man's body, leaving his own unprotected. All her patient could think of was that he couldn't return a body all mangled with arrows to his friend's loving family.

Before long, Lirienne had tears in her eyes and, soon after, her cheeks were drenched. This happened much too often, but there was nothing she could do about it.

Lirienne had to halt her healing once more in order to rebuild the barricade to protect her thoughts. She strained to push back the anguished memories and construct a stronger mental shield. Once she had done so, she continued her work, but the image of the dead man was etched onto her brain now, along with a terrible sense of grief, and nothing she could do would erase it. She worked diligently at healing while she held off the need to cry great, gasping sobs.

She shaped and extended the bones of the arm, reconnecting

the broken fragments and making everything more solid. The muscles in the arm, too, needed to be regrown, long enough to reconnect the torn parts. The detail was excruciating, and her energy and ability to focus were almost gone now. She trembled as fatigue set in, but she wouldn't let the supervisor have the satisfaction of seeing her collapse.

With a gasp, Lirienne withdrew from her patient's body, her psyche thin and threadbare from having experienced everything the soldier had shared.

She signaled his waiting comrades to come over and they lifted him away. Her mind reeled with images of battle. She shook her head in an effort to dismiss. It was to no avail. She needed to leave.

Lirienne raced out of the infirmary as fast as her short legs could take her. Daria waved goodbye, but Lirienne was unable to acknowledge her in her haste.

She paused in the outer room where the healers rested. Leaning against a wall, she tried to recover her composure. She breathed deeply, managing to get the shaking under control. In the healers' recovery room there was a table overflowing with food—breads, cheeses, fruits and sweets. Her guard was waiting there, helping himself, but he stopped as soon as he saw her. She didn't blame him for sneaking a snack. Healers were exempt from the latest food-rationing rules, but almost all others were required to follow them. She should eat now, but she had no appetite even though she had done much work and was extremely weak. She couldn't eat, not with images of war, blood, and death spinning in her head.

CHAPTER EIGHT

Lirienne left the College with her guard in tow. It was late afternoon as she wandered back toward the palace, infected with the turmoil of her last few patients. She was still weak from her work and from not having taken any food. The day, however, was too beautiful not to lift her spirits.

Lake Gerlamaine spread out like a sheet of smooth glass for leagues to the east. The path she walked traced its edge. She smiled at the smell of spring in the air as she basked in the steeply angled sunshine. She couldn't help but be uplifted by the sun's brilliance reflected on the water.

Upon the level plane of the lake's mirrored surface lay a multitude of rectangular patches in many shades of green. These were the floating gardens upon which her people grew essential food crops. Without these gardens, the masses of people who crowded the city would starve. In fact, the whole country of Kalad was brimming over with citizens.

Maru-trained gardeners tended these plots. Working all day in the sun, they measured the quality of the soil, its composition, moistness, and the integrity of the islands of dirt. They monitored the health of the crops they planted with their bare hands laid upon the soil, reaching out, connecting through their sensitive fingers, sensing their plants growing moment by moment, coaxing them to flourish with their thoughts and maru. It was much like healing.

Her father had learned this art in his youth. She'd never seen him wear the sage green robes of the Gardeners Guild and found it difficult to imagine him dressed in any Guild colors, neither the taupe robes of the maru-trained miners nor the steel gray of the warriors' order. The thought made her grin. Her own order wore silver. Almost everyone in Kalad wore the robes of their order, and everyone, except her father, had an order. The king never belonged to a Guild, although he had maru gifts. For a second, she wondered what his other talent had been, for everyone usually had a major gift and a minor one. A guarded man, he had never shared that information with her.

The path veered away and climbed gently. Lirienne slowed her pace. At the crest of the rise, she paused to look down onto the barracks and drill yards of the military compound on the other side. There, soldiers exercised, and others, recently returned from the front, took some rest. There were also Castillonians there, captured and held captive as a result of the conflict her brother had started and her father had continued. Lirienne was tired of watching people die because of it.

The Castillonians were different from her people. They were taller and more muscular. Their skin was bronzed by the sun, which had no effect on the pale Hilliri. An occasional emissary of the countries to the west might appear in court, but otherwise the Hilliri of Kalad and the Trillas (the word the Mundatar used for themselves) stayed on their own sides of the great river. Only Castillon was on the Hilliri side of the great river, and she knew many resented it.

She had learned their language as part of her education. It was the common tongue used in many lands; places not yet touched by war.

The people of Castillon were unusually tall, even for Trillas, with skins tanned by the hot sun of their land. The people there, both men and women, wore their dark hair long, plaited in sections, and woven through with bright-colored ribbons.

The image of these strange folk fascinated Lirienne. In her land, everyone wore their respective, drab guild colors.

As Lirienne wandered down the other side of the hill, she noticed a group of soldiers on the path ahead of her, leading an assembly of Castillonian prisoners, heading toward the compound. The prisoners were an unfortunate-looking lot; their clothing soiled and in tatters, their heads hanging low as they plodded along in single file, heavy manacles connecting ankles and wrists. Several were injured and bleeding.

There was one among them who was taller than the others and more tightly bound across the chest as well as at the wrists. She imagined that this one might be the Slasher, though she couldn't say why she thought so. She felt no pity that he would be sent to the dungeons to wait until the end of the war, unable to bring victory to his people. He might even be put to death for his crimes. It would be vindication for Talora's early demise.

She caught an angry shout from somewhere nearby and

recognized Valran's voice. She saw his compact frame outlined by the sun as he came down from a small hill up ahead, his platinum hair tied in a tight top knot in the fashion of Hilliri soldiers. He approached the group of soldiers under his command, barking orders she couldn't hear from a distance. She hurried forward so she could greet him before he passed through the compound gates.

A soldier broke from Valran's group and turned back toward the captives. He began kicking and punching the nearest one, who then collapsed. Many of the other Hilliri soldiers descended on the fallen man and his comrades, kicking and shouting profanities, their rage infecting one another.

As she neared the scene, red haze suddenly covered Lirienne's vision. Her thoughts shifted back to the memories of her patient. The brutality of the battle, the desperation of it, the terror of dying, and the grief over a fallen comrade, all enveloped her. She gasped, bending over, clutching herself.

Her guard moved to her side. "My lady, are you ill?"

Lirienne waved him off, but the sound of arrows thudding as they sank deep into flesh filled her ears. She tried to tell herself it wasn't what was happening now, but the sounds of the captives being beaten overlapped with the sounds from her memories, or rather, her patient's memories.

She was desperate for the noise and visions to cease. The brutality had to stop. The war must stop.

As she took a step forward to intervene, her guard blocked her way. She looked around him at the melee. Some of the captives tried to protect their fallen comrade, while others who were more loosely tied attempted to use their shackles as weapons, fighting back. More soldiers joined in until the whole group was in the skirmish, brutishly harassing the weakened, chained captives. Yet the sound in her ears was still from that earlier scene in her patient's memory.

Valran joined the fray, aiming directly for the Slasher. It took the help of a few others, but they managed to force the tall man to his knees, and finally onto his side. He fell, struggling and crying out as hard-booted legs kicked deep into his flesh. Tied up as he was, he could do nothing to defend himself. Eventually, the soldiers lost interest and shifted their focus to other captives who were still standing.

The hatred and violence terrified Lirienne. The sound of boots breaking bones and of the Trillas men crying out made her shrink back. If only the world could be silent for a while. An urge to take action charged up within her. She wanted to move forward but her guard still blocked her way. No matter, she would force her way around him if she had to.

A quick shove and she was through. The man was so surprised that he didn't resist. She ran up to where her brother stood over the fallen body of the Slasher. Valran looked very pleased with himself until he caught sight of Lirienne, then his expression turned to annoyance.

"What are you doing here?"

"Stop them! Stop them right now. Please!" She flung herself at him, clinging to his arms, trying to push him away from the man. She was trembling, confused by her memories and what she had just witnessed.

Valran thrust her away from him, standing his ground. "These are prisoners of war, Lirienne. They aided the Slasher in his evil work." He pointed with his chin at the tall man on the ground at his feet. "He deserves no mercy. I won't withhold the payback my soldiers are due."

"Payback?" Lirienne shook her head in confusion.

His expression ignited with fury. "There is no way we're going to let him live, Lirienne, not after all the things he's done. Not after Talora. He's going to die, preferably the slow and very painful death he deserves for causing the deaths of so many of our people. You shouldn't watch this. Go back to your chambers and rest."

Lirienne looked down at the Slasher as he lay curled up on the ground with his eyes shut tight. His chest rose only slightly as he breathed. Soldiers were still kicking him. The image of her patient protecting the body of his friend overlaid with that of the Slasher. She wanted all of this anger and pain to stop.

Lirienne slipped off her gloves. She touched the man on the wrist with her bared hands. Instantly she made contact with his broken body. With her abilities, she could sense the life force bleeding out of him. He was leaking like a pot with holes in it. He would die of his injuries if left unattended. That was wrong. No matter who he had killed, her people should treat their captives the way they would want to be treated had the situation been reversed.

Overlaid on her mental image of his broken insides, Lirienne felt the terror of her earlier patient during battle. She wanted to protect this man, save him from harm, just as her patient had wanted to help his comrade. She wanted desperately to silence the harsh sounds of beatings all around her. The Slasher's vital signs diminished. Panic rose in her. If he died, his people would want revenge and the war would never end.

She felt her power engage. Everything shimmered around her for a brief moment. Then... it all disappeared.

CHAPTER NINE

The scent of pine wafted up Lirienne's nostrils. She was lying on the ground. A padding of dry needles from last fall pricked through the thin cloth of her robe. Water burbled in the distance. She wondered about this. Apparently, she was in a forest near water, though she couldn't recall how she got there.

She turned her head to one side. A Trillas man lay beside her just out of reach. She thought about moving out of his way, for he frightened her, but she was too drained to move, too tired to care. She drifted back into slumber.

She woke again, this time to find the sky dark. A display of stars filtered through the branches above her. A soft moan startled her. The prisoner was still nearby. She recalled what had happened and who the prisoner was. It was the infamous Slasher, and she was alone with him in a dark forest.

Terrified, she pulled herself up against a tree, as far away from him as she could manage. At least there was a carpet of short grass to cushion her there. She stared at his prone form. His eyes were closed and his breathing shallow. She realized that he needed healing if he was going to survive, yet she was afraid to go near him.

Drained beyond anything she had ever experienced, the very thought of rising seemed impossible. She cried, looking up at the stars. It was a terribly stupid thing she had done. She had transported both herself and this stranger right across the river. She knew this could be done using maru, but she'd never been taught how, nor had she ever attempted it. Somehow, on instinct, she had accomplished it, but at a great cost.

She remembered thinking about the place they were now in, a place she had spotted long ago. It was across the river from Kalad, in one of the provinces of the Mundatar, but not the one this man came from. His home, Castillon, was much farther south, where the river met the sea. All she could recall was that she had wanted desperately to get away from the violence. It must have happened then; in the frenzy of the fighting she had pushed them both here with her power.

The man groaned again. She began to reach out but checked herself. He might hurt her, even though she had saved him.

He was still, his chest barely rising. If he was unconscious, he couldn't hurt her. All the stories of his terrible deeds flashed into her mind. How could she help such a man? Yet she had argued for mercy with her brother. She could hardly remember why.

Slowly, she rolled onto her side and crawled across the forest floor until she was close enough to touch him. Her heart pounded as she opened his shirt and placed her hand on his chest. Mental contact was instantaneous, but his mind felt strange, though his body seemed ordinary enough, if over large.

The Mundatar were supposed to be nothing like the Hilliri, though. She knew they lived short, brutal lives, and were careless in their affections with their women, often floating from one lover to another without commitment. Lirienne shuddered to think of it. The Hilliri only married once in spite of their long lives and were reserved in their affections. Still, it wasn't for her to judge the worthiness of a patient to receive healing. That was not what they taught at the College, so she continued.

She assessed his injuries, sorting out what damage was worst, but she was spent. The cost of their transport had been too great. She couldn't afford to use any more maru.

She had been impulsive, and it wasn't the first time. What would happen to her now? Releasing a captive of such infamy might be seen as sedition or treason. Would she be allowed to return or would she be in danger? Would her family protect her or use her as an example?

She rolled onto her back and stifled a sob. She had managed, in one capricious minute, to save this murderer at the expense of her own position and possibly her life. She lay there for a while, waiting for her maru to replenish. In time, even without food, it would rebuild.

The stars overhead gave fair light to the space around her—a small grassy clearing surrounded by pines and patches where the cast-off needles formed spongy piles. The trees created areas of deep gloom nearby, accentuating the bright spaces between them. She looked up again, letting her mind wander, watching how the empty branches of the tree nearest her jutted out in various directions. Farther up the trunk though, groups of needles swirled around each limb making a soft covering.

The scene calmed her. The beautiful garden at her chambers

often made her feel the same way. But despair rose in her as she realized that she might never see that special place again. Still, the calm of this glade, with the shushing water nearby and the delicate sounds of the night brought her some tranquility.

Her gaze shifted between the distant branches and the nearer ones. It was odd how the lower branches lacked needles, yet the upper ones were fully covered. She closed her eyes, giving in to her weariness.

Lying back, she lifted her arms over her head and pressed her bare hands into the nearby trunk. Lirienne could sense maru flowing up and down the length of the tree. There was maru everywhere; she knew that, of course. She could sense it in the other trees around her, in the ground beneath her, and in the man who lay beside her.

She looked again at the stranger. She sensed his maru, even from here, but only dimly. She knew that meant he wouldn't live much longer, not without her help.

She touched the supple carpet of tiny blades of grass and watched them sway as they sprang back. There was a way to acquire maru, but the College Masters had taught that it was dangerous and difficult to draw maru from other things and refused to show their students how to do it.

Lirienne froze at the thought, her hand hovering just above the grass. Holding her breath, she placed her palm lightly on the ground, compressing the tufts. They were insignificant enough that she doubted it would do much harm to try. She closed her eyes and tried to sense the maru, as if she was healing a body.

Her fingers warmed with the contact. She sensed maru under her palm. Taking felt wrong, hurtful, and it required more concentration for her to reach out and draw in what was there, but she did manage to collect a small sample. With her waning strength and a patient in need, Lirienne would not hesitate.

She turned to face a tree. She sensed its maru was more substantial. She touched the rough bark—the coolness of it came first, then the warmth as she drew maru out from it. It was easier this time, the maru almost leaping to her hand, into her body, warming her cold insides. It strengthened her trembling arms.

It flowed even faster now, flying into her like a lightning strike, sparks pricking sharply as it flowed up her arms and into her torso. The unpleasantness made her want to withdraw, but at the same time, she desperately needed to continue. The power filled her until she felt taller, larger, greater somehow than she had ever felt before.

She trembled again, only this time it was with the brimming excess of maru that filled her. She must stop, but she couldn't. Her hands wouldn't move. A pressure built behind her eyes. It frightened her. The world began to blur, and Lirienne finally fell, her grasp of the tree broken as she lost all thought.

46

CHAPTER TEN

I t was light again when Lirienne woke once more. Morning had come and she felt whole —strong, in fact. She pushed herself to sitting from where she had fallen and leaned against the tree once more.

She rested there for a minute, savoring the strangeness. She had taken life force from a tree. Glancing up at its branches, it surprised her to see that it was now only a dry, lifeless husk, blackened as if struck by lightning. It made her shudder, but then, it was only a tree.

The time had come to do what she could for the man she had swept away from almost certain death. Looking over, she was relieved to see that he was still clinging to life. Lirienne rose to her knees. She inhaled the sharp pine-scented air until she felt steady. She approached him again; this time with a healer's assessing gaze. One eyelid was swollen to double its size. His lips cut and bruised. She found a smooth, undamaged spot among the many purpling bruises on his chest and placed her bare hands there.

As she touched him, the world spun briefly then settled, as it always did. Closing her eyes, she followed the awareness of her arms through to her hands, then beyond herself, into him. Searching the pathways of his blood and sinew, seeking out the places where things were awry, Lirienne made a mental inventory of all of the man's injuries, prioritizing them. There was little time left, having waited so long. Starting with the worst damage, she worked quickly. At least, she now had the power to do it.

An artery in his shoulder bulged dangerously. It hadn't burst, but it would if the flow of blood kept up its force. Lirienne shored up the walls that surrounded it by multiplying strong, healthy cells. She calmed his heart to reduce the pressure until the healing set.

There was a crack in his jawbone and in one arm, damage to one of his kidneys, and many broken ribs, the result of being kicked by hard boots. As Lirienne knit the bones back into place, she encouraged his body to repair itself by stimulating cell growth. She took her time, nudging and knitting, then breaking up the swelling in the muscles that surrounded the breaks. She silently cursed the soldiers and her brother for providing her with such an enormous task.

As Lirienne worked, the stranger warmed. She kept her mental barriers up to block stray thoughts from slipping through. The last thing she wanted was to explore the mind of a murderer.

Lirienne checked his life force once more after she had dealt with the last broken bone, and when she saw that all was well, she withdrew her awareness until she was no longer linked with him.

She shivered. Again, she realized, she had come dangerously close to the limit of her store of maru. Healing this patient taxed her more than doing several others. She considered tapping another tree, but the blackened husk of the first one reminded her of the intensity of the experience. She sat back and rested. She needed food, but there was none around. She felt drab and listless. She recalled how well she had felt when she woke this morning—strong, healthy, and bright. She craved the return of her strength. Looking about, she saw hundreds of tall pines all around her. What harm would there be if there were two blackened trees in the forest instead of one? She would be more careful this time.

She reached out again, this time to a different tree, and began to siphon maru. Although she was more prepared for the intensity of the draw, Lirienne still struggled to stop when she had enough. This time, she managed to do so sooner. With a sharp pang of regret, she pulled away from the tree somewhat short of satisfied and still tired from her healing work.

Lirienne shivered as a thought occurred to her. Such great evil could be done with this knowledge. She battled fatigue and fear for as long as she could, and fatigue finally won.

CHAPTER ELEVEN

When Lirienne opened her eyes again, the world was full of brilliant light streaming down into the clearing. She must have slept for hours, for she felt well and truly rested.

Propping herself up using her elbows on her bed of pine needles and loam, she took in her surroundings.

Across the clearing lay the prostrate form of the man she had rescued. His chest rose and fell in regular intervals. Memories of the last few days flooded back into Lirienne's mind.

He was the Slasher. She wanted to run far away from here, far from him and from all of her troubles. While she had saved him from a certain death, she didn't imagine she was safe in his presence. How he must hate the Hilliri to have attacked unsuspecting soldiers as they walked through the dense forest, or even worse, while they slept in their tents. He was rumored to have killed as many as fifty at a time. Lirienne could find no honor in such actions.

His hands were still chained. So far, he hadn't moved. Not even a twitch, which meant she might have time before he woke to figure out what to do.

Hearing the splash of water nearby, she elected to locate the river and orient herself. In the light of day it wasn't difficult to find the Eraldis River. It was flush and overflowing with meltwater from the ice-topped mountains in the north.

Lirienne thought of washing herself, for she was covered in dirt and bits of decomposing pine needles had worked their way into her hair and clothing. But as she approached the river's edge, a chill radiated off the water and she realized it would be too cold for that.

She contented herself with sitting near the edge and scooping up handfuls of water to splash on her face. As she leaned over the riverbank, she spotted the spires of her city through the trees on the far side.

Home. It wasn't that far away, but given her situation, the possibility of returning felt hopelessly remote. She needed time to think about how to proceed. She leaned back and looked up at the blue sky overhead. Clouds floated by.

Would her family protect her if returned? Sometimes it was hard to know their minds. They would certainly be angry at what she had done, but it wouldn't be the first time she'd been impulsive.

Suddenly, her view was filled with eyes of brilliant blue, framed by long dark lashes and bronzed flesh. A flutter of panic grabbed her, and she scrambled back from the Slasher. He was still in chains but had managed to flip his bindings to the front. He furrowed his dark brows.

"Can you understand me? How did I get here, and where are my soldiers?"

Lirienne shook her head, terrified of his nearness and unable to release her voice.

He was so tall and muscular. He had spoken in the common tongue of the Mundatar—Trillas, she corrected herself—but with the thick accent of Castillon. His voice was deeper and more resonant than she was accustomed to. Being small, Lirienne felt fragile and delicate in his shadow.

Perhaps he sensed this, for he leaned back, giving her some space. Lirienne relaxed slightly.

He looked down at his chained hands and his chest through the shreds of his shirt. He shook his head in confusion. "How is it that I'm no longer injured? Last I can recall, I was a prisoner in Kalad, but I think we're across the river in Argentia now."

Lirienne heard his voice soften and she had calmed enough to find her own voice. "I'm a healer."

She spoke the common tongue of the Trillas passably. She rarely had the chance to use it. The Trillas weren't allowed to move freely about in Kalad. No doubt her accent was as odd to him as his was to her.

"I brought you here a few nights ago."

The man stared at her.

"I could only take one person, and you were the one receiving the worst beating. I'm sorry I couldn't help the others."

She looked up at this stranger, examining his face. He wanted answers. He needed to understand. She realized the Trillas knew little about maru and how the Hilliri used it. He wouldn't comprehend.

"But we're on the other side of the river, in Argentia. We were in Kaldene City when..." He shook his head. "You brought me? How?"

"As well as healing, I have the ability to transport."

His mouth dropped open. He stared at her, eyes narrowing, pulling back a step. Perhaps she should have said less about her abilities.

A sharp pain needled her in the stomach. A loud gurgle followed. How long had it been since she'd eaten? She sat up, waiting for her strength to return.

"We're going to need food," he said. "I will set some traps to see if I can catch something for us to eat. Can you... release me from these?" He held up his hands with the manacles and chains binding them.

Lirienne didn't have the key, but she could probably remove his bindings the same way she transported. It was a risk, freeing him, but she needed food soon, and she had no skills to acquire it for herself, other than gathering a few berries. She couldn't survive on maru siphoned from trees alone.

She reached out a hand and touched the cold iron on his wrists. She imagined the assembly piled on the ground. She drew her maru like water from a well and applied it to the vision.

The man gasped.

Lirienne opened her eyes and saw that she had indeed removed his chains.

He rubbed his wrists, then trained his bright eyes on her and spoke solemnly. "Thank you. I owe you a debt for your assistance, my Lady Savior. I will need some time to set traps and start a fire."

Lirienne blushed at his naming of her. "I'm going to gather some berries. I saw some earlier along the riverbank."

He lowered his head. "When I have found some food, I will return. Will you be all right here for a while? These woods are hunted often so there shouldn't be too many predators about."

Lirienne concurred.

He turned away and dashed off into the thicker part of the forest. In a moment he was gone.

It seemed he had some appreciation for the effort she had expended to bring him back to health. For now, circumstances forced her to trust him. She stumbled along the river's edge, looking back occasionally, not quite sure she had made the right choice, wondering if he would even return to her or flee instead.

After hunting for a while, she managed to collect a small handful of berries. She had probably expended more energy in gathering them than they would provide in nourishment.

As she inched along the soft riverbank, collecting a final few, she came to a muddy section where she had to step back a little and walk around. Upon turning toward the river, she chanced onto a large bush, hidden under a shrub of another kind. She stepped right up to the ledge overhanging the water and was obliged to walk out onto the soft sand of the bank in order to reach the large supply of blueberries available on this one bush. It was muddy here too, and her shoe stuck while she leaned toward it.

As she tugged her foot out of the muck, the shoe remained stuck. Her foot slipped free, however, and she overbalanced, going forward toward the shrubs. They were prickly and she wanted to avoid landing on them, so she twisted to fall to one side, into the water. She landed awkwardly with her wrist striking a rock and she cried out in pain.

She curled the hurt hand into her chest and held it with the other, but a heavy surge of water swirled into the little inlet where she'd fallen and overtook her. The sudden chill made her gasp as the current swept her away down the swift-flowing river.

She shouted out as loud a cry as her small voice could muster and struggled to swim back to shore as the current dragged her along, but the river picked up speed, edging her out into the center where the flow was even faster and the water deeper. Lirienne began to shiver uncontrollably as the cold penetrated her body. Her teeth chattered. Her hands went numb. She was too far from shore to swim back now and getting more tired by the minute as she floated downstream.

Somewhere in the back of her mind, she knew the process. She was a healer, after all, and had studied such things. She felt light and sleepy. That was a bad sign. Even worse, she was too far out to reach any overhanging branches. She looked back and saw the spot where she had fallen in as it became more and more distant. She passed the place where she had viewed the spires of her city. Then she passed beyond the city limit and was now somewhere in the countryside to the south. Small farmhouses dotted the open landscape here, but she saw no one.

A piece of wood floated nearby, and she reached out a hand to grasp it. She pulled herself up on it, its buoyancy supporting her. She fell asleep several times as she floated. Leagues, it seemed, were rolling by, but she knew she had only minutes to get out of the frigid water, and no strength left for the task.

She laughed at the irony. Knowing exactly how she was going to die, exactly what was happening to her body, yet unable to do anything. She went over the details. When the shivering stopped, things were progressing. When she became sleepy, it wouldn't be long. She might do something rash, something inadvisable as her mind shut down to preserve her strength. It didn't matter now, but she would have liked to return home. So many still needed healing. She would have liked to see what she could've done to stop this awful war.

It would have been nice.

CHAPTER TWELVE

"Hold on to me!" A deep voice called to her. "I'll help you to shore."

Lirienne lifted her head up from the wood she clung to, seeing bright white teeth flashing against bronzed skin fast approaching as she drifted. Bare to the waist, the Slasher gritted his teeth. He swam out, nearing her as she drifted along. Taller and heavier, he had better control in the swift-flowing water. As he neared, he held out his hand and she grasped it with the last of her strength. He slipped his arms around her back and held her fast against his chest. Lirienne continued to shiver, her teeth clacking together as she pressed against his warmth.

Judging by the angle of the sun, it must have been late afternoon when Lirienne woke to find herself wrapped in a torn and dirty shirt and covered in a pile of dry leaves. Still shivering, but less than before, her hands and feet ached. A strip of cloth wrapped her sore wrist.

The man kneeled down to inspect her. She wished she knew his name, but asking him would mean sharing hers, and if he knew who she was, he might make her a hostage to gain some advantage in the war. He held out something on a stick. Lirienne sniffed. It was meat, something small, cooked over a fire. What animal had he caught? Her stomach grumbled with the temptation of food even though she didn't know what it was. It had been hours, or perhaps even days, but she couldn't use her hands. They were too stiff from the cold, and her wrist stung when she tried to open her palm. Noting that she didn't take it, he broke off a chunk and held it up to her lips. She decided it was important to eat it, despite her aversion. No longer in the palace, she could not expect the same things she had had as a princess.

It was difficult to chew since her teeth chattered so much, but the food went down well and nourished her. She ate several small bits in this manner until her trembling lessened. Food, she knew, would help her warm up, but receiving it like this embarrassed her. She looked up at him, the Slasher, a name she could no longer use, and smiled. He had called her his savior.

"You came back."

"I went looking for some food, and once I had made a trap and caught something, I started a fire. It was a good thing I headed back upstream, or I would never have spotted you."

Lirienne wrapped the large shirt tighter around herself. She realized, with a start, that it was his shirt she wore, not her own clothing. She looked up to see him redden.

"Your wet clothing prevented you from warming up. I hope you will excuse me for taking the liberty. It was necessary and I had very little to work with."

Lirienne shook her head and waved a hand. It was the correct treatment for hypothermia; the wet clothing would have kept her chilled. As uncomfortable as the thought was, she was grateful that he had known what to do.

He licked his lips, searching for words. "Castillonians are a sea-faring people. While working on the fishing boats as a boy, I learned how to treat exposure to cold."

Lirienne nodded, still too addled to talk much. She knew she was staring but couldn't help it. The infamous Slasher. She was at his mercy now, but rather than take her life, he had risked his own to save her. It wasn't how she was used to thinking about the Trillas, and certainly not about this one in particular.

"You need to rest now that you've eaten something," he said. "I'll check the traps and see if I can get a little bit more for later."

He left her to rest. She dozed, drifting in and out, shivering all the while and thinking about the man who had rescued her. He certainly was not what she expected. She didn't trust him entirely, but his honorable behavior allowed her to relax a little. Whatever he was, he wasn't a threat to her. He'd had too many opportunities to kill her or take advantage of her, and he had only been kind and respectful.

He returned and sat by the fire, spitting another small animal and setting it to roast.

Lirienne lifted herself up to sitting, wincing from the stabbing pain in her bandaged wrist while doing so. Her hands had stopped trembling. She calculated the worst effects of her exposure had subsided. A warm bath would be so nice right now, but of course, it wasn't going to happen.

"I believe we're even now."

He looked at her sidewise. "Does this mean we aren't going to be friends?" He grinned, which looked rather foolish.

She could use a friend right now.

He chewed on a blade of grass while he turned the spit. The meat sizzled. It was starting to smell very good, though she probably didn't want to know what animal it had come from. She eyed her new friend. He returned to her side with a fresh piece of roasted meat, which he offered her on the stick. She took it and began to nibble. He watched her as she chewed.

She looked over at him as he stared. "Does my eating amuse you?"

He shook his head. "No, I'm just thinking... trying to figure out how to free my men."

Her stomach turned at the thought. She drew the food away from her mouth and sat up straighter. "You'd set them free so they can continue to attack and kill my people?"

He blinked in surprise and his mouth dropped open.

She continued, her anger spooling up. "I want to see an end to this war, not an escalation."

He lowered his head and played with a stone on the ground. After a moment, his eyes returned to lock with hers. "No one wants war."

Lirienne shook her head. It surprised her that he spoke with such passion. "I was under the impression you liked murder and mayhem, and the more deaths, the better."

The man froze. "You think I like killing? You're mistaken. I wish I could be anywhere else, doing anything else, but I was ordered to defend my people and my country against invaders."

Now it was Lirienne's turn to be tongue-tied. "But—you attack people when they are unaware, sleeping, or simply walking about. That isn't an honorable way to fight."

He turned his bright eyes on her and looked very sad. "It's the only kind of war Castillon can fight against your people. We are outnumbered, out trained, and out supplied. What I do evens the odds just a little bit. It may seem brutal to you. If I had options, I would do things differently."

Lirienne left a space of silence to think. He was more a man of honor than she had ever considered. She had never thought of how much better the army of Kalad was organized and equipped than the Castillonians, nor how few the Castillonians numbered. Nor had she considered that her people had invaded Castillon in the first place. They used maru to fight as well, a huge advantage over the Trillas who had none. If his liege lord commanded him to fight, he was duty bound to obey. He had even found a way to overcome great odds to defend his land.

But he had said one thing that resonated strongly with her. That he didn't want to fight... that he wanted to stop the war.

CHAPTER THIRTEEN

Two days of rest and feeding did much to improve Lirienne's outlook. She stayed close to the fire, taking advantage of its heat, and when her clothing finally dried, she headed into the woods to change and returned with the shirt that the Slasher had lent her folded up in her arms.

He was sitting across from where she stood in front of the fire. Still bare-chested, he tended the flames as he cooked.

Lirienne wrinkled her nose. "Squirrel again?"

"They like my traps. There are a lot of them."

Lirienne reached over and held out the shirt. "Thank you for the loan. I'm sure you would like to have this back."

He looked up at her, and she noticed his cheeks redden. He slipped the shirt on over his head and wriggled it down onto his chest. He licked his lips and cleared his throat. "I apologize again for the way—"

Now Lirienne was blushing. "It's fine, really. Thank you for saving me."

She took her place across from him once more. For a while, neither Lirienne nor her companion spoke. She watched him through the flames, observing his graceful movements, despite the length of his limbs.

He'd been nothing other than thoroughly polite and solicitous to her. She was certain he was noble born—he had to be, with his education and manners—and the fact that he played a major role in the defense of his land. Doubtless, he presumed the same of her... but what was his name, and who was he really? She wished she could ask him, but that would be dangerous.

***

Lirienne was still tired beyond what she had expected. She thought about draining another tree but pushed the idea aside. To do so, she would have to slip away unseen, but she was too unsteady for that. Instead, she enjoyed the quiet of the forest—

only birdsong and the sound of rushing water to fill the silences. Kalad was crowded with people, making silence a rare and precious thing.

As her companion turned their next meal on its wooden spit, he observed her often, looking down only occasionally to check the meat for doneness.

"How does it work, your healing?"

Lirienne smiled. "The power is called maru, and it's applied using the mind, to shape and fix the parts of the body that are damaged."

His thick brows furrowed. "You mean you just think and it all works... everything gets fixed?"

Lirienne shook her head. "You make it sound so easy, like a wave of the hand, but it's very difficult and requires years of training and a thorough knowledge of the body's workings."

"So, you are highly trained then. But it still seems like magic."

Of course, it would. Lirienne thought about a different way to explain. "You have healers too, in your land? They know how the body works and what to do to repair damage. It's the same, only we use maru to effect it, rather than cutting with knives and patching with a needle and thread." Lirienne played with a strand of her hair as she spoke. Healing was all she knew. At least she knew it well. "But our maru is greatly limited. We are only allowed to apply it under certain circumstances."

He sighed and stretched out. He had the longest legs she had ever seen, although his arms were almost as impressive. His hair was dark—so different from the Hilliri. Yet, when she watched him now, he seemed correct.

She shifted, uncomfortable as much with the hard ground as with the direction of her thoughts. Others would think her mad already, having stopped the beating of captive Trillas. Most of the Hilliri actively hated the Mundatar, or at the very least, thought of them as little better than beasts. She had heard of this man's exploits, of how he dropped out of nowhere and wreaked havoc on her people, leaving a trail of bloodied bodies wherever he went. A scene of bloodstained horror filled her mind; the one the soldier had imprinted on her that had led to all of this. She blinked and shivered.

"Are you cold?"

Lirienne shook her head. He had been kind and helpful. How could he also have done all of those terrible things? She knew that he had, because she had seen it in his mind when she was healing him, even though she set barriers when she worked. As usual, she'd had difficulty keeping them up, and when she slipped, his memories of all the people he'd killed had seeped in. The men he held in his hands as they died, and the women he made love to as well. Lirienne blushed. Her sensitivity made it possible for her to see it all, even though she would rather not. But to love and hate so intensely must be terribly destructive. She had not delved deeply into his psyche, for it had been his body that needed immediate care, but surely, she thought, his mind would tear itself apart. Yet, he didn't look like a man on the brink of an emotional collapse.

She met his eyes and shivered again at their intense blueness.

He looked concerned. "Are you sure you're all right?"

Lirienne watched the flames dance. The dying fire crackled as its heat reached a knot of resin which burst into a spray of sparks. One landed on Lirienne's ragged robes. Her companion pounced, extinguishing it with his bare hand. For a moment, his face was close to hers. She held her breath and pulled back from him.

He sat back as well.

Lirienne organized the tatters of her gown. "You are very gallant. I suppose this means I owe you another life saved."

"Are we keeping score now?"

She reached out and took his hand to check for burns. In a moment of inattentiveness, she accidentally touched his palm with hers and their minds forged an instant link. She tensed, annoyed that she had neglected her barriers again. As their eyes met, their minds examined one another's. Lirienne sensed his respect and interest. She released his hand and broke the connection, turning away.

This isn't right... isn't natural, she thought, but those thoughts belonged to other people—people like her tiresome, proper sister. Hilliri and Trillas did not mind-speak to one another.

He looked puzzled. "What just happened?"

Lirienne covered her mouth with her hand. "Forgive me. I accidentally forged a mind-link between us when I was checking your hand. It happens when I touch someone without wearing my gloves." The gloves had been lost days before.

He shifted his weight backward. "Are you saying that you can hear what goes on in my head?"

Once more, she'd managed to let her guard slip. When would she learn? She couldn't blame him for finding it disturbing. It made most people uncomfortable, even the Hilliri who all shared these abilities. But it cost them to keep their thoughts barred away.

It kept them from connecting with one another in the deepest, most enduring way.

"You can hear what I think as well, unless I take special care to create a block." She wondered what he had 'heard.' Sometimes it would be just emotions and impressions, other times there would be words.

The impulse to yawn crept over her and she gave in to it.

He shifted once more, to be solicitous. "Do you want to rest now? I can keep watch for a while."

Lirienne hadn't thought about watches, but he was right. There was no reason to believe it was safe in this forest. "Please wake me up to take a shift. You need to rest as well."

He agreed, and Lirienne stretched herself out beside the fire across from him. She turned her back toward the heat, but even without facing him, she felt his eyes on her, and her mind wouldn't release her from the memory of his thoughts.

"A man usually expects his thoughts to be his own," he said.

Lirienne realized he might be finding her just as dangerous as she found him. "I'm sorry. I must try harder to keep my mind blocked."

He softened. "Rest, please, my lady. I didn't mean to complain."

CHAPTER FOURTEEN

irienne woke suddenly. It was the middle of the night. For a moment, she had no idea where she was. She looked around for danger but saw none. Her companion was still there, his body propped against a tree, his eyes focused on the distance. Dark curls tumbled over his brow and across his foreign face. Regardless of his strangeness, his presence reassured her. She knew he would protect her.

She stared up at the canopy of pine trees. Their scraggly dark branches laced together in the gaps, making a pattern through which the starry sky beamed. Life seemed simple out here in the middle of nowhere. There was only the two of them, a forest and a river.

He shifted his gaze to her and smiled. "You've rested somewhat, my lady?"

Lirienne stretched out. "You should have a turn to sleep now. You must be tired."

He shook his head, rose from his place, and headed out into the thick of trees.

Lirienne followed. "Where are you going?"

He stopped a short distance from the fire and crouched down, staring at the ground. "Just checking my traps."

Lirienne noticed a contraption made of several sticks and a heavy rock at his feet. It looked as if it could easily be knocked over, but as she studied it, she could imagine how it would fall, trapping a small animal under the rock, knocking it out. The roughly cut twigs fit together perfectly. She realized with amazement that he had made this without tools.

"Where did you learn how to make such a device?"

He lifted the rock and checked under it. Nothing. "My older brother taught me wood lore when I was a boy." His face closed up and his expression became flat.

Lirienne reached out and touched his arm. "I'm sorry I asked."

He turned his head away to hide his face. She could see tension in his jaw line.

"The war?"

"Yes."

The war affected everyone. Facing toward the firelight now, she caught the sadness in his eyes. She wanted to cheer him up, but it wouldn't have been right. Sometimes it was necessary to hold onto sadness. "You see why I want to stop it?"

"I would have it over as well, but I'm not sure how to make it happen. People are angry. Every time someone like my brother dies at the hands of your people, it fires up their fury and makes them want to fight more."

Lirienne thought of Talora and recognized that this was happening on her side as well.

He looked away from the fire once more and wandered farther into the brush. The starlight was intense on this cloudless night, illuminating his path through the woods. He stopped again, crouching down to check another twig-and-stone trap.

"That captain who caught me, the one who looks like he might be your kinsman... he killed my brother. I found him dead, and that man had just left the house." The muscles in his jaw worked harder.

Lirienne could hardly draw breath. "I'm sorry. He is my brother."

He continued on, deeper into the woods. Lirienne followed as best she could, falling behind him with his long strides.

He spun around to glare at her. "He killed my brother and his woman in their bed while they slept."

All air compressed out of her lungs. Lirienne struggled to calm herself.

He closed his eyes and breathed in. "She was with child," he said softly.

Lirienne, who valued lives and tried to save people every day with her healing, couldn't speak. Losing a child was a great tragedy.

He wandered further.

She reached out an arm. "I'm sorry. I wish I could do something. I'm sorry."

He looked up at the sky. The brightness of the dome of stars lit the whole forest in between the branches of the trees. A shadow fell on his face and she couldn't read his expression.

"Then help me free my men from their prison. Return me to Kalad, somewhere near where they are being held, and I can do the rest."

Lirienne cast her gaze out into the darkened forest. She couldn't do what he asked, no matter how much she owed him. No matter what Valran had done to his brother and his brother's wife.

"I can't help you. Not with that."

He frowned. "I don't understand. You said you wanted to do something."

Lirienne shook her head. "I freed you when you were being beaten. It may have been at great cost to my own position, I don't know. If I return to my home, my family may be able to protect me, but there are limits. I don't know how I will be received after what I've done."

He stared at the stars for a while, then looked down at her. "I didn't think of that. I'm sorry." His dark brows furrowed. "But I can't return home knowing they are being held captive and are likely to be put to death. I must try to help them."

Lirienne looked away from his stare. She swallowed hard. "Yet, if you free them, they will go back to fighting and killing. You will be consigning me to days of exhaustive healing as I try to undo the damage they will continue to inflict on my people. The killing will never end."

Anger flashed across his face. "Yet by not doing anything to free them, I am consigned to live with the knowledge that they died and I did nothing, although your people had attacked my land, and my people only tried to defend themselves."

Lirienne stared at her companion in frustration. He was right, but then so was she.

He walked back toward the fire. She followed him, not knowing what else to do.

His posture changed then. He held out a hand, entreating her. "I don't want you to suffer. You have been more generous than I have any right to expect. It makes a difference. I understand how this war has affected you, how you suffer when you heal soldiers, and how the war has forced you into a tedious life of mending broken soldiers. I would like to help change that."

Lirienne leaned forward to listen.

He chewed his lip. "If you help me now, I will work with you to stop the war."

Lirienne's heart leaped at the thought. "Can you do that? What influence do you have?"

He paused, thinking, keeping his stare steady on her. "To convince you, I have to tell you who I am, and that would put me in greater danger. You must promise me you won't change the plan once I tell you."

Lirienne's heart pounded as she considered that the balance of the world might be tipping in her favor. Who could he be? She didn't see any other choice than to agree.

"I give you my word."

He swallowed hard. "I trust you. I think you know I wouldn't harm you, and I believe that you wouldn't harm me either."

She agreed.

He dropped to his knees, but he was still able to look down at her. "I am Lorenzo Calimero, son of Carlosi, and heir to Castillon."

Lirienne shook her head in denial. She almost grinned. It was too perfect, too symmetrical. "Then it's only fair that you know who I am as well."

Lorenzo tilted his head in puzzlement.

"Lirienne, youngest daughter of King Tarkhan Godehera."

He shook his head and laughed. Lirienne laughed too.

"Perhaps we can do something, daughter of Tarkhan. Together we may yet stop a war."

He had called her his savior, but in the end, Lirienne believed that he might be hers.

CHAPTER FIFTEEN

The tree turned black within seconds. A smoky, charred scent filled her nostrils. Lirienne felt wonderful as she absorbed the maru from it, filling up to almost overflowing, this time with practiced skill. It was the third time she had done this, and it was starting to get easier. She felt aglow, as if the maru could shine through her body like a light, but she knew it was an invisible power. Her companion would be none the wiser.

She returned to the clearing where Lorenzo was stamping out the fire. He swept the waste from their cooking into a shallow hole and covered it with dirt. Looking down at the wreck of her robe, Lirienne realized she would have to go to her room first and change in order for her ruse to be effective.

Lorenzo dusted off his hands on his filthy pants.

They were both a ragged mess.

"Are you ready?" he asked.

"Yes. We'll go to my chambers first, where I can get a fresh robe."

Lorenzo looked down at her. "What do I do now?"

Lirienne smiled. "Just take my hand. I'll do the work. You're just coming along for the ride."

Lirienne wished she were more confident than she sounded. She had only done this once—twice if you counted the manacles. If she understood the theory correctly, all she had to do is keep an image of where she wanted to go firmly in her mind, reach into her store of maru, and push herself there. Lorenzo just needed to be touching her to come along. This was her minor talent, the one other thing she could do besides healing. It had come to her late, as often was the case with secondary gifts.

She wrapped her hands in a strip of cloth from her ragged robe. This would have to do. She held out a hand to Lorenzo, who took it gently in his own. His strong hands dwarfed her tiny ones. He watched her from his towering height, something she wouldn't grow accustomed to quickly, and waited. She closed her eyes and brought the image of her home into her mind. The chambers were large and airy, with an enclosed garden. She would aim for there. She spent a great deal of time out in her garden, exploring the plants and flowers, soaking up the sun during the day or the stars at night. She knew every corner and wasn't likely to miss.

Her store of maru, brimming over from the tree she had wasted, was there for her to dip into and apply to transport. She exhaled, her body strong and bright. She took a measure from it and pushed herself into the other place.

For a moment, it was cold and dark, unlike the forest clearing they had stood in. After several heartbeats, the world brightened, and she could discern the grey walls that surrounded the garden and smell the fresh dirt and growing things. Lorenzo still held her hands in his; his mouth opened wide and his eyes popped with amazement. He released her hands, and she held a finger up to her pursed lips. They must not alert the palace guards to their presence.

"Wait here. I won't be long." She indicated a tree-shaded bench in a corner where he could remain undetected. He saluted her and left, crouching uncomfortably low to prevent detection over the high walls.

He was too tall for her world.

Lirienne slipped into her chambers. Everything remained as she had left it several mornings ago when she had gone off to meet Lord Pirvan and had then been called in to work an extra shift. So much had changed since then.

She found some water and a clean gown and rushed through the effort to appear normal again. For the ruse to work, she had to appear perfectly ordinary.

She would have to transport them to the jail, for there was no way to wander the halls undetected, not with a very tall Trillas in tow. Also, should she be found, there would be questions and possibly consequences. She had disappeared for days and taken a prisoner with her.

From her bedroom, she transported, this time imagining the dark corner of the hall near the jail and conveying herself there. The drain was much less than the previous time, which made sense. The distance traveled wasn't far. She still had maru enough to fetch Lorenzo and return after she assessed the situation.

She listened to the sounds in the hallway. In the distance, she heard footsteps and a door open and close. More footsteps sounded from another source and direction. She waited, trying to determine where the walker was going. She realized there were two pairs of steps. They were coming closer.

She flattened herself against the wall, knowing she was hidden but still feeling exposed. The steps passed by, right behind her wall. The jingling of a sword belt with its metal links and buckles was loud in her ears.

"The king has decided what to do with our captives."

Valran! The voice was so familiar. Lirienne resisted the temptation to reveal herself and seek his help.

"Yes Commander. What has he ordered then?" This voice was male, but not one she knew.

"They're all going to be executed for crimes of war. It will be done publicly, at midday."

The voices drifted off as they passed out of range. It was late morning now. There was no time to spare.

Lirienne made quick work of locating the prisoners. They were all locked up in the same cellblock, a long hallway with numerous separate chambers lining its length. She entered, wearing her veil, and demanded to see the soldiers to assess their health, and the guard, nervous of the presence of a healer, granted her access without question. The silver robes were often an easy passport to entry where others might be barred.

Only one of the prisoners appeared unable to travel, having a broken leg. Another was weak from internal bleeding, and she dealt with both of these easily. The looks on their faces when they felt their pain disappear in moments amused Lirienne.

At each cell, she whispered quickly to the captives to be ready to leave should an opportunity appear. She felt as if she needed to repeat herself, for each of them just stared at her as if she had spoken a language they didn't know, but Lorenzo had assured her they all spoke the common tongue and would understand. It seemed they were simply incredulous that a Hilliri woman would help them.

After slipping back into her room, she returned to the garden and Lorenzo. He sat on the ground in the corner, crouched low enough to remain undetected.

"The bench would have been adequate." Lirienne chided him for sitting on the dusty ground.

"I wanted to be absolutely sure. If anyone finds me here, I suspect I'm as good as dead."

She had to agree. "We have to hurry. An execution order is set for noon. They will come and move the prisoners a little while before to take them to the public square where it will be done. We must release them before that happens or it will be too late."

Lorenzo looked up at the sky to determine the sun's angle. Lines of worry appeared on his face. "We're almost out of time."

Lirienne grabbed his hands in her freshly gloved ones. In a blink, they were both back behind the wall in the prison. Lirienne leaned against it for a moment. She had become dizzy.

Lorenzo shook his head, as if to clear it of fog. "I'll never get used to that."

Lirienne looked up into his bright eyes. "Remember your promise. You won't kill any of the guards."

"I don't have any weapons in any case."

Lirienne peered out from behind the wall. The hallway was empty save for one guard by the entrance to the jail. What she was about to do gave her pause. Working against her own people and using maru against them felt all wrong, but she could see no other way. These were the tools she had to work with.

She signaled to Lorenzo to remain in place, then covered her face with the veil, stepped out into the passage, and walked up to the soldier. She attempted to move confidently, as if she belonged. When she arrived in front of the man, she waited expectantly for him to acknowledge her.

The man's eyes widened. "You again? Healer, are you here to check more of the prisoners?"

Lirienne blinked.

The soldier stepped aside to allow her entry. As she passed by, she slipped off a glove and touched the back of his neck. The man's eyes bulged as she reached into his mind and locked up his muscles so he couldn't move. Lirienne felt a pang of guilt at using her abilities in this way. She had taken a healing tactic and used it for other purposes. A quick twist of the nerves in one area of his brain froze him so that he would remain stuck that way for a while as she hurried to open the cells. She left him facing a wall so he couldn't see what she was doing and so that she would not have to see his face. Snatching the key ring clipped to his belt, Lirienne called back quietly to Lorenzo to come.

He crept into the cellblock and helped her open the doors. With his presence, the prisoners followed them willingly and with delight. They had all thought him dead the day she fled with his broken body. Lirienne reached the back of the block and unlocked the last of the cells. The man with the interior bleed was still pale, but he colored up as he recognized his leader and cried out in surprise.

Lorenzo shushed him, but the damage was done.

There was a shout from the doorway. The guard became unstuck and ran out to alert the others. Lirienne estimated it would take a few minutes for reinforcements to come, but almost immediately she heard several pairs of boots stamping along the corridor outside.

She glanced at Lorenzo who looked back in panic He was thinking, devising a strategy to escape.

The Castillonian nearest the door cleared his throat to get Lorenzo's attention. "That commander and several others are coming down the hall. We're stuck in here."

Lorenzo shook his head affirmatively and turned to Lirienne. "My lady, can I avail upon your power one more time? I just need to get out into the hall behind them."

Lirienne wasn't sure what one unarmed man could do against three, but she grabbed his hand and thought again about the little hiding spot just outside. She had enough power for that, if not much more. She pushed, it was dark, and then they were there.

The world spun as she felt them arrive. She looked around the corner to watch as Lorenzo leapt out into the hallway and crashed into the last soldier in the group from behind. Lirienne heard a sharp crack and the man went down. Lorenzo reached for the one in front of him who hadn't reacted yet; giving him a hard blow to the head, he was down as well. This left her brother who had just drawn his sword and was in mid turn. Lorenzo was taller and heavier by far, but Valran was armed. Lirienne pulled back behind the wall to hide, but she had to know what was happening.

She peered out again as Lorenzo tripped Valran with one of his long legs and knocked him in the head. For a moment, she panicked, thinking Lorenzo would kill her brother.

"Don't!"

Lorenzo looked back at her and signaled agreement.

The others were pouring out of the prison door now, dazed and uncertain of what to do. Lorenzo picked up the unconscious Valran and carried him into the first cell, locking the door.

Then he gave orders to his men to gather close. Lirienne realized she needed to tell them the safest way to leave. She joined them in the hall and pointed toward an exit. It would lead out behind the palace to a quiet area.

"That way is a door, just on your left. It will be guarded by a soldier, but likely no more than one."

Lorenzo came to her and looked down. She felt small beside him. He took her still-gloved hand in his. "Thank you for all of your help, my lady. Where and when shall we meet again?"

Lirienne pulled off her glove and spread her fingers to make contact with his palm. "Show me an image of the place where I will find you." She dropped her shielding.

A small house at the edge of a Trillas town appeared in her mind, then a room inside, its sparse furnishings humble but distinct. A wood-framed bed with a wicker chair pressed up against the wall beside it. It was clear enough to allow her to travel there.

"When?" she asked.

Lorenzo gave a fleeting look at his men. "A fortnight? At starbright."

Lirienne assented. It would be the brightest night of the month. "Farewell, Lorenzo. Be safe."

"And you, my Lady Lirienne. Farewell." He dropped her hand and turned to follow the others down the hall.

CHAPTER SIXTEEN

A prickly vine swung in Lirienne's face, startling her as she popped into her intended destination in her sister's private garden. She had refilled her maru at one of the trees growing in a palace garden. A dead tree might disappoint a gardener, but few knew the secret of stealing maru, making it unlikely anyone would conclude what really happened here.

She looked around the ivy-covered brick walls. This unit held four suites, each facing a different direction for increased privacy. Each suite of rooms had its own entrance and private garden. The garden, accessible only from inside or through the one small gardener's gate, was unoccupied.

Stepping around the vines that hid her, she crouched low so no one would see her head from a window or balcony in an adjacent building. She pulled her veil back over her face and crept along until she reached the entrance. Opening the door a crack, just wide enough to squeeze through, Lirienne stepped into the living room and looked about. Selana wasn't there. She would wait for her.

Lirienne slipped into a closet in the entrance, where Selana's cloaks and warm things were stored. It smelled of wool and fur, which tickled her nose. She held her breath until the urge to sneeze passed, then cracked open the door to watch the front entrance.

Lirienne settled on the closet floor and, after a while, drifted into a light slumber. She woke frequently, always with a start, then after remembering where she was, drifted off again. As time wore on, she started to get very hungry as well.

After waiting for hours, the door finally opened, and Selana entered. She removed her coat and left it on a chair by the door.

Lirienne sighed with relief and slipped out of the closet behind her.

"Selana?" Lirienne kept her voice low so as not to surprise her sister.

Selana whirled around. "Lirienne!"

Lirienne waved her hands downward. "You'll alert the guard."

It looked as if Selana hadn't slept in days. Her pale amber hair was dull and unkempt, and her robes badly creased.

Selana crossed her arms and frowned. "I should indeed. You've done an awful thing, freeing that criminal."

Stepping across the space between them, Lirienne touched her sister lightly on the arm, and Selana dropped her pose to pull her into an embrace, holding her for a long while. While they were often at odds with one another, they were still family.

Moving back a little, Lirienne stood while Selana examined her face.

Her sister stroked her hair back with her finely gloved hand. "Where have you been?"

Lirienne swallowed. "It's a long story."

"Val is livid, and Father won't even speak about it." Selana shook her head in dismay. "Did you really free that horrible creature? How did you manage to get him away with an entire unit surrounding you?" She began to pace the room, then froze, turning back to Lirienne. "I don't know how you are going to keep from being locked up, or worse!"

"I know, Selana, and I'm really sorry I made you worry so much. I don't even know what to say. I saw Val's men beating their prisoners so badly I thought they were going to kill them."

Selana grimaced, her hands balling into fists. "It would be no more than they deserved, filthy Mundatar."

It wasn't going to be easy making Selana understand. Most people thought the same way. She considered those early moments when she had taken Lorenzo away, and what had gone through her mind.

"I know you will find this hard to understand, but when I saw him... he was bleeding... dying. I couldn't just watch or walk away. I'm a healer. I didn't even know how, but I transported him away."

For a long time, Selana just stared at her. Lirienne wouldn't have believed what she'd done either, before now. Then a flicker of surprise crossed Selana's face. "You found your second gift."

Lirienne hugged her sister. It felt good that they were no longer competing, at least for the moment. "I need to talk to Father."

Selana shook her head. "He's furious with you. He's been raging and pacing for days. He has soldiers searching all over the city for you. I can't believe they couldn't find you. They're everywhere."

"I was across the river in Argentia."

Incredulous, Selana shook her head again. "I'm not sure he'll talk to you at all. He's likely to throw you in a cell and leave you there for a long time."

Lirienne looked up into her taller sister's face. Her pinched expression was so typical. "That's why I was hoping to find you here. You can calm him down enough so that he'll listen to me." Selana's art of manipulation had useful purposes.

A sharp vertical line surfaced on her sister's brow. "I'm tired of fixing up your messes. I wish you'd just behave yourself instead of always getting into trouble."

Dropping her arms from Selana's waist, Lirienne looked aside for a moment.

"What would you have me do? They were going to beat their prisoners to death. If Valran were captured, would you want him treated that way at the hands of his enemies?"

A moment of silence passed between them. Selana raised her brows. "You have a point, I suppose. I just wish you had found a way to save the day without breaking the law. What you did could be seen as treason, and by rights, Father could even order your death, although I doubt he would go that far."

The thought chilled Lirienne. She had been impulsive, she knew that, but she still felt she had done the right thing. "I hate this war, Selana. I hate the fighting, the death, everything it represents. I'm tired of patching up damaged soldiers too."

Selana rolled her eyes and raised her arms in the air. "Can't you simply do your job and heal people and deliver babies?"

Lirienne kept her expression neutral, though her mind boiled. Of course Selana would see it that way. She thought little about others, only about how they inconvenienced her. If only it were that simple. Lirienne must get back into their father's good graces or Kalad would have Ice Queen Selana to rule them.

CHAPTER SEVENTEEN

Lirienne stood at the door of her father's study, waiting to be let in. She smoothed her robe in an effort to dry her sweating palms.

An elderly servant in the king's livery greeted her. Noran, one of the palace stewards, had known her since she was a small child and had always been kind. His eyes were sad as he opened the outer door.

Selana waved her inside. "He's waiting in his study. I'm afraid he's in quite a mood."

Lirienne looked wide-eyed at her sister.

Selana's eyebrows rose. "I tried, Liri, I really did. It wasn't easy to get him to calm down even a little."

Lirienne held back. "What do you think he'll do?"

Selana shrugged. "Who knows? Be thankful you're his daughter. At least he will likely spare you from the worst options for that reason alone."

Lirienne worried nonetheless. For as long as she could remember, her father had always been a hard man.

Noran pushed the heavy inner door open and waved them inside. The king stood with his back to them, staring at the portrait of his late queen, Lirienne's mother, above the mantle. His body was stiff, his demeanor colder than usual.

She hung her head, clasped her hands in front of her, and waited. Hold your tongue, she warned herself. Apologize as if you really mean it. The second part was Selana's advice, and Lirienne's life depended on it.

Her father turned abruptly. He stared without comment for a long time and then sat down at his desk. He shook his head then looked up at her. "What have you to say for yourself?"

Lirienne stepped forward. "I'm very sorry, Father."

He tapped his fingers against the dense wood of the desk as he thought. Pursing his lips, he bobbed his head as if he had decided something, and then took a deep breath. "Lirienne, I've had enough of your flighty behavior. I gave you a deadline to find a husband, but instead you did this."

"I was working on that, and I will continue to, Father."

Her father's eyes bulged slightly. "What in the world were you thinking? The Slasher is the most dangerous man in all of the Trillas lands and the three Hilliri kingdoms!"

"He didn't harm me, Father."

The king huffed.

"Thank the Guardians. You were lucky."

There was honesty in his words, especially the mention of their deities, and it struck her that her father had actually worried about her.

"He could have held you for ransom, ruining the gains we have made in the war."

He was right, of course, but Lirienne needed to tell him the whole story.

"I knew that. I never told him who I was." Not until the very end.

Her father's gaze bore down on her, challenging her to look away. "Explain how and why you took him."

Her life hung in the balance now, and she could ill afford to be cagey.

"I was at the infirmary all morning. While healing my last few patients, I was having difficulty with my barriers, and one of the soldiers who was frightened and delirious broke through. An onslaught of troubling battle memories besieged me. I struggled to cope with his emotions. Somehow, he left the images imprinted on my mind. Later, when I encountered Valran's team and they started beating up their captives, my patient's horrible memories came back and overwhelmed me. All I could think of was getting away and stopping the beating."

The king listened, stone-faced. Gone was the slight softness he had shown earlier. "And?"

Lirienne had no idea what he thought of her explanation. "I saw the Slasher taking the worst of the soldiers' anger. I didn't know who he was. I was confused and terrified. The memories drew me into another time and place. I had no idea what I was doing, no idea that I even had the ability."

The king's eyes narrowed. "You transported him and yourself across the river?"

Lirienne nodded. The lump in her throat cut off her voice. It was a huge thing that she had done, but it could happen that way sometimes when a need arose. Only then would an ability assert itself.

Her father leaned back thoughtfully. "You found your second talent."

"Yes."

"What happened across the river? You were gone for several days. We sent out searchers but couldn't find you. No one thought to look outside of Kalad."

Lirienne swallowed to clear the lump. "At first I was terribly drained, so I had to rest for a long while." She would not speak of how she had drained the trees. "When I was strong enough, I looked after his injuries. He was almost gone by then."

The king tilted his head forward and crossed his arms. "You drained yourself transporting and healing a Mundatar? Foolish child!"

Lirienne's face heated. "I thought about how I would have wanted the Castillonians to treat our people if they were their captives. If they had caught Valran, for example. I felt I could do no less."

"The Mundatar are hardly deserving of the same treatment."

The heat spread from her face down her arms. She refused to engage in this argument. "I repaired the damage done by the Hilliri soldiers. When I was done, I was spent once more. I had to rest again for a long while. When I awoke, I went foraging for food in the forest, but I slipped and fell into the river."

Her father's eyes flickered. He must care, though he worked hard not to show it. "That could have been fatal. The waters are still icy this time of year."

"I have no doubt I would have died, but the man you call the Slasher had awoken by then and he came to my rescue. He dredged me from the chill waters, bare-chested and frozen himself, and wrapped me in his shirt until I was warm. He made a fire and trapped animals for food. He cooked them and fed me until I had recovered."

Now the king's eyes were wide. "The Slasher saved your life?"

"Yes, he did."

Again, the king's eyes flickered. "It hardly matters when he has killed hundreds of our own. I am glad you're safe, Lirienne, regardless of your misdeeds. I don't see a need for a public display. We will say that you were captured and managed to break free. You will have to do some penance for your misdemeanors to appease me, though. And you will have to work to earn my trust again."

"Of course, whatever you wish, Father."

Lirienne wanted to ask about the war, why they were fighting, and when they could stop, but she knew now was not the time. Later, when her father was in a gentler mood, she would make her inquiries.

The king thrust his chin outward, a sign, Lirienne knew, of his growing impatience and discontent. "Since you are having difficulty understanding why the Mundatar are our enemies, Lirienne, I will arrange to have you practice your craft on the front lines. You are much too shielded here from the real effects of their work. You will see how it really is, how the Slasher and his men work, and the damage they wreak."

Selana, who had been standing behind Lirienne, stepped forward. "Father, Lirienne is a gentle woman. The front is no place for her."

"I've made up my mind, Selana. You'll find there's more steel in Lirienne than you think. If my son can work his trade on the front lines, then my daughter surely can as well." He glared at Selana and she backed away. "Unless, of course, you want to join her there to keep her company?"

Selana shook her head. "They have no use for gemstones and jewelry there. I can offer nothing to help the cause."

"Good, you recognize your limitations. You are no fool."

He turned back to Lirienne who was still trying to absorb the decision. "We've talked enough. I have work to do. You will leave tomorrow with Valran. You are all dismissed."

Lirienne and Selana backed away and headed for the door, but Valran, whose uniform was in an appalling state, blocked their way. Lirienne halted.

Valran stepped further into the room and addressed the king. "Excuse me for being late. There was some trouble in the prison."

The king frowned. "Explain."

Valran rubbed his forehead and flattened out his hair. "The Castillonians have escaped."

The king scowled. "How is that possible?"

Valran shook his head. "You know how clever the Slasher is. I have no idea how he managed it."

"The Slasher? How? Did he come back and free his men?"

Lirienne felt bad for her part in this ruse. Valran would be chastised for the escape she had enabled.

"I only saw him for a moment before he knocked me out."

The king shook his head. "You let a key captive be freed on your watch as well as all of the others?"

Valran's face dropped into stony seriousness. "I will recapture them all, Father, especially him. I promise. If it's the last thing I do."

CHAPTER EIGHTEEN

A sharp metallic tang filled her nostrils. Everywhere Lirienne looked, she saw blood. She shook her head. The field triage healers hadn't done very much for the soldier they brought her. At least they could have stopped the worst of the bleeding or given him some relief from pain. She wondered if she could save this one.

A month had passed since Lirienne travelled to the front and already she was exhausted. Soldiers were brought in every hour, each one worse than the last. When she closed her eyes at night, she saw red.

Although Lirienne could patch up these soldiers who had gone with their swords and spears off to war, it felt so pointless. There was no way to measure all the costs of war just by the number of casualties. The value of each individual was incalculable. Those who lived were often damaged in body, but also deep in their spirit. They would require a kind of healing that few were capable of performing. To Lirienne, there was no cause noble enough to justify all this death.

She straightened and disengaged her hands from the patient she was working on. She was done with her task of stopping the internal bleeding. The supervisor of the local healers, a man named Dor, came over to continue her work, repairing the torn muscles, and another came to wrap the remaining wounds, which were being left to heal on their own. In order to conserve energy, the healers had agreed to repair only the most critical injuries, leaving minor ones. They worked in teams, each person performing one task repeatedly, moving from one patient to the next. There were not enough healers to repair all of the wounded soldiers. The youngest students performed the wrapping of the lesions that remained. Some wounds would eventually heal on their own; others were left for the healers back in the city, if the soldier lived through the long trip. Try as she might to follow these procedures, it was difficult to stop when she could see the pain in her patients' eyes.

"Who is next?"

Dor pointed to another bloody body on a stretcher. "This one here."

Lirienne dipped her soiled hands in the clear water of a basin, scrubbing them with soap until they were clean and rinsing them in a second basin.

She turned to the next soldier. Her fingers began to twitch. She lifted her hands up in front of her, spread out the digits to see their condition. They were raw and chafed and they trembled.

She hungered to fill up on maru at a tree, but blackened trees all over the camp would be noticed. This now-familiar yearning concerned her. What did the taking actually cost? She pushed aside the thought of the wondrous sensation it gave her, and tried to ignore the shaking. There were still so many who needed her.

Dor, however, caught sight of her and came over. "You are done for today. Go rest."

She heard the gruffness of his tone. Had she failed in some way? "I'm sorry."

Dor changed his tone. "You didn't start this war, little bird, and you can't patch up every soldier injured in the fighting, although I suspect you might secretly wish to."

He was right. Lirienne didn't like to accept defeat. She usually lasted longer than this.

Dor nudged her out of the tent, and she went to rest in her bed for a while, though she was too excited to sleep. Tonight was starbright, and she hoped to see Lorenzo.

When night fell at last, she rose and dressed in warm clothing. The army encampment was a tidy village of canvas tents, hundreds of them, lined up row upon row, creating streets and avenues.

Before they parted, Lorenzo had placed a clear image in her mind of a room in a small house somewhere in Castillon near the border.

Of course, she needed to replenish her maru before leaving. She ached to fill up, which made her stop for a moment. This new sensation was becoming more frequent. She would take note in the future should she feel this way again. A short walk into the forest nearby brought her to a well-hidden tree suitable for her needs. When she was done, she felt an awesome strength complete her. She called up the image Lorenzo had shared with her: a humble shack nestled in the woods. She gathered up her strength of will and pushed.

Seconds passed while she remained in a black, airless emptiness.

She tried to breathe but coughed instead. There was no air in this in-between space. As the moments passed in the dark and her desire to breathe grew, Lirienne clamped down on the panic rising within her. Empty space pressed against her ears. She wanted to scream. At last, a dim light blossomed around her as she appeared in a tiny bedroom in a small hut.

She gasped for air as soon as she realized she had arrived. Her knees buckled. The room began to spin, but before she could fall, strong arms caught her and swept her up. Lorenzo was here, waiting for her.

He eased her down to the bed. "My lady."

He crouched down and leaned his crossed arms on the edge of the bed. She turned to see his bright eyes sparkle in the dim candlelight and caught a flash of his white teeth. As the room stopped moving, she was able to sit up. He took her hand and held it.

Lirienne smiled to see him well. "I'm so glad to find you here," she said.

"My fighters weren't happy I left them, but I chose this house for a reason. They won't question or follow me here."

Lirienne looked about the place. It was a modest home with few furnishings: a bed, a chair, a table, a wash basin and a single window, just as he'd shown her when she'd taken the image from his mind. Yet there had been a hint in his thoughts of a strong emotional attachment to this place. "Is there something significant about this house?"

Lorenzo turned away. "It was my brother's."

Remembering how his brother had died, Lirienne now understood the sadness that clung to him. She wished she could help him, but she knew little of how to help this kind of hurt.

Lorenzo's somber mood lifted. "I will never get used to the way you can travel. It's a wonder."

This reminded her that she must check her maru. It had dipped significantly, but not dangerously.

He dragged his fingers through his tangled curls and sat down beside her on the bed. She noted the bright ribbons woven through many of his strands of hair. His blue eyes drew Lirienne's gaze. She waited for him to be ready to talk, but he stayed there looking into her eyes until Lirienne had to glance away. There was something about this man, enemy of her people, which drew her toward him. Her heart pounded as she realized where her thoughts were taking her. It was dangerous territory.

Lorenzo cleared his throat. "I spoke with my father."

Would the belligerent Lord Carlosi agree to cease fighting? Lorenzo looked unhappy—apparently not.

Lirienne arched an inquiring eyebrow. "I take it that didn't go as we'd hoped."

He shook his head. Lirienne noticed his muscles stiffen and his hands ball into fists. He sighed and released the tension. Poor man, he was as frustrated with his father as she was with her own.

"And you?" he asked.

Lirienne chewed on her lip while selecting her words. "I was able to speak with my father about what I had done, but he sent me to the front to work as a punishment. I couldn't speak to him about anything else—not while he was still so angry with me."

"It was a gamble. We must find others to work with us. I think my father would listen to almost anyone else but me."

Lirienne knew exactly what that felt like. "My brother returned to the front with me. I can try to talk to him, though I'm worried he won't listen either."

"Don't give up on him without trying, Lirienne. He may surprise you."

Lirienne had no idea why Lorenzo would think so, but it was a generous thought, which surprised her.

He grinned. "You're puzzled. You think that he will continue to hate me because of my role in his wife's death. I also have equal reason to hate him because of my brother, but I don't."

"Why not?" Lirienne wondered how the man could be so forgiving.

Lorenzo looked out the window, up at the stars. He smiled and took Lirienne by the shoulders. "I realized I had to look past what happened to my brother—to forgive the one responsible, or I would spend my whole life mired in that bitterness. It's the only way to make peace, and the only way I can have peace of mind. If you can show your brother how the hatred affects him, you can, perhaps, make him see how important it is to give it up."

It surprised Lirienne that Lorenzo would be so generous in his thinking. He gave her brother credit for being capable of the same viewpoint, an admirable quality. Lirienne wasn't sure Valran could manage it, but she would try.

"We have a lot of work to do. We should meet again soon."

Lorenzo smiled. "We've only just begun. We can try to return here next starbright to plan more, but I may not be able to make that meeting if I have other orders."

"I have to work scheduled shifts too, and I can't appear uncooperative or my father will hear of it and be angry with me. There's no way to communicate to make other arrangements."

Lorenzo shook his head. "Not unless you can do your mind thing from a distance."

Lirienne smiled at this. Of course, she couldn't. "No, but if either of us is unable to come on the next meeting night, we can always try again on the following starbright."

Lorenzo looked into her eyes with a solemn expression and bowed low. "Until the next starbright, then, my lady."

Lirienne's heart fluttered at his elegant manners. He was every bit a gentleman and a noble soul. Why couldn't she find a nice Hilliri nobleman with the same characteristics?

CHAPTER NINETEEN

When Lirienne transported back to the encampment, she nearly collapsed. Whatever maru she had siphoned from the tree before leaving hadn't lasted as long as it normally would. Worse, it left her drained and thirsting for more. She wondered if doing this might cause her some kind of harm, but concluded that her mission to stop the war had priority over her own safety.

The starshine was intense on this particular night in the cycle, and she was easily able to get her bearings. She'd materialized in a wooded area just outside the camp perimeter, where she selected a tree and placed her bare hands on it, preparing to take another draw of maru.

As she shifted her awareness into the tree, she hungered for the extra charge its maru would give her. She plunged in and began to draw up from the tree's well of power, but as it entered her, she noticed it "tasted" odd. Lifting her hands, she broke contact and cut off the flow. Food and drink would have to do. She wasn't going to touch that strange stuff tonight.

She tidied her hair and wrapped her cloak around her. Nights were still cool, especially near the canyon at the border. The winds whipped through there and brought the temperature down much lower than elsewhere. She slipped into the darkened side streets of the makeshift village, keeping to the shadows as she made her way back to her tent.

As she lay in her bed, sleep refused to come as her thoughts revolved around the day's events. Lorenzo's generous belief that her brother could change his mind continued to surprise her. Similar to their father, Valran had an unyielding mind, but he did behave honorably most of the time. She understood his bitterness over the death of his wife, and she had difficulty imagining him putting those feelings aside for the good of his nation, or even for his own sanity. It made Lorenzo all the nobler, even a little wiser, his youth and Trillas origins notwithstanding.

Lirienne caught herself at the idea. Had she really thought the

Trillas less noble and intelligent than the Hilliri? It was a rather superior attitude now that she thought of it. It was common among her people to believe they were better in most ways than the Trillas, but Lirienne hadn't really believed it—or had she?

Her thoughts wandered back to Lorenzo. He had looked after her in the woods—saved her from the dangers of the swift river. He'd been solicitous when she was weak. He had listened to her and taken her seriously despite the fact she probably looked like a child in his eyes. And he believed that her brother could be noble enough to set aside his anger for the sake of peace. He was a better man than most of the Hilliri men she had met during her search for a husband.

When light first pressed in through the canvas of her tent, she gave up on the idea of sleeping at all. She rose to wash and dress. There were no servants here, but the solitude was welcome. She had her thoughts to occupy her.

She continued to consider the discussions of the night just past while she polished the dust from her boots. Walking through the forest had deposited a good deal of soil on them. A voice outside her tent shook her out of her reverie. She poked her head out. A messenger waited.

The stern man handed her a folded paper, bowed, and left.

She unfolded the note and read a cross message from her brother. She was late for their weekly meeting. Her musings had made her lose track of the time. She'd forgotten her regular engagement. He would be angry. Valran's patience with everyone was short these days, and he was already irritated with her for needing his supervision when he'd rather have avoided her altogether.

Lirienne splashed water on her face and adjusted the folds of her silver gown. She covered her face in her veil to remain anonymous as she walked through the encampment.

Valran's pavilion served as both his sleeping quarters and his workspace. A large desk piled high with maps and books took up one corner, with a number of camp chairs strewn about for meetings with his staff. Off in the back was a curtained section where he slept and dressed. In the center of the space, a large table where he took his meals filled most of the area. This morning it was set for two.

Lirienne took her place across from her brother. She opened a cloth napkin and laid it in her lap. "Good morning, Val. Thank you for the invitation. It gets lonely here sometimes."

Valran looked up from his reading. "Are the other healers not friendly?"

Lirienne considered how to answer. "We're really too tired to waste energy on small talk."

A servant came in and poured out cups of hot tea. She might not have servants, but her brother was a commander here. Valran tilted his head in dismissal and the servant left.

"I didn't realize they were being worked so hard."

Lirienne tested the tea with a little sip. It was still too hot. She picked up a roll and buttered it instead. Baked yeast breads were a luxury only a prince might enjoy in this place.

"You must know the numbers of injured," she said. "Why are you surprised?"

Valran shook his head. "I guess I really have no idea what it takes to perform healing tasks."

It didn't surprise her. The guilds didn't share much of their knowledge, issues, or limitations with outsiders. She knew just as little about warfare.

"Val, I've heard several explanations for why we're at war, but I'm still struggling to understand. What is it all for?"

Questions like this were Valran's favorite. He loved to teach her about his world, as if she were the younger sibling, even though they were twins. Everyone treated Lirienne as if she were younger, most likely because she was smaller.

Valran swallowed a sip of tea and cleared his throat. "It's like this... Kalad is very densely populated. While we don't have many children, the Hilliri are very long-lived, and over the years, our land has been getting full, and there are fewer and fewer good places to grow crops. Castillon is very sparsely populated, although it's hard to imagine why, with the Trillas bedding each other with great frequency." Valran cleared his throat and continued. "There is also the matter of the Hilliri colony that has settled just inside the border of Castillon. They help legitimize our claim. The people of Alterra are quite peculiar, but they serve a purpose. They decided to settle there to live differently from the way we live in Kalad, but really, they're just a bunch of oddballs. The Castillonian Trillas are recent arrivals from elsewhere. They only settled those lands in the last hundred years. We need the land more than they do, and so we're taking it. They can always go back to where they came from."

Valran tilted his cup to finish the tea and placed it back on the table. Lirienne reflected on what he had said. Anyone in Kalad would have said the same thing. This was nothing new, yet as

Lirienne listened, it shocked her how haughty it sounded—that the Hilliri deserved the land and the Trillas didn't.

"Isn't there a precedent regarding whoever had the land first to consider? I mean, how would you feel if the Trillas decided they needed some of Kalad and came in and took it?"

Valran's eyes narrowed. "Lirienne, don't tell me the time you spent in the forest with that bandit has made you sympathetic to his side."

In an effort to cover up her feelings, Lirienne chuckled. "No, silly, the Slasher is a real brute, why would you say that?"

"Then why didn't you bring him back to me? We could have kept him and the rest of his crew. The war would be half over by now, just by your doing that."

Lirienne dropped any pretense of humor. Instead, she let her mouth hang open and pressed her hand to her chest. "I set him free because he demanded it. By the Guardians, he was twice my size! And Valran, I can assure you, no one wants to see this war ended more than I."

A scowl set into her brother's features. "You mean to say that you would rather not be healing soldiers? You would rather be setting broken bones of clumsy children and delivering babies? It seems so . . . unimportant." He shook his head, baffled.

Lirienne reached out and touched his hand as it rested on the table. Both of them were fully gloved. "Val, you see the glory in war, but from the side of the healer, it's all carnage, blood, and death; the soldiers that survive are often shattered in mind as well as in body. Fighting brings out the cruelty in soldiers too. Haven't you noticed?"

Valran shot up from his chair and slammed his fists on the table. The utensils jumped and clattered, and Lirienne flinched.

"I see that you are weak, sister. You let that—that villain convince you to betray your own country. It's time you took control, took ownership of your actions, and made sacrifices for your people."

Lirienne stood and stared at her brother. He wasn't especially tall either, so she didn't have to tilt her head overmuch. "This is about Talora, I think. You don't usually get upset over such things."

Her brother exhaled and rounded his shoulders. "You knew it was him, Lirienne. You should have done it for me. It would have made things right between us."

She reached out and clasped him by the shoulder. "I would

have, Val, if I could. I'm sorry." She waited, allowing silence to fill the space between them. "But you need to let go of your hatred of this man. It will eat away at your heart until you become bitter and can't enjoy life any longer."

Valran stared at her for a long time. He swallowed. "I will enjoy life again, sister, once I have the Slasher's head sitting on a pike outside my pavilion."

CHAPTER TWENTY

Lirienne's knees gave out the moment she appeared in the little Castillonian home where she met Lorenzo.

It was getting worse, she was certain. The maru she took from the trees had less and less effect, requiring her to take more each time. Increasingly, she pulsed with desire for it, especially at night, reliving the rush of it filling her body with power when her strength ebbed.

Lorenzo caught her in his long arms and held her. "I've got you."

"Oh!"

She clasped his sleeve. He would hardly notice her weight. He was so strong, and she so light. Standing up, Lirienne straightened her hair and clothing with one hand; the other, she realized, was still clutching Lorenzo. He kept his arms around her. His proximity made her cheeks redden.

Lirienne cleared her throat. "I don't know why, but traveling like this is draining me worse than before."

Lorenzo shook his head. "It's amazing that you can do it. I'm just worried you'll end up somewhere else one day, and I won't be there to catch you."

He released her from his grip. There was a twinkle in his blue eyes. She liked that he found humor even in awkward situations.

"I was never trained to do this. I'm still learning." She turned to observe him. His hair was sleep-mussed and he looked tired. "You've been busy."

The comment didn't require a reply; it was simply a statement of fact. He raised his eyebrows. "How could you tell?"

Lirienne suppressed a smile. "You forget I work as a healer in your enemy's camp. The injured are brought to me every day. It's a good way to tell how well a war is going, exhausting as it is."

Lorenzo stared at his boots. "I'm sorry, but I have to follow orders, at least until I can convince my father to give me different orders."

Lirienne nodded. "I spoke to my brother."

Lorenzo glanced at her out of the corner of his eye. "Oh . . .

and how did he take your proposal?"

Lirienne stared at the ground now. She had hoped for better. "Not well, I'm afraid. He has made it a personal goal to take your life in revenge for his wife's death. He says he won't rest until he has done so. And he's angry with me for letting you go." She released a breath. "I'm sorry. I don't know what to do now. There is no one else to ask. What if he succeeds, Lorenzo? You must be careful. You should have seen how angry he was." A wave of cold came over her and the weakness flared up again.

Lorenzo examined her silently, then he reached out and touched her hair. "You would miss me when I'm dead then?"

Lirienne clutched his sleeve. "I'm an outcast now. You're the only one who really understands."

There was more, but she couldn't speak of it. No one would understand, not even he.

Lorenzo cocked his head to one side observing her. His eyes traveled over her features. She wondered what he was thinking. She leaned in toward him and shivered again.

He began removing his jacket. "Are you cold?"

She waved him off. "It's okay. I'll be fine. The trip has drained me more than usual." Her words drifted off as she spoke. The thought of finding Lorenzo's dead body made her want to weep, and her weakness made it worse.

Lorenzo was now by her side, wrapping the jacket around her shoulders. He held her close, and she leaned into his embrace, resting her head on his chest. Lirienne sniffed as her eyes began to water.

Pulling away enough to see her face, Lorenzo looked puzzled. "You would weep for me, my lady?" He stared at her for a long moment. His eyes appeared darker in the dim light.

"I would miss your daring river rescues and camping skills." She forced a grin, but she knew if he were gone, a terrible emptiness would set in. "Would you miss me?"

The question made him fluster. As he searched for words, something must have come into his head, for a look of realization came over him and he opened his mouth. Then he closed it again. She could tell he was gathering his thoughts, so she waited until he was ready to speak.

He took her by the shoulders and knelt down to her level. "I've been struggling with how I feel when you leave here. My nights are full of dreams of you. I can't stop thinking about you. I know it's foolish, Lirienne. Your people would think you as mad as mine would think me."

Lirienne blinked, trying to follow this confused confession. Her face flushed as his meaning became clear. "Are you suggesting we stop this war by creating a family alliance?"

A Trillas and a Hilliri. This strange attraction might serve their purposes. She looked at Lorenzo's tall, lean body and then down at her own tiny, delicate one, wondering how compatible they really were.

Then Lirienne thought of her brother and his revenge. And of her father who would never forgive her for the transgression, but Lirienne had to think of herself and her people first.

Lorenzo's eyes followed hers. He lifted her chin with a finger. "There has been a tension between us. I have sensed it. Is it not the same for you?"

Lirienne agreed, but the thought of everything he implied terrified her. Did she dare defy her father? And marriage between the two peoples had, to her knowledge, never occurred. Could there even be children? Where could they safely live? So many questions, and she had no answers, only desires that threatened to change everything.

Lorenzo stared at her, waiting. "I would protect you, Lirienne, on my honor."

There was honesty in his assertion, and she believed him. He had protected her already, many times. As he stood there making his astonishing proposal, she could actually imagine them being together. She knew that the qualities she had searched for in her suitors and never found were in ample evidence in this man from a different land and culture.

He took her hands in his as he waited for an answer, but Lirienne could find no words. It took a long while to make up her mind. All of her life Lirienne had acted to satisfy her desires. She studied healing even though her father disapproved. She had refused unsuitable suitors when others had tried to convince her to accept them. Here was another challenge, another choice others might view as wrong. She understood this well, for she had reminded herself more than once that he had killed Talora. An act done in war, yes, but her family would not be able to forgive such a choice. In spite of this, her whole being cried out for her to accept Lorenzo's outlandish offer.

He was the man she wanted. Was she bold enough to take that

path? After a long pause, and a long time watching Lorenzo's bright, questioning eyes watching her, she knew the answer.

She kissed him full on the lips. It was the most brazen thing she had ever done with any man. Lorenzo, no stranger to love, artfully took the lead, cupping her face in his hands and then lingering about her neck as he deepened the kiss, eventually winding his hands down to her waist where he held her cradled against his body.

Lirienne lost herself in the sensual pleasure of his touch. The Hilliri seldom removed their gloves for any reason, making skin-to-skin contact a rare and euphoric experience. Lorenzo traveled his lips down her neck and lingered at the intersection of her shoulder. She wanted to tear his shirt off, and press her hands into his flesh, but she pulled back.

Lorenzo released her from his gentle embrace and watched her intently. There was a joyous smile on his face. "I am besotted with you, Lirienne Godehera, but I believe I am in luck. It appears to be mutual."

CHAPTER TWENTY-ONE

Lorenzo laid his head on Lirienne's chest. He slung his arm around her waist and pulled her tightly against him. They spread out on the bed, both fully clothed, in the upstairs room of the cottage. They had talked for hours, making plans and learning more about each other. So far, they had skillfully sidestepped the subject of marriage, but they were running out of other topics to discuss.

Lirienne toyed with his hair, swirling the curls up tighter and releasing them. "I love your curls. My hair just falls straight down."

Lorenzo lifted his hand and caressed her hair. "Yours is so fine and soft, like a newborn baby's."

He pushed himself up to meet her face to face and kissed her gently. His touch made her dizzy. She couldn't help but want more.

Finally, he came up for air and kept his face close to hers. "Well, my love, shall we plan out how we are going to do this?"

Lirienne sat up. Marriage discussions shouldn't be held in a horizontal position. "You really are serious about this? You think it will work to stop the war?"

"If you come live with me in Castillon, then how can your family plan to attack us? They might harm you."

Lirienne swayed her head from side to side as she weighed that thought. "This all assumes that my family cares about my well-being."

Lorenzo propped himself up on his elbow and turned to Lirienne. "Surely your family cares about you, even if they don't show it often. They are connected to you. Family bonds are deep in the blood."

Focusing on the wall behind him, Lirienne tried to think of how her father and brother would react. Obviously, they would be very angry, but once it was done, there would be nothing they could do. When the Hilliri married, it was a private affair. The parents had to abide by the couple's decision, however sometimes they didn't. If a daughter chose a man who was abhorrent to the family, they might keep her away from him. They might not force her to leave her new husband, but financial leverage could be applied to make the girl do their bidding.

Lirienne refocused on Lorenzo and smiled at him. Being here talking with him was wonderful. He listened and showed interest, a rare quality among the noble sons of Kalad.

He smiled back. "Tell me about your marriage rites. What are the Hilliri customs?"

"There's not much to tell. When a couple has decided they want to be together, they simply make each other a pledge."

Lorenzo looked puzzled. "Alone? Is there no one to officiate, no public ceremony? Does the family attend?"

Lirienne couldn't help but laugh. It was such a silly idea. The family could never be present when lovers pledged to share their lives. It was such a personal, intimate thing. "Goodness, family? I should think not, especially when the pledge is sealed by their first night together."

"Oh, I see."

But she could tell Lorenzo was having a difficult time with the idea. "Tell me what you do in Castillon. Obviously it's very different."

Lorenzo rolled his eyes. "Much different. In Castillon, there is always a public ceremony. Our village Sibyl performs the rites that bind the couple in the eyes of the Guardians, and everyone is there to witness it."

Lirienne made a face as if she had tasted something bad.

Lorenzo held up a finger. "But wait. There is no public bedding, if that's what you're thinking. That happens after, and I assure you, there are no witnesses."

Lirienne sighed with relief. If their two cultures were different, at least they weren't completely opposite.

Lorenzo toyed with her ear. She cocked her head as he found a ticklish spot. "But I must say I like the idea of a private pledge . . . and of course, what comes after." He waggled his eyebrows.

Lirienne pushed him away. She had difficulty with his unconcealed desires. The Hilliri, who made choices for life, did not engage in casual intimacy. There were rumors about the Trillas and their proclivities, but she had no idea what the truth was. If they were to marry, she had to be sure there would be no other women in his life afterward, for she would know every secret every time she touched him and their minds linked. It was already a strange sensation when she caught flashes of Lorenzo's past lovers, and she had only kissed him. She realized she would have to be direct about it.

"Are you going to continue to bed other women after we are wed?"

Lorenzo laughed, tipping his head back as a throaty chuckle emitted from his chest. Tears sprung to his eyes. When he settled, a silly grin still fixed to his face, he cleared his throat and tried to look serious. "My lady, a man may sample from the crops in the fields, but when the harvest comes in, he knows it's time to visit the granary instead."

The simile was rather preposterous. Lirienne laughed in turn, and Lorenzo joined her. It took a while to quiet after this. Each time one stopped, they looked at the other and broke out again in belly laughs.

Finally, they both managed to control their outbursts at the same time and ended by staring at one another in all earnestness. Lorenzo leaped off the bed and crouched down on one knee, taking her hands in his as she sat with her legs dangling off the bedside.

"Lorenzo?"

He gazed at her with sober intent and wrapped his fingers around hers. "Lirienne Godehera, Lady of Kalad, I pledge thee, on my honor, to be thy husband and lover, and to eschew all others from this day forth." He blushed a little with the last part. "If you will have me."

He waited, expectantly.

A rush of warm thoughts bathed her as she considered his words. He didn't know her traditions, but he was right on target with the sentiment. He would do. He was more than right.

"I accept your oath, Lorenzo Calimero of Castillon, and give mine in turn." Lirienne reversed her hands so that they were on the outside and Lorenzo's were underneath. "I, Lirienne Godehera, pledge to you my oath, honoring my ancestors and my family, to be your wife, faithful in all ways, until my dying day."

"I forgot about that last part, but of course this is a forever pledge."

Lirienne shushed him. This was a serious moment, although she could hear her family in her mind telling her it was a foolish, ill-advised action. Worst of all, it reminded her that she was likely to live a great deal longer than he was. She shut down the obtrusive thought.

There was nothing left to say. It had all been said, and with such earnestness that Lirienne flushed with pleasure at the thought that she had chosen well, no matter what others might say.

Lorenzo looked puzzled. "Is that all then? We're married?"

Lirienne grinned. She took Lorenzo by the wrist and pulled him up to her. She wrapped her arms around his shoulders and kissed him without reserve. "Almost. There's just one more thing."

CHAPTER TWENTY-TWO

Lorenzo climbed back onto the bed all the while kissing Lirienne. She fumbled as she searched for his shirt edge. When she had it in her grasp, she worked it up his torso and over his head, laying bare the smooth hills of his chest. She sat back on her heels and observed him, taking in the interesting landscape.

Dark hair sprinkled his chest, something that Hilliri men didn't have. It grew in a thin line down the middle, heading toward his waist. As a student of medicine, she knew about men's bodies, and so far, she had seen nothing too different in Lorenzo from any Hilliri man, although he would be considered nearly a giant.

She tugged at his belt. It was an intricate affair with a clasp and hidden release mechanism. Lorenzo flicked it open with a large finger wedged in just the right spot, and the two halves dropped to the bed.

Before Lirienne had the chance to proceed, Lorenzo began working the many tiny toggles of her robe. He released them one at a time with one hand—they went all the way down to her ankles—while the other lifted away the silver fabric.

By the time he had completed this task, Lirienne could scarcely keep her hands to herself. She pulled on the waist of Lorenzo's breeches, working them down over his hips. Lorenzo interrupted her with kisses as he pulled her robe away from her shoulders and off her arms. She was bare to the waist now, save for a thin shift that covered her torso. The fine fabric pulled across her breasts, and Lorenzo honed in with his hands.

It was unbearable—all this fumbling. It was taking too long. As much as she desired Lorenzo, this was uncharted territory for her.

Lorenzo worked the shift up and over her head. Completely bare now, she shivered, more from fear than cold. Lorenzo pressed her against him, and she warmed, though doubts still circled her mind, preying on her confidence. As he held her, she felt her smallness magnify. He could kneel and look her in the eye. His shoulders were so broad and muscular; his hands massive as he caressed her back. Lirienne wondered how this was going to work, but there was no going back. He didn't appear to be concerned, so perhaps she shouldn't be either.

Lorenzo pushed her back a little so he could look at her. "Lirienne, I swore I would protect you. I would never hurt you either. Won't you trust me?"

Did he know what troubled her? He'd had many lovers before, perhaps he knew women better than she imagined.

He kissed her lips, then traveled down her neck, lingering at her shoulders and then went further down where he toyed with his tongue over her breast. When he had lingered there long enough, he continued down. A fire smoldered between her legs. He arrived at the scene of the blaze with tongue and lips, working over the moist places no man had ever encountered. She groaned and bit her lip as pleasure warmed her.

Lorenzo probed deeper, plying her most sensitive place until she saw spots under her eyelids and her breath went ragged. A hoarse sound emitted from her throat as she tensed and then relaxed.

The house was still. Lorenzo, however, was not done. He slipped from his breeches and tossed them on the floor. He began again, working his hands over her body until every place had awoken and was alert. Lirienne blushed as she thought of all the things Lorenzo was doing to her. She wanted to respond in kind but had no experience to guide her.

A thought came to her unbidden. She had experienced enough of intimacy through mental links with patients to know how things worked, and what was pleasing to a man. A Hilliri man, at least. Her healing abilities also gave her some knowledge that might be useful. As she was currently ungloved, her ability to sense Lorenzo's thoughts and physical responses was available to her. She dropped all barriers and reached for his surface thoughts.

Lirienne caressed Lorenzo's splendid chest as she kept contact. He wouldn't be aware of her mind grazing just under the surface of his thoughts. As she massaged his muscles, she felt him relax and realized that he too had been tense.

He kissed her fingertips. "Your healing touch is useful for other things, I see."

Smiling coyly in response, Lirienne turned him over and worked her way down the muscles of his back. She eventually landed at his buttocks. The skin there was smooth and unblemished and pale compared to his bronzed torso. His chest rumbled in pleasure at her ministrations. She paused, taking the time to enjoy every one of his sensations as if they were her own. It was most curious to share his pleasure.

"I hope you don't mind. It's an advantage for one who has had no experience in this."

Lorenzo breathed in deep and released the breath. "You're doing just fine, my love."

Lirienne returned to her massaging. She tugged him, urging him to turn over. Then she worked her way around to the front. He hissed when she took him in her hands, making her grin. Lirienne handled him carefully, gauging each touch by the response to the last one. At last, he pulled her hand away.

He stretched himself out on the bed and pulled Lirienne on top of him. She eased herself down over him and discovered her fears were unfounded when he slid easily into her. She let out a sigh of wonder at the sensation of being filled. He held her there, unmoving for a long moment, his breath ragged but steady. She pressed her hands onto his chest to prop herself up and began to sway.

No sensation had ever felt sweeter in Lirienne's life. If this was how it would be between them, she was glad. He shifted his hips to meet hers, and a steady aching movement began, leading toward a long rise in tension. She lost track of time as the rhythm continued. An ache was building in her bones, and Lorenzo's thick muscles tensed. Like in a dance, her fingers interlaced with his, his mind aware and opened to hers. Finally, she dropped all of her barriers so he could share in her thoughts too. His eyes widened in wonder as he sensed her pleasure. He thrust quicker and rougher now as his resolve for gentleness frayed in the face of his own need. Lirienne didn't want tenderness at this moment. She only needed relief from the tension that overwhelmed her.

As she crested the heights of that terrible ache, she longed for release, but Lorenzo slowed his pace, threatening to delay her final pleasure. Lirienne's breath was ragged now as she gripped his shoulders, digging in with her nails. Lorenzo grasped her hips and guided her to a few final pushes. White hot sparks flashed behind Lirienne's eyes as she gasped and cried out, trembling momentarily before collapsing in his strong arms. They lay still for a long while as their hearts returned to their normal rhythms; their fingers still entwined as their minds kept contact.

Lirienne drifted off but returned to awareness as Lorenzo shifted her to his side. With faces almost pressed together, they stared into one another's eyes.

"You see, there was nothing to fear, my love. Are you not

pleased?”

A smile spread across Lirienne's face. She nuzzled his nose with her own. "Indeed. My new husband has shown his true worth this night."

CHAPTER TWENTY-THREE

Three more soldiers were carried into the infirmary. Every bed was full; most already had two patients where there should only be one. The porters looked around, unsure where to put their charges.

Supervisor Dor scanned the room for a place. Then he shook his head. "There's no more room. Grab a sheet and lay them on the floor by the tent wall."

The porters bowed and went to work. Things were getting worse instead of better. Still, she smiled when she thought of her plans. Every moment brought her thoughts back to Lorenzo. Her husband—what a strange new thought.

Weeks had passed. The war was still on and mounting in destruction. If they had any plans to stop the fighting, they were surely failing in their task.

Dor turned his gaze on her and frowned. "Lirienne, I can't believe you already look tired. You've only been at work for an hour."

She shook her head. She was sleeping more than usual, but the extra rest didn't seem to help. "I feel like I'm carrying around a pack full of stones all of the time. I keep checking my levels, and I'm okay to work, but then I get drained so fast." Perhaps the maru she had taken from the trees had tainted her own source.

A line appeared on Dor's forehead. Everyone was tired. Everyone was overworked. He had dismissed her early for the last four days though, which was unusual.

"I don't like your color today. Finish up with this one and go rest."

Lirienne looked around at the injured waiting their turn. A sorry lot; who would help them if everyone took extra breaks?

Across from the surgery, the army had erected a smaller tent with cots to rest on and food for the healers during their breaks. Lirienne nibbled dried apples while lying on a cot. She stared at the canvas ceiling as the feeble daylight filtered in. What had changed? She used to be the last one to finish.

Curling up into the rough wool blanket, Lirienne drifted into thoughts of her beloved. His father, Carlosi Calimero, Lord of Castillon, lived in the main town of Madrezza, situated right at the mouth of the great river in the south. Lorenzo was planning to speak with him. A sort of king in his own right, Carlosi was the one leading the fight on the Trillas side.

Lirienne knew that Lorenzo was one of Castillon's war leaders. He masterminded a variety of plots that saw him drop out of his hiding place in the trees to slay soldiers before they ever got out onto the field of battle. He also had dispatched soldiers while they slept in their tents—although this no longer happened since Valran posted additional guards in the camp. It was hard to reconcile this kind of vicious attack with her gentle lover, but she knew how outnumbered and outmatched the Castillonians were. These were the actions of the desperate. She could hardly blame them for not playing by the standard rules of war.

She wanted so much to see him again, to press herself into his arms. She imagined him tucked in beside her on the cot, then thought it silly, since he was much too large to fit on it, even alone. Still, if she could see his blue eyes and wide smile, she would be content.

She heard shouts outside the thin tent. Her brother Valran barked orders. His voice was getting closer.

Then his head popped through the flap. "You're resting again? Are you avoiding your work?"

Lirienne blinked at the bright light streaming in from outside.

"You promised you would be a paragon of virtue in exchange for—never mind. I expect nothing less than your fullest effort."

No one knew why she was here except her brother.

"I have been working, but the supervisor ordered me to rest when I started to weaken. He didn't complain to you, did he?"

"He doesn't know your abilities, sister. You should be one of his greatest assets here. The College usually refuses to send us their better healers."

The chill between them hadn't altered. Valran looked frustrated. No doubt he had a lot on his mind.

"I'm trying, Val, but I just haven't been very well."

Valran stared for a moment. The sharp lines of his face didn't soften with care as they once would have. Lirienne missed his warmth.

"Get Dor to check you out. Despite your antics, I'm fairly certain Father would be livid if anything happened to you."

Of course he would, Lirienne agreed. He would miss having

her to order about.

There being nothing left to say, Valran departed.

Lirienne's stomach churned. She wondered if it was the food, or that her brother had disturbed her calm. The tent began to turn. She squeezed her eyes shut, but the spinning wouldn't halt.

She should ask another healer to check her, but she had so much trouble keeping her barriers up. There were too many things in her mind she couldn't afford to share. No one could learn why she was here, about Lorenzo, or the taking of maru from trees. Sometimes, when it was quiet at night, she would check her own body in the same way as she would check a patient. But she couldn't heal herself—that would require far too much maru and take more concentration than any healer could manage. If she found something wrong, she would have to ask for help.

Allowing her breathing to go shallow, Lirienne monitored the rise of her chest as she drew in and expelled air. She slipped into a state of meditation, the red undersides of her eyelids connecting her to her flesh. With her mind, she followed the pathways of her blood and nerves until she reached an area of disturbance. It wasn't unhealthy, just not usual. A tiny clot, a bundle of nerves, a throbbing flow of blood led her to a surprising presence: the tiny, growing form of a baby.

At first, Lirienne couldn't reconcile the truth. It wasn't as if she didn't know how it happened. She was a healer and certainly knew about such things. Her mind just refused to connect cause and effect. Somehow, she hadn't believed it could happen, not between two such different people. Now she felt foolish for not believing it possible.

Again, she had fallen into the same way of thinking as most Hilliri. They believed the Trillas were very different. If she could conceive a child, then it was proof that they were more alike than the Hilliri wanted to admit.

Denial wasn't helpful, though. She had allowed herself to be drawn in by Lorenzo's captivating charm, his directness, and his passion for life. This was what she had searched for and never found among the eligible men of Kalad. He had swept her away, so she hadn't thought about prevention, which was possible—a simple adjustment using maru—but now it was too late.

She might be small, but Lirienne was no child, and she recognized the truth of her situation. She couldn't stay in Kalad and bear a child fathered by the country's worst enemy.

She curled up on her cot, wondering what she was going to do.

The long silver robes would conceal her predicament for a month or so, but eventually her growing belly would be obvious to all.

Sometimes, a Hilliri woman would find herself in a situation where her parents didn't approve of her husband. They would prevent the husband from seeing their daughter, hoping that she wasn't pregnant already. Often, though, the daughter would slip out and find her man. She would return when she was well into pregnancy. It was hard to argue with an imminent birth, and the unwanted husband would be reluctantly accepted. It wasn't as if the woman could marry another. That was taboo.

In her case, there would be no returning, no accepting. Lirienne had to leave. She couldn't go to Lorenzo though. They weren't supposed to meet yet. He would be somewhere out in the forest, in an enemy camp, leading his fighters to defend their land. She had to wait until the next starbright, a fortnight away. Meanwhile, new life grew inside her, a tiny miracle that she and Lorenzo had created from their love.

She wanted, more than anything, to be with Lorenzo at this moment, to share this news. She craved his strength to fortify her, his enthusiasm to warm her, his presence to comfort her. Without him, she was alone in the world with no one to turn to. For the sake of their baby, though, she would have to find strength, at least until she could return to him and they could make plans to leave together.

CHAPTER TWENTY-FOUR

It was a relief when the day Lirienne and Lorenzo had planned to meet finally arrived. The sky had grown progressively brighter over the last few nights. The day before, Lirienne had seen the middle star, the one that only came out a few days before starbright which was the one night of each cycle when the cloudy atmosphere surrounding the world was at its thinnest and a veil of a thousand tiny points of light filled the sky.

Lirienne was the last person in the healing tent, finishing with a patient who had taken longer than most. A borderline case that anyone else would have "pitched". Lirienne couldn't allow herself to judge him unworthy when his injuries were still within the carefully monitored limit of her abilities.

Dor frowned at her. He looked more tired than usual. "How much longer will you be?"

Lirienne hummed under her breath as she worked. "Another quarter hour. Why don't you go on? I can clean up when I'm finished."

He nodded absently, waved, and left.

Lirienne straightened the moment he was gone. In truth, her patient's healing was complete. She had only pretended it wasn't to see if she could get a few minutes alone, and it had worked.

Dor's fatigue had made him careless. He didn't know why she was here, but he had been ordered not to leave her alone and had kept that order up until now.

Lirienne called for help from the soldiers waiting outside and they brought the patient to another tent to rest. She went to the break tent to clean up and eat a little. No one was there.

She slipped off her silver robe and tucked it under a cot. Underneath, she wore a plain gray dress. The others had left a little food behind for her, which she stuffed into her pockets.

Listening for sounds of someone coming, she waited, but luck was with her. After she finished stowing the food, Lirienne grabbed one of the heavy woolen blankets to wrap around her shoulders. The days were warmer now, but it could be cold at night. Peeking outside, she observed that the camp was relatively quiet at this late hour, and the healing tent was close to the perimeter. Lirienne walked purposefully out into the night air. There were camp helpers about, guild-less people who had little talent with maru, who worked at the more mundane chores. Without her silver robe, she hoped to pass as one.

A soldier approached her, yawning. She tensed as she passed him, but he wasn't interested.

Walking a little farther, she reached the edge of the camp and looked about. She slipped behind a large tent filled with snoring people.

Once she was outside the camp circle, shadows enveloped everything around her. The sky filled with a cloak of stars, making navigation easy, but also making it easier to spot her pale hair as she waded through the woods. She covered it with the blanket just to be extra careful. No one would look for her until dawn, when she didn't show up for her next shift.

A pang of guilt struck her. Her absence would make more work for the others, and possibly lower the level at which patients were pitched. She balled up her fists in frustration. She wasn't the only one responsible for the health of the soldiers. If the generals didn't send soldiers out to fight, they wouldn't come back injured in the first place. If only the College would send more healers to the front, and if only they would test the healers before dismissing them from their shifts, to be sure they had given all they could to their work.

She passed through a denser section of the forest. She needed to put some distance between herself and the camp before she attempted to transport away. She didn't want anyone to notice that blackened trees were becoming more frequent in the area, so she had to spread out the locations from which she selected trees for this task.

Fatigue began to slow her, but she couldn't tell if it was because she was unused to walking, or the healing she had done, or perhaps her current condition. She would stop soon, rest, and select a tree.

She hoped that Lorenzo would be at the house when she arrived. She was eager to tell him the news and eager to see him again. The walk had tired her though. She shivered, sensing a fever. More maru would definitely help, even if it was tainted and unsavory. She didn't relish the thought, but there was no other way.

She selected a strong, healthy tree and placed her palms flat against the rough wood. She tapped the tree, taking as much as she felt she could bear.

It was so delicious. It was a relief to sense the strength flow into her after weeks of being drained. She loved the pulsing sensation as it charged her, thickly flowing, until the maru filled her to the brim. For a moment, Lirienne panicked, thinking that the added maru might be harmful to her baby. She was so tired she hadn't considered this before. She snapped her hands back from the tree. Even a baby had maru, so it shouldn't be harmful, but the doubt troubled her.

What was this doing to her? Each time, she wanted to draw from the tree until it felt as if she shone like the sun with the strength that it gave her. Only her fear kept her from doing so.

Gathering up her wits, she called upon the image of the little bedroom in the hut where Lorenzo's brother had died, in the town not far from the fighting. She would find Lorenzo there and give him the news. With only a slight push of her will, she tapped her over-brimming maru and transported herself there.

This time Lirienne was careful to take a deep breath before she went, so that when she arrived, she still had air in her lungs. She looked around the room, a bare place with only a bed, a night table and a single chair as furnishings. No one was here. But nothing had changed either. Lirienne was unfazed. He might come if she waited for a while. She sat on the chair and rested, although she had maru aplenty for the return trip.

After an hour, doubt crept into Lirienne's thoughts. What should she do if Lorenzo didn't come? How long should she wait for him and what should she do if someone else came instead? She jumped to her feet and headed downstairs. No Lorenzo there either. She lifted the curtain from the window, thinking he might be outside. The position of the house was a little way from the rest of the village. She let only one eye peer through the gap. There was no one. No one was outside in the distance either. Perhaps everyone was camped near the front lines. She let the curtain drop and searched the room. It was probably safer upstairs where she could remain unseen. She could transport away if anyone came in.

Back to the upstairs bedroom she went. She paced the length of the room as the hours passed, thinking of all the unpleasant things that might have happened to Lorenzo. He could be injured and unable to get here, or perhaps be in the middle of a battle.

On the other hand, he might have been called back to Madrezza to report to his father.

After waiting half the night for him, Lirienne reluctantly decided to return to the encampment. It made her sick to think of having to wait another month before seeing Lorenzo again, so she hunted through the house until she found a sheet of parchment, a pen, and some ink. She wrote him a brief message. In it, she suggested a new, secondary time they could meet in just two weeks, if their primary time wasn't possible. She didn't tell him about the baby. She would wait until she saw him again.

She placed the note on the pillow and with a quick thought and a maru backed push, she was back in the woods just outside the rows of tents. It was still dark enough to slip back to her tent undetected.

She attempted to get some rest before her next shift, but she drifted in and out of a troubled sleep, dreaming of battles, wounded soldiers, and death. She also dreamed of healing. Each time she looked down at her next patient, a moment of shock passed through her to see that it was someone she cared for. One time it was Valran and later on it was Lorenzo. She tossed aside the blanket and rose. This kind of sleep offered her no rest.

CHAPTER TWENTY-FIVE

Two weeks later, Lirienne tried again to meet with Lorenzo. Her heart lifted at the thought of seeing him, only to sink when she arrived at the house to find it empty. A layer of dust had accumulated on every surface with no traces to signal anyone had been there. When she checked the bedroom, the note was still on the pillow. Lirienne didn't know what else to do, so she waited an hour, and then reluctantly returned to her tent.

Every day Dor had more questions about her waning energy. Although she tried to avoid him, it was his duty to ensure the healers in his charge were well enough to perform their work, and she was clearly flagging.

He asked her to have one of the women healers she worked with check her, but Lirienne couldn't allow that. It would reveal the secret of her condition. As it was, she could only hold him off so long before Dor would go to speak with her brother on the matter. She had to find Lorenzo and go away with him soon. If she stayed, she would eventually be obliged to reveal her pregnancy, and then the dreaded question of the baby's father would create another disaster.

If she couldn't find him or learn what had happened to him, she would spend the next month going through all of the possibilities for why Lorenzo hadn't come until she went mad with worry. And what if he didn't show up the next month again? The thought left her desperate.

The wait seemed especially long until the next starbright, although it was only another two weeks.

When the night arrived, Lirienne scented a storm in the air. Without thinking, she went off into the wood and drew maru from a tree. It filled her but left a gnawing gap-like hunger in her belly.

Lirienne could only hope that this time Lorenzo would be there. If he wasn't, she didn't know what to do. There was nowhere else to go.

As she materialized into the dark upper room of Lorenzo's

house, she gasped for air. It wasn't the travel that made her cough. Smoke filtered into the room from the ceiling. She ran to the window to peer outside. The ground below was empty. Rain poured down. Lightning brightened the sky and the outdoors became as brilliant as day for a second. The windows rattled a few moments later as the thunder reverberated. Darkness returned. More smoke filled the room, making her cough, and a wave of heat washed over her. As the room flashed with brightness again, she realized that lightning must have struck the house. It was too dangerous to stay here. With her maru, she jumped the short distance into the bushes just outside the house. From there, she watched the building light up as the flames consumed it.

She sank down to the ground and struggled with her tears. How would she ever find Lorenzo now?

Mastering herself, she concluded she must try something new. Lirienne searched her memories for another place where she might find him, since it was obvious he hadn't returned here, and now he couldn't. They had talked of Madrezza, the town where his father lived, and he had shared a brief glimpse of the place he called home, a large manor on the hillside. Remembering the images he had shared as they lay together, their hands clasped, their minds mingling, Lirienne had an idea. The only picture that might be strong enough for her to fix upon was one of his personal rooms in that place. It was a long way off, and the dilemma was that the trip might deplete her of maru. Who knew what dangers might greet her there, and where she might refill in order to flee should she need to.

She puzzled about this for a while, getting wetter as the rain came down, reviewing the scant information she had on the manor and its surroundings. The images available to her were of a portrait hanging on the wall in Lorenzo's room, a window, a desk, an upholstered chaise, and a rug. Lirienne tried to remember what was outside of Lorenzo's room. Had she seen a tree? If so, she could flee out to it in a short hop and draw what she needed to return to the Hilliri camp moments later.

Her robes were drenched with rain. It was time to leave.

Closing her eyes, she imagined herself on the bed in Lorenzo's room, in the sumptuous house on the hill.

In a flash, she was there. Lirienne opened her eyes with a start and looked about her surroundings. It wasn't the room she had envisioned. The scent of turpentine and linseed oil assaulted her nose, reminding her of a time long past when she sat for a portrait. The scent made her gag and her head began to spin. Instead of the sumptuous furnishings of a wealthy family home, there were painted canvases stretched on frames leaning against a wall, a table full of brushes and jars, and a bed with an old, worn quilt. Lirienne filled with despair as she realized she wouldn't find Lorenzo here.

She was clearly in someone else's home, but whose house and where? Was there danger here? She scanned the room. Several panes of glass let in a faint glow of dawn. Her mind furiously tried to make sense of what she saw. A large portrait hung above the bed. This must have been why Lirienne had ended up here. She probably had imagined the portrait in Lorenzo's room inaccurately. The sitter in this portrait, a Hilliri woman, looked almost alive, as if she might stand and walk away at any moment.

Something about the woman's features struck Lirienne as familiar. Seeing a familial resemblance, she smiled. As she had said to Lord Pirvan, she was likely related in some way to all of the noble houses of the Hilliri. At least the portrait indicated the home belonged to someone Hilliri. Perhaps she had traveled to a place she knew—the home of a relative somewhere in Kalad. Nothing around Lirienne felt familiar though. The house was too modest. Thinking of her safety, she moved toward the window. Enroute, she tripped and knocked over a chair. Her heart fluttered at the sound. She cringed as it echoed throughout the room.

A shuffling sound came from behind the door. Someone was in the house. The doorknob squeaked as it turned. She swung around and began tugging at the window to escape. The homeowner could be either friend or foe, she didn't intend to stay and find out. Pulling at the sash, she tried to lift the pane on its channel, but it wouldn't budge. With a creak of hinges, she knew that someone had entered the room. Cooking odors wafted in.

She swung around, pressing herself back against the window. A Hilliri woman stepped in and straightened in surprise, letting out a yelp. Belatedly, Lirienne realized she should have transported outside, but now that the woman was looking at her, she couldn't. The woman held back, breathing hard. Her brightly colored, homemade clothes were very unusual and, oddest of all, her hands were bare.

The woman blinked. "You frightened me. Who are you? And how did you get in here?"

She eyed Lirienne with surprise and suspicion. She spoke well, without a clear regional accent to help Lirienne guess her present location. Even if she was a stranger, Lirienne was happy to have found a Hilliri woman. She was a trespasser here, but not an enemy.

"I didn't mean to intrude. I'm sorry. I was cold and the house looked nice," Lirienne babbled, sounding frantic and distressed. "I should have knocked. It's just that I'm completely confused."

The woman didn't appear to be a threat, nor did she seem overly threatened by Lirienne, but she kept her distance.

Lirienne needed answers though, and she needed to find Lorenzo. "Where am I?"

The woman relaxed a little. Lirienne was so petite she was hardly fearsome. "You're in the village of Alterra. You haven't answered my question yet."

"I'm Nia," she lied. It was better not to say who she really was. That would be much more dangerous.

The woman tilted her head and smiled. "I'm Adina. I'm the local healer."

She spoke as one who knew many kinds of people, some of whom might not be in their right mind. She probably had figured Lirienne to be one of them. Her gray eyes were bright in the filtered light. Her smooth, weathered face a sign of age among the long-lived Hilliri. Lirienne thought she looked kind. Adina said she was a healer, which relieved her somewhat. She wondered why the name of the village seemed familiar.

"I don't know that village. Is it in Kalad?"

Adina frowned. "How is it that you don't know where you are?"

Lirienne searched for something believable to say. "As I said, I am lost."

It wasn't the best answer, but Adina let the response go. "This village is fairly new. It's in Castillon, not too far from the border of Kalad."

Lirienne's mouth dropped open. "What are Hilliri doing in Castillon?" The moment she asked, Lirienne remembered the settlement her brother had mentioned.

Adina kept her face calm, though a twitch appeared at the corner of her mouth. "We established Alterra to live in exile."

Lirienne hadn't understood why anyone would want to live in exile. "Castillon belongs to the Trillas, but if Kalad wins the war, your village will be in Kalad once more."

Adina cleared her throat. "That may be true. Kaldene soldiers have already infiltrated our village, but they haven't kept more than an occasional watch on us. When we first came here, we were on the sufferance of the Lord of Castillon. He will not likely defend us, though. We can only wait and see what happens."

Lirienne heard footsteps and a door unlatching. A man entered the room and stood beside the woman. "Adina, you didn't tell me we had a guest!"

She turned to the man and then back to Lirienne. "More like an intruder. Nia, this is my husband, Ergin. He is a painter. Ergin, this is Nia."

He was tall and thin, with silver hair and sharp, pale green eyes. He gave a deep and formal bow, incongruous with the rustic setting. "At your service, my lady."

The formal address surprised her. Dressed as she was, there was no reason to think that she was anything but common.

Adina looked at her. "She hasn't said yet what brings her here."

It was hard to think of something that would satisfy them that wouldn't either make them fearful or cause them to judge her. Lirienne decided it was best to stick as close to the truth as possible.

"I'm in some trouble back home."

For a young woman that could mean a number of things, none of which would be a danger to others.

Adina stared at Lirienne for a moment. She peered at her husband, who inclined his head, as if she had spoken, then turned to Lirienne. "You may stay here with us for today."

Lirienne blushed. "I couldn't . . ." She had invaded their home, and they invited her to stay.

Her expression must have looked puzzled, for Adina reassured her. "You did say that you didn't have anywhere to go. We can't send you back out alone without shelter."

Lirienne felt warmed, yet ashamed. She hadn't told them her real name or anything about how or why she had appeared in their home. She looked up at the portrait again. The man's name was familiar. Then it came to her.

"You're Ergamine Lotreah, the painter!"

His eyes twinkled with delight. "I see you recognize my portrait of our late queen. You're familiar with my work, then?"

For a moment, Lirienne could only blink. He'd just said that the portrait was of her mother—the mother she had never known. She worked to school her features to stillness. She recalled the portrait in her father's study, done by another artist, but compared to this work, it seemed stilted and harsh. Ergin clearly had great talent.

"Indeed, I am," Lirienne said.

She stared at the painting for a moment longer to collect her thoughts. The work was rugged, loose brush strokes done with a relaxed hand, yet it evoked something fleeting of the person behind the frozen smile. "She's wonderful. I almost expect her to stand up and step out of the frame."

Ergin looked up at his painting. "It would have hung in the Royal Palace, but I painted it just before she died. The king refused to accept the work when I brought it to him. He said it looked too much like her and he couldn't bear to look at it. It was one of my best works, so I kept it."

A lump formed in Lirienne's throat as she thought of her mother, sitting for a portrait during what would be her last days. Lirienne wanted badly to know something about the woman who had brought her into this world, but to risk revealing her identity was foolish.

"Was she . . . kind?"

Ergin looked upward and shivered. "Indeed, to her very core, or her likeness would never have graced the walls of my home. I keep it to remind me that warm and generous people are still born among the Hilliri."

"Ergin, please . . ." Adina chided her husband. "We live here to be away from Kalad and the oppressive social rules there." She turned to Lirienne, examining her, evaluating.

A loud gurgling made Lirienne clasp her stomach.

Ergin smirked a little. "You must be hungry. We should get you something to eat."

Lirienne smiled, relieved she had found somewhere friendly. They seemed like good people, if somewhat odd.

While the man left, the woman sat down beside her on the bed. "Is there something I should know about why a young woman would be wandering around in the forest on the wrong side of the border?"

Lirienne didn't want to answer, but she couldn't let them think something worse had happened. "My husband disappeared, and I can't go home to my parents. They didn't approve of him." It was a common enough story and it wasn't all that far from the truth.

"So you wandered into Castillon and found a village near the border?"

Ergin entered with a tray, which he placed on the bed beside

Lirienne. Hot porridge transported sharp spice scents up to her nose. She wolfed down spoonfuls, unable to keep herself to a well-mannered pace. It had been a long time since her last meal.

Ergin watched her. "Our guest is hungry, my dear."

Adina looked over at her husband knowingly.

Lirienne glanced up from her bowl and reddened. Would Adina guess her predicament?

CHAPTER TWENTY-SIX

The next morning, Lirienne woke late, much revived. Freed from healing for a time, her energy rose in response. She stretched out and stood up. A breeze wafted through the open window. There was warmth on the wind, a sign that summer was indeed upon them. Her gaze returned to the portrait of her mother. It was wonderful to see her likeness and hear Ergin's stories about her last night, but she worried her hosts would notice the resemblance and ask questions.

Still, she was safer here than in the army camp. She would have to try to find news of Lorenzo, too. A delay was the most likely reason for his absence, but it was hard not to wonder if he still lived. Of course, if someone in the Kalad army had killed him, there would have been celebrating in the encampment at the news and she would have heard by now.

There was a knock at the door.

Lirienne opened it and Adina popped her head in. "Good morning. I hope you were comfortable last night." She slipped inside and closed the door.

"Indeed. Once again, I must thank you for allowing me to stay."

Adina sat in the corner chair by the window. "You indicated that you left your family and weren't planning to return. Are you planning to stay here in Alterra?"

Lirienne looked down at her toes. She didn't know where to go.

"Is it possible?" she asked. "I have to figure out what to do, and I am hoping to find someone who can tell me what happened to my husband."

"You must be worried about him."

Lirienne shook her head. "He's resourceful. I'm sure he'll show up eventually."

"I hope so." Adina looked up at the portrait.

Lirienne had tried to put her fears about Lorenzo aside, but all her worries flooded back at Adina's question. Tears welled up in her eyes.

Adina dropped her kitchen rag and wrapped her arms around

Lirienne. "You're safe here, Nia. No one is going to send you away if you don't want to go."

Lirienne could hardly believe such affection from a total stranger. She accepted the embrace and slid her arms around Adina in return. A lump caught in her throat and she sobbed a little.

After a time, Adina released her and grinned. "I know what you need . . . some pie! Let's make one. I have a bowl of strawberries we can use."

"I can wash and slice them. Please allow me to help. You've done so much for me already."

They went into the kitchen where Adina showed Lirienne the cutting board and a basin of rinse water, then handed her a sharp knife. While they worked—Adina rolling out the pastry dough and Lirienne preparing berries—they talked and sang childhood songs. Lirienne relaxed as she laughed at the silly rhymes and meaningless tales. Adina also told her stories about her grown-up sons who were working abroad, one as an architect and the other as a bridge builder.

Lirienne mused on what her child might grow up to be one day, imagining him a tall, dark-haired man with blue eyes like his father. Perhaps he would be a healer as she was. She liked that idea, but then the thought occurred to her that he already had a place as heir to Castillon, though that particular journey would be arduous. She puzzled on that thought. When had she realized her baby was a boy?

After dinner and the pie, which was excellent, Lirienne joined Ergin and Adina as they walked to the village common. She hadn't been outside yet, so everything was new to her. The forest thinned in the area they had settled, but the homes—small wooden structures with bright painted shutters—were sheltered under the tall canopy of trees. As they walked, the growth thinned out even more to a cleared area where emerald grass carpeted the ground and a starry sky opened up above them. Ergin said there were about thirty families here. Goats grazed and chickens pecked the ground by their feet. Inexperienced with livestock, Lirienne kept her distance.

A crowd gathered at this twilight hour. Oil lamps hung on posts around the perimeter of the area to give light. After several families joined the gathering, Lirienne realized no one wore guild colors. Instead, they wore bright shades of fine homespun mohair, decorated with needlework. Everyone looked different—

remarkably individual. They wore their hair in a variety of styles too. All of this, she realized, was intentional, to distinguish themselves from the people of Kalad, and from each other. It was a defiance of the conformity she had known all her life. She understood what they were working to achieve here.

Ergin, the apparent leader, called everyone to order. They stood in a circle in the middle of the common with Ergin at its center. He introduced Lirienne as Nia, and people called out to welcome her.

"Thank you for sheltering me."

Ergin continued. "We come together to remind ourselves of the reason for our exile, to recall what we have left behind and what we have acquired here in exchange."

A young girl stepped forward. "I left behind an inflexible guild school where I couldn't learn. Instead, I now learn all of the time, in everything I do."

Lirienne couldn't tell by the usual methods what her profession was.

Others nodded in agreement. Lirienne had experienced that inflexibility too, at the College of the Marukar. So many times when she'd asked for explanations, her teachers simply told her to accept how things were and not question, but the "why" felt meaningful and the need to know wouldn't let go of her.

A woman stepped forward as the girl returned to the circle. "I could never express my emotions. It wasn't acceptable to speak my mind. Now, I speak of all my joys and fears and people listen and appreciate me for it."

Lirienne also understood this. Many times she had tried to make herself heard, only to be treated as if her ideas were peculiar and didn't matter.

It went on like this until everyone had taken a turn. When it was over, they discussed a little bit of business—which person would be doing what over the next week. Apparently, they worked collectively—growing food and making clothing and crafts for sale—and everyone shared the harvest and the money. Lirienne didn't mind helping out to earn her keep, but she wasn't sure she would like it if she painted as well as Ergin and had to share the profits from her artwork.

As they wrapped up their meeting, a group of five soldiers from Kalad stepped into the clearing, startling Lirienne. Quickly, she covered her head with her wrap to hide her identity, lest they notice her and drag her back to her brother. Her heart pounded as their presence filled the common with bristling attitude.

Their leader cleared his throat. "Mayor Lotreah, a gathering in the village center doesn't seem wise considering there is a war going on at your very doorstep."

Ergin stepped forward to speak with the man. "Commander, we meet here every week to organize the operation of our village. We won't let your battles keep us from our business."

The soldier pursed his lips as he considered the response. "That may be, but we cannot ensure your safety if you continue."

Ergin bowed a little and lowered his head in concession. "It will have to do for the moment."

The soldiers turned about, marching back down the central path toward the unseen border. The commander scanned the crowd as he passed. Once he reached the outskirts of the village, Lirienne released a breath and pulled her wrap back around her shoulders. She would have to be careful here or someone would recognize her and notify her brother. By now, they would have noticed she wasn't in the encampment and her brother would be searching frantically for her. If they found her, she would be in bigger trouble than before.

When the gathering was over, Ergin walked arm in arm with Adina toward their home. Lirienne kept a little distance. She didn't want to be an ever-present bother to the nice couple who had taken her in.

As they approached the house, Ergin asked Lirienne what she thought of their village.

"I agree with you that society in Kalad is very rigid," she told him, "I like that you've tried to do better."

She thought of her own circumstance. While she had to accept responsibility for her actions in freeing a prisoner, the penalty seemed harsh. Working as a healer with the army during war was not for the faint of heart. The College normally only allowed those who volunteered to do this work, and Lirienne had certainly not volunteered.

The villagers reminded her more of Lorenzo than of anyone she knew back home. She sensed that the Trillas had fewer social rules and more freedom to speak their mind. The Hilliri, burdened by their gifts, their abilities, their long lives, and their extraordinary sensitivity, were afraid of getting too close to one another.

"When do you paint, Ergin?"

"When the mood strikes me. Sometimes I work for hours, and

then I even forget to eat. That's when it's the best." He grinned.

Lirienne thought that her host had a particular quality about him, something she had never seen before. He seemed more alive, alert to every stimulus. He was in tune with people, time, and the world. It was quite remarkable.

"You don't look like you miss your home at all, Nia."

Lirienne looked up at the stars through the clearing in the canopy of trees. Out here in the forest, there were no city lights to dim her view. The sky was full to overflowing with points of light. It was beautiful.

"No, I think I have come to the place where I should be."

CHAPTER TWENTY-SEVEN

Everyone had to work to make sure there was enough to go around. They put Lirienne to tending the goats. Although she had no experience with animals, it turned out the beasts liked her and followed her about, which meant they weren't running away as much as usual.

Perhaps it was the fact that she was expecting. Most of the goats were female, and they were almost all pregnant as well. These were special goats; their hair made wool that was beautiful, warm, and highly valued. At this moment, though, they looked rather peculiar and skinny from recent shearing. Their odd rectangular irises and leftover wisps of curly hair gave them the appearance of vagabonds. They bleated mournfully, inconsistent with their playful dancing.

She didn't have to do much but make sure that none of her charges strayed too far from their grazing grounds. They ate whatever grew on the forest floor, denuding an area after grazing there for a day, obliging them to move on to another location. This made her worry that soldiers might cross her path as she wandered about in the forest, so she wore local clothing borrowed from the villagers and kept a shawl to cover her head and face if needed.

The goats were fun to watch as they leaped about, prancing from rock to rock and over one another. She sat on a large boulder and looked out over the herd.

She had a few companions in this task: a young girl named Bethna and her smaller brother, Kinal. She took the opportunity to get to know them while they kept watch. They chattered on about the personality of this or that nanny goat as they petted the calmest ones.

Apparently, goats mostly bore twins. Lirienne smiled at this, for she was a twin too. This breed also grew hair at an amazing rate. Even though they were all but naked, her young companions assured her that the goats would be ready for shearing by the end of summer. Lirienne asked her young colleagues as many silly questions as she could think of to pass the time.

"Does it hurt them to be shorn?"

Bethna laughed and shook her head. "They're really hard to catch, but once you have one, they cooperate."

The boy cocked his head at that but kept silent.

"And you collect their wool to make clothing?"

Kinal grinned. "Yes, and to trade."

Lirienne smiled at them. Adults would have been much more impatient with her questions.

Since the grounds near the village were stripped of vegetation and it would take time for more to grow there, they led the herd north toward the border, where the land became rockier, and the trees were stunted by the shallow bed of soil in which they grew.

Finally, they came to the great canyon that was also the border with Kalad. It was a mighty scar cut deep into the land from east to west with a thin line of blue at the bottom. It had kept the two cultures isolated from one another for many centuries. This river flowed into the Eraldis, in whose chill waters Lirienne had almost lost her life. Recently bridges were built to span the chasm. They once facilitated limited trade between both countries, but now they only brought soldiers from Kalad into Castillon. Thankfully, those bridges were a good distance west of here. She wasn't likely to encounter any soldiers this far from the main roads, although they were frequent visitors in the village.

The wind whipped into a rage at these heights, making Lirienne's hair dance.

The goats, stripped of their only protection from the elements, clung together for warmth. They backed away from the edge, thankfully knowing better than to creep out on the exposed cliffs. The undergrowth grew thicker among the gnarled trees anyway. Lirienne counted quickly to see if she had all of her charges in sight.

With a sinking heart, she realized her count came up short. She thought of a dam who had already kidded, and her two little ones, who hadn't been seen in a while. She signaled to her companions that she would head east from where the herd huddled, along the side of the canyon. If she didn't find the missing goats there, she would return and head out in the opposite direction. Kinal looked concerned, but Bethna only smiled.

Lirienne walked along the ledge. Her bright, borrowed mohair robes lifted awkwardly with the shifting wind. She pulled her cloak tightly around her. She stepped carefully, keeping an eye on the ground. Along the path, she noted a few gaps where the ground appeared to pour away down some hidden hole. These shapes were always long and narrow, and always parallel with the edge of the canyon. She wondered what had made them. As she lingered along the cliff, she thought about what might be at their depths.

Curious, she left the path and went over to the edge of one particularly large slit. She saw light down in the middle of the hole, which surprised her. She had expected darkness. She followed the line of the cliff until she came to another one and saw that it too had a light shining through the middle of its depths.

What witchery was this?

Just then, she heard the bleat of a mother goat. She scanned through the trees and spotted the missing dam and her two kids, born early in the season. They were close to one of the holes.

She approached them slowly so they wouldn't bolt, concerned that they might misstep and fall into the hole. Who knew where they might end up if they did?

The mother goat had other ideas, though, and the moment she discerned that Lirienne had come close enough, she nudged her two charges forward right into the deep gash in the ground. In a moment, the three goats disappeared through the gap. Lirienne cried out, too late to stop them from falling to their doom. She rushed up to the edge of the hole and looked down.

Bright blue shone back at her. She shook her head in disbelief. How could the sky be underground? She noticed the long cut widened at the far end, where it appeared there were layers of stone, much like steps, carved into the sides of the gap. At the bottom, a length of stone floor stretched out, and at the far end, she could see more of the blue. The hole led to a lower-level cavern that looked out on one side to the canyon wall. It was a cave with a window.

The nanny and her kids blinked their strange eyes as they looked up at Lirienne. She called out to them to come, but they remained in place. Reluctantly, Lirienne took a step over the edge and climbed gingerly down to their level.

When she reached the ground below, the goats gathered around her, nibbling on her clothing. She petted the mother, chiding her for wandering off. The goat rubbed up against her hip. This, Lirienne realized, was goat affection. She petted the horned head and scratched between her ears, eliciting rhythmic bleats of goat happiness. She thought of the climb back up the rough stairs. The goats would be able to manage with no problem, provided she could convince them to come, but she would have to be especially careful. She peered over the canyon extending in front of her.

Perhaps there was another way out?

She approached the cliff edge. The whole side of the cave opened to the canyon, but its position somehow kept the wind out. There was no way to leave by this route, so she turned back to the stairs. As she approached the back of the cave where the light barely penetrated, she noted a hole that led into what appeared to be a tunnel. Judging by her position, it should lead to one of the other holes along the path. She followed it for a short distance until it opened out onto another similar cavern with another tunnel on the far side. The holes were linked up in a chain.

As she explored this second cave, the goats joined her. It was similar in structure to the first, but instead of a line of steps, a long, slightly angled ramp of stone and earth led up to the ground level above. Since the goats appeared to be following her again, she lifted the hem of her robe and began a careful ascent.

The going was rough as the surface was soft and slippery in places and hard and bumpy in others. The steady climb upward took strength and balance. Her breath came in wheezing gasps as she stumbled along, wishing the stairs had been safer, but in the end, a lesser incline was the more rational choice, no matter what it was made of, so she continued. The goats skipped along beside her, getting ahead when she slowed.

She navigated her way up through the opening in the ground back into the sunlit forest, breathing heavily as she settled herself down on the nearest fallen log. The mother goat snuffled at her neck, licking her salty skin.

"You are a lot of trouble, miss!" Lirienne said to the nanny goat as she scratched her head, but she was glad to have found this place and learned its secrets.

CHAPTER TWENTY-EIGHT

Lirienne rubbed her belly. It had grown over the past three months, and her baby moved increasingly, keeping her from resting at night. Yet her strength grew with her baby, for she no longer spent her days draining herself of maru to heal dying soldiers. It was a relief not to see blood and broken bodies everywhere she looked, and to look forward to holding a little wonder in her arms very soon.

She learned many new things while attempting to contribute to the village. She cooked, gathered food, sewed clothing, and much more. It pleased her to be busy. It helped her keep her mind off what might have happened to Lorenzo. In her daydreams, she imagined Lorenzo's expression of delight when she would tell him of their child.

At the next starbright, she went to the village where the house had been and waited in the bushes, but Lorenzo did not show. After that, she realized there was no point in returning. Doubts threatened to overwhelm her. She couldn't stop imagining Lorenzo lying on the forest floor somewhere, his lifeless body crumbling with time and exposure. Then she recalled how clever he could be, and how long he had already avoided capture and death in this conflict, and her hope rekindled for a while.

She worried she would have to raise this baby on her own, but she was running out of options for where to live once the child was born. She doubted the people of the village would accept her after the birth of such a strange child. Certainly there was no place for such a being within any of the three kingdoms of the Hilliri. She imagined the words they would use, Mundatar being the kindest of them. She had always thought she would go to live with Lorenzo at his home in Madrezza once the war was over, but without him, she had no idea how his people would react. She was certain they wouldn't take her in without him present to substantiate her claim.

She thought of her family but dismissed the idea. Appearances were important to a king. If she remained in Kalad, assuming they would even take her back, she would be forced to give up the child. She could never do that, and even if she could, no one would want her child. She also was sure she couldn't live without knowing what happened to him.

As summer became fall, she missed Lorenzo all the time. She listened when soldiers came by in case they spoke of the Slasher. Her hope gradually was replaced by acceptance. He was most certainly dead now. Many nights she huddled in her bed and wept for the loss of him. Bitterly, she realized their dream was gone. There would be no peace either.

As cold fell over the world, the issue of her baby's birth became unavoidable.

One day, while Adina sat beside her, darning some mittens, she turned to her with her quiet, gentle manner. "We haven't talked about your baby or what you want for the birth. I hope you'll allow me to assist."

Lirienne slumped. She was sad all of the time now that Lorenzo was probably dead. Adina was a calming presence and a skilled healer. She would welcome her aid, yet she could imagine her friend's kind features turning to horror as she held up a newborn baby with dark hair and bright eyes. Ergin and Adina were warm and accepting people, but it was beyond reason for her to hope that they would welcome such a child.

"I already owe you so much, Adina. I know it's too much to ask."

Adina tilted her head and smiled. "We are friends now, Nia. To welcome new life into the world is one of the most rewarding tasks for a healer. I hope you will allow me to support you in your journey."

The false name stung every time a friend spoke it, and now it pricked her. Lirienne understood what she meant, having assisted in numerous births, but it was unlikely that anyone would be sympathetic to her choice of husband. He was the enemy, and his people were considered inferior to hers.

She knew how to deliver a baby, and she believed she could manage on her own, but she would have to leave before the weather turned.

"It's getting chilly these days. Will it snow here?" she asked.

Lirienne had no idea what this time of year was like in this land. It was much further south than Kaldene City.

Adina shook her head. "It mostly rains in the winter. It hardly seems like winter compared to the hills outside of Kaldene City."

An image of the whiteness that blanketed the world on those

days when snow fell in the city came to Lirienne's mind. The layer of brightness obliterated sound, but the cold seeped into the drafty palace rooms and all the fireplaces in the world couldn't drive it away.

"The wool will keep us warm enough, I should think," Lirienne said.

Adina concurred. "Yes, definitely. It's an amazing material."

It would be shearing time soon, when she would be able to see the fruits of her labors harvested. Lirienne was glad that her goat herding efforts would be helpful to the people of the village. She wanted to leave something of worth behind in exchange for what she must take.

She rose to see what Ergin was doing. He was painting. It was fascinating to watch him work. The man was a brilliant artist. Lirienne could sit for hours, observing him mixing and applying paint. Perhaps one day when her predicament was resolved, she would commission him to paint a family portrait of her and Lorenzo and their baby.

Then she remembered that Lorenzo was likely already dead. She held back the tears that threatened to fall.

Ergin placed his brush on the table and turned toward Lirienne, examining her. "Would you sit for me, Nia? The heart-like shape of your face is somewhat rare, and I do so admire those cheekbones."

Lirienne blushed and chewed her lip. It was more than she could have asked for. "I would be honored."

That Ergin found her face interesting made her blush. She took a chair from the corner and placed it opposite him and sat down.

Ergin moved the canvas he was working on aside and grabbed a board and a creamy sheet of paper. He swapped out his brushes for some charcoal.

Lirienne mused while he sketched. Ergin was well traveled and knowledgeable on many subjects and many questions came to mind as she sat for him.

"Do you have a map of Castillon? I am curious about the sea, is it far from here?"

Ergin, immersed in his drawing, murmured, "It's a fair ride, perhaps four hours from here to the shore."

"And to get to one of the Trillas villages near there—is it much further?"

Ergin smudged a line with the tip of a finger, making it softer. "Well, the main town is Madrezza, which is at the mouth of the river Eraldis to the east. That's about another three hours ride along the coast. There's not much in between. Castillon is half empty, as it was only settled in the last century. It's very far from the rest of the Trillas-populated lands."

He tossed her a folded paper. She kept her upper body still for him as she unfolded the sheet to find a handmade map of Castillon sketched on it.

Looking up from the drawing, Lirienne met eyes with Ergin. "Did you make this?"

Ergin grinned in affirmation as he examined her features before returning to his work. "It's an old thing. I had it for years when I lived in Kalad. We used it to decide where we would settle when we came here."

Looking over the crisply inked parchment, Lirienne imagined Ergin and Adina and a few others coming to this glade with only a cart full of goods to get them started. It was a bold thing they had done—a dangerous thing.

"Do you know where the fighting is?"

"Yes, of course. When I go to Kalad to sell my work, I always take a route to avoid the fighting, although it costs me in time to detour around it. There is a Hilliri-controlled border outpost here that I use for crossing." He put down his charcoal and rose to look at the map, pointing to a spot at the border to the east of the village, at some distance from Alterra.

"Better to be safe, I suppose."

Lirienne had many questions to ask, and Ergin had abandoned his sketch for the moment, so she stood and spread the map out on the table beside him.

Ergin pointed to an area to the west, near the border between the Eraldis River and Alterra, passing the main road and two secondary roads, but falling short of their town by a good piece. "The fighting is mostly just along here. Kalad tries frequently to gain ground southward into Castillon, but they often get pushed back north to the canyon by the Castillonians. I wouldn't have thought the two sides evenly matched, but the Trillas always manage to find ways, even though they are poorly equipped and few in numbers. They keep Kalad from making any real advances. I suppose it helps that they know the ground better."

Lirienne stared at the map, thinking to commit it to memory. It might be useful.

Ergin returned to his chair and his sketch, and she settled back into hers. An image was beginning to form on his paper.

"I'm saddened that Kalad would use our presence here as an

excuse for aggression," Ergin went on. "The Trillas are different from us, but really, I suspect not in any important ways. They don't deserve this war."

Lirienne realized that Ergin was sympathizing with the Castillonians. For a moment, she was tempted to tell him the full story about her and Lorenzo. However, it occurred to her that people often say such things, but don't really mean them. She couldn't risk banishment from the only place that was safe for her right now. But she must decide what to do and do it soon. There wasn't much time left.

A heavy rapping on the front door echoed through the house. Ergin rose to answer it. Lirienne peeked out from her room. She caught a flash of steel gray and realized it was an army patrol. Her heart fluttered. It didn't happen often, but she still had to guard against detection by the soldiers who patrolled the village. Lirienne closed the door as quietly as possible, leaning against the wall and holding her breath. If they entered the house, she should be prepared to transport away to somewhere safe.

She heard Ergin answering the soldier. "No, we haven't seen a short young woman. Of course, we will inform you right away if one shows up in the village."

When the outer door closed again, she finally released the air she was holding. The tension made her dizzy. Her family must be worried, sending out soldiers to find her. She regretted not being able to tell them where she was, but there was no way she could imagine returning to them, ever.

CHAPTER TWENTY-NINE

The leaves turned color and it was finally shearing time. The goats had indeed grown shaggy as the summer faded. Their wool would be important both as a trade good and to keep the residents of Alterra warm throughout the cold season.

Bethna and Kinal, with whom Lirienne tended the flock, gave her a demonstration. They each had a set of clippers, which they put aside along with their gloves, and ran to grab a nearby animal. After catching a goat, they would caress its head and neck until it went limp before cutting off the matted layers of long hair with the shears. If done correctly, it came off in one large piece. The job looked simple enough.

Bethna handed Lirienne a spare pair of shears and went to work on a smaller goat on her own. Lirienne caught one of the dams that liked to follow her and petted her head. The goat appreciated the petting but showed no signs of sleepiness. Lirienne began to clip at the shaggy coat anyway. The goat wriggled and ran off, leaving Lirienne with a tuft of hair in her hand and a bare patch on the goat's side. Lirienne chased after it and sat down on top of it to hold it as she worked. She looked over at the other goat herders. Each one of their goats seemed to close its eyes shortly after they began to caress its fluffy head. Their goats seemed so relaxed and easy to work with compared to her own captive.

When she saw Lirienne struggling with her goat, Bethna grinned. She enjoyed watching Lirienne's struggles. Hot spots burned on Lirienne's cheeks.

She turned to Kinal, who was successfully managing a rather large goat. He was almost done, and a thick sheet of sheared hair lay beside the drowsing beast. He looked back at Lirienne, but with some measure of what appeared to be guilt. There must be a secret to this job which Bethna had intentionally neglected to tell her.

Lirienne wondered what she had done to produce such intransigence, then decided the girl was simply young and probably enjoyed feeling more capable than Lirienne. "Why aren't my goats sleeping like yours?"

Bethna shrugged, feigning dumbness. Kinal stared at his sister, and then at Lirienne. He focused on his work with renewed effort. Lirienne gritted her teeth. She refused to accept such unkind treatment. She stood, letting the dam free, and brushed off the excess hair that clung to her robe. "I guess you'll be shearing the whole flock without me then." She made to leave.

Bethna's mouth dropped open.

The boy, having released his latest victim, followed Lirienne as she walked away. "Wait!"

Lirienne turned and waited.

He opened his mouth to speak, but at first, there was no sound. "We . . . we put them to sleep using maru."

Lirienne's eyes widened in surprise. She had little awareness of what uses others had for the power outside of her own healing abilities, but she had put many a patient to sleep while working on their injuries, so she assumed it was essentially the same thing with animals.

Kinal caught a kid and knelt beside it. "Here."

She watched as he petted it and its eyes closed.

"You make them think of heaviness, of whiteness, like snow. Then they fall asleep."

Lirienne raised a brow. Of course! They did this without gloves. She should have figured it out.

"That's it?"

Kinal nodded.

Lirienne smiled at him. "Thank you. I'm not sure why your sister didn't want to tell me."

The boy chewed his lip. "Dunno. She can be bossy sometimes. I think she preferred it when it was only her and me doing the tending."

She had spoiled their routine by joining them. "Well, there are a lot of goats to shear. I think we'd best get back to it. I'm sure your sister will be glad she has fewer to work on this year, even if it means she has to put up with my presence."

She caught the goat that always followed her. Following the boy's instructions, she managed to put it to sleep. It didn't take much maru to accomplish this. Then, it was much easier to clip off all of the hair. It took a few tries for Lirienne to figure out the shearing technique, but after that, she was able to remove a whole coat in one piece as the others had.

The pile of hair grew as she worked, and her arms and back

began to ache. After a time, she found that she had become almost as efficient at the job as the others. She was pleased with her efforts. It wasn't quite like healing, but the results were similarly satisfying.

She continued to work all day, catching the goats, putting them to sleep, and clipping off their heavy coats, until she had a great big pile beside her. Occasionally she would look over and notice Bethna had been watching her, though the girl looked away as soon as their eyes met.

Spiteful child, Lirienne thought to herself, wondering what she had done to make Bethna dislike her so much.

CHAPTER THIRTY

The sky turned ink-dark and clouds roiled. A cold dampness lingered in the air. Restless, Lirienne felt like the baby was doing summersaults inside her. She could do little but sit and try to find a comfortable position. Her body ached from the day's work.

Adina popped her head into the room. "Dinner's ready."

"I'm sorry," Lirienne said. "I meant to offer to help tonight."

"You spent the day tending the goats."

It was true, she had, and in the cold weather this made her more tired than ever, but their wool would be a great help to the villagers in the coming winter months. It assuaged her guilt as she privately stocked up on supplies and dried foods for her confinement.

She had decided that once the time was near, she would leave the village and live in the forest on her own. It wasn't the best plan, but she couldn't think of anything else she could do.

She had tried to learn as much as she could about how to live off the land and had stored away items she thought she might need. When she had a free moment, she headed over to the string of caves where she had found the goats back in the spring. It was far enough from the village that it wasn't likely they would find her. She stashed as much firewood and as many blankets as she could, as well as a small chest filled with food, which she locked against vermin. So far, it remained in good condition.

They sat in their accustomed places at dinner, Ergin at one end of the table, Adina at the other, and Lirienne along one side. She had come to love their quiet ways. They didn't talk much, but Lirienne sensed other methods of communication took place. She knew that they couldn't communicate mind to mind unless they touched, yet they were quite remarkable in their synchronicity. She guessed that they had been married a very long time, though she could only wonder how old they must be.

She was grateful for their help and friendship all these months, but she had too much affection for them to test their goodwill with her truth. It was as much for their sakes as for her own that she endeavored to leave.

She decided that she would go tonight. All signs pointed to her child being ready to be born in a few weeks at the most. She couldn't risk waiting any longer. Later that night, she would flee to her new residence: a cave looking out over the canyon dividing the two nations.

The house was quiet when Lirienne awoke in the early hours. Outside, darkness covered the forest, but a glow in the sky indicated that dawn was not far off. She listened to the sounds of the sleeping home to make sure no one was awake. When some time had passed, she decided it was safe to travel. She had stowed a packed bag under her bed. She didn't have much, other than some warm clothing for the winter months she had been preparing under Adina's guidance.

Knitting was new to her and she laughed as she made the stitches so tight that the garment had to be undone and restarted three times before she found the right touch. She looked at others' work with much admiration after that. She did all the plain garter stitch of a sweater top, and when it came to the hem, she passed it over to Adina, who quickly added a few rows in a multi-colored floral pattern. The result was rather pretty, so she made another for good measure, and a skirt, with the same pattern repeated on the hem.

There were baby clothes as well, but those were gifts from Adina and the other people of the village. Lirienne wasn't skilled enough yet to navigate tiny sleeves and pant legs.

The clothing the Alterrans wore was so different. In Kalad, guild robes in drab colors dominated. Robes were always full length and belted, which allowed for little revelation of the figure beneath. The garb of the Alterrans was colorful and shapely, as the knitting tended to cling to the body. The patterns and decoration added another personal touch, and the dye colors were significantly brighter than anything society approved of back home.

Lirienne began to identify people in the village by their clothing and realized how much anonymity traditional Hilliri clothing provided. Each Alterran stood out as someone unique.

As she stuffed the last items into her bag and swung it over her shoulder, she took care not to make noise. She stepped carefully, cautious of loose boards and creaky door hinges, moving ever so slowly.

As she shut the front door and stepped into the forest, she breathed in. Her deception done, she could walk now with ease. She looked up to see the stars between the trees. A thick band of clustered points showed her where she should walk. She tightened her cloak around her and headed toward her new home.

As Lirienne neared the ravine where the chain of caves was located, she slowed her pace. By now, her eyes had adapted to the night, but it wouldn't do for her to twist an ankle walking on the uneven ground or slip accidentally and fall into one of the caves lurking below.

She soon spotted the first sunken holes. She kept to the cliffside as she headed east along the ravine edge, watching the line of cave openings on the ground beside her under the trees. The cave she had chosen was at the end of the chain, the one farthest from both the front and Alterra. She recognized the outline of the rugged stair she had first used to get into the cave. Her body was more ungainly now, so she had to take great care not to slip and fall as she descended. She wished Lorenzo could be here. He would offer to help her, balancing her weight against his own strong body. But that was not her story. She resigned herself to being on her own.

As she reached the bottom of the natural staircase, she took a long breath and turned to the opening. It was morning now, and the light of the bright blue winter sky beamed in from the large aperture. She sat by the ledge and took in the scene, so beautiful and so peaceful.

The ravine, etched out by flowing waters over millennia, had grown over with vines and moss. The winter turned these red or brown, but they still showed signs of life, if dormant.

Creeping out of the house without waking anyone and trekking through the forest in the dark had strained Lirienne. She went to her stores and brought out a sleeping pad and blanket and settled down in the back of the cave for a rest in her new home.

For a long time, she couldn't sleep. She was unused to the stillness of the wild and the quiet shuffling of other living things. The hugeness of what she had done engulfed her and made her wonder at the wisdom of it. If only she could have found Lorenzo. They could have lived here together. She would have to be content to live here with her baby instead.

CHAPTER THIRTY-ONE

Lirienne opened her eyes, disoriented at first, thinking she was still in Ergin's house. The sun beat down. Her mouth was parched and her stomach rumbled. She sat up abruptly before she realized where she was. The ravine view out the large hole in the side of the cave confirmed that she had indeed run away.

Taking stock, Lirienne was glad to recall that she had food and supplies and was well equipped for her next few months. What she would do once it was gone, she didn't know. So much was uncertain. Hiding out here in the cave was the only solution she could manage, but it was far from ideal.

She moved to the chest where she kept her food and found some dried fruits to nibble for breakfast. She needed water, though. She hadn't thought to bring any with her on her final journey as there was a spring nearby. She could fill her canteen there, and she had a larger container for storage.

As the day became warmer, Lirienne sat near the ledge overlooking the ravine and soaked up a little sunshine. She looked over the edge and thought of her future. It seemed bleak with Lorenzo likely dead, and she and their son forced to live alone in the woods. Even the baby's impending birth could not lift her mood. Yet she still harbored a tiny hope that something would change, otherwise she would have elected to leap from this high place and let the canyon take her life.

She knew she should eat meat if she could find some. She recalled the traps that Lorenzo had made in the forest after he had rescued her from the river. She would try to set up her own. It should be considerably easier since she had tools this time.

A wave of longing flooded through her. Tears sprang from her eyes as her thoughts went to Lorenzo. Perhaps the changes in her body made it worse. Emotions could be in turmoil during pregnancy, and the mingling of grief with anticipation left an ache in her heart every day. She made her traps as he had done, with a stone and a few twigs, hardly even looking at her work as the tears made it difficult to see. She wiped her eyes with her sleeve and returned to her cave.

A week of this simple life of trapping, tending fire, and collecting water made the days blur into each other. The season was advancing, though, and she had no doubt there would be strong signs of winter shortly. She would have to devise some way to shelter the cave opening from the elements. Once the wind turned cold and shifted directions, it might not be so still inside her new domain.

She built walls from thin boughs, woven together and thatched with vines and grasses. It was all she could find. She propped these up with thicker branches bundled together and strapped into a triangle shape for stability. She laid the thatched parts on one side. It was an imperfect solution, but it would at least cut down on the amount of wind that would be able to enter her new home.

At night, she sat by the open fire pit, carefully feeding it bits of kindling. She would have to collect as much as possible to store for the winter to come. Already, she had a good-sized pile that she had prepared over the last few months before settling in.

This life was silent. She missed the company of her friends in Alterra, and her family in Kaldene City. She sometimes spoke her thoughts aloud, just to have an excuse to use her voice and hear speech. She felt silly at first, but as time went on, she grew accustomed to it. She would even answer her own questions, as if there were another person present. She pretended Lorenzo was there to keep her company. She talked about their baby, how he moved about, becoming more restless now as his time to be born grew nearer.

Once, she spotted a soldier. He was patrolling near the edge of the territory they typically covered. He had stared out over the forest where the string of caves began. She slipped behind a slender tree and held her breath. After a while, she dared to peek out and check. He had gone by then. It brought on a fresh pang of guilt that her family didn't know where she was or if she still lived, but there was no way to tell them.

Another time, she heard goats bleating. She worried more about them. They might go to her, being familiar with her scent. She ducked back into her cave and tried not to move for a long while. She realized then that she missed the goats too, and even the surly girl and her brother who had tended them with her.

A few weeks after she moved in, she started to notice contractions. This was normal, and she was glad she possessed a healer's knowledge, or she might have panicked. This was the body's way of preparing for the main event. They made her uncomfortable. Sometimes she couldn't sleep because of them, so she paced the length of the cave, taking care not to go too near the opening in the dark.

At last, she woke one morning and felt the dampness of the first snow. It seeped into her body and left her tired and sore. She stayed in bed most of that day, watching the white stuff fall from the sky. Just before dusk, she rose, collected some water, and checked her traps. She caught mostly squirrels, but they were nourishing. It pleased her to know that she had earned her meal from her own devices. It wasn't something a princess usually had to do. Lirienne didn't feel like much of a princess anymore.

She watched the sunset out of her cave opening, the sky all red and gray and purple as the light faded. The fire crackled and sparked as she added soft wood branches containing resin, feeding the flames so that her meat would cook. Occasionally it would sputter as the fat melted away. As the meat browned, she realized she wasn't hungry. In fact, the scent of it was making her sick. All of a sudden, a wave of nausea sent her rushing to the ravine edge where she bent over and emptied her stomach.

She stepped back from the edge, taking care not to slip and fall. She sat, trying to take a calming breath, but as she released the air from her lungs her whole middle compressed sharply, making her curl up into a ball. Once the sensation had passed, she stood and returned to the fire, only to find that her clothing was soaked below the waist. As a skilled healer, Lirienne knew well that her time had come. Her baby was about to be born.

CHAPTER THIRTY-TWO

Lirienne returned to her bed and piled the covers over her, as many as she could find. Then she attempted to relax, using the techniques that the Masters of her College had taught her. She would need to keep herself calm and controlled so that she could monitor her own progress.

For a long while she stayed beneath the pile of blankets breathing slowly and forcing herself to relax each time a wave of pressure and pain came upon her. It was difficult to manage with the cold pressing in on her. She knew this process; she had been through it many times before, helping women bring their children into the world. She practiced the correct way to breathe so that she could ride out the contractions that came like waves crashing upon the shore.

Hours passed as Lirienne did nothing but concentrate with all her might. She drifted in and out of sleep. She was tired, and the fatigue of concentrating so hard for so long wore on her. Nothing she had ever done had prepared her for this.

By dawn, as the pale glow of the rising sun filled her cave with limpid light, she had scarcely slept and she was colder than before.

The contractions were closer together now, an indication her labor had progressed. The pain, fatigue, and cold made Lirienne irritable. She knew she couldn't go on much longer.

She must have dozed off again despite her pain, for Lirienne woke with a start and found that the fire had burned out and her cave was growing cold. In her weakened state, she didn't have enough energy to start a new one. Perhaps her blankets would be enough to keep her warm.

Thirsty as well as hungry, she reached a hand out and caught the strap of her canteen. Yanking it toward her, she opened it, only to find it was almost empty.

***

Unable to keep her eyes open, Lirienne dozed again, slipping in and out of consciousness. As the morning progressed, her cave warmed a little. As she stared out at the view, she wondered if she would survive this. She wondered how she had been so foolish as to think that she could do this on her own. Now her baby's life was at risk as well as her own. Once more, she thought of Lorenzo and wondered how he had died, convinced that he was indeed dead. Perhaps when she died, she might see him again somewhere beyond this world.

The lore of her people spoke of the Guardians, beings of great power who watched over the world as a gardener tends his crops. It was believed that the spirits of people who passed on were gathered by these Guardians and brought somewhere safe and comfortable to rest from the great burdens of life.

It would take a Guardian coming to her right now with his or her great power, assuming that there were healers among them too, for Lirienne to survive this day.

As she stared out of the open side of her cave, licking her dried lips, she thought she heard a familiar sound: the bleating of a goat. Lirienne laughed, thinking her mind was losing its grip on reality.

After a moment, she heard the bleating of two not-so-small kids as well. Perhaps she wasn't hallucinating yet. She turned to look at the back wall of the cave where the stairway cut naturally into the stone. There stood the goat that she had rescued from this cavern in the spring with her two full-grown kids gathered around her. Behind them on the stairs stood Bethna and Kinal.

Lirienne tried to prop herself up, and opened her mouth to call out, but only a croak escaped.

The children looked at each other and then back to Lirienne.

She tried to call out again, putting in more effort. "Help!"

Her weak voice barely carried across the large cave, but they seemed to have heard. Kinal smiled at Lirienne, but Bethna looked as if she had seen something rotten and tugged her brother back up the stairs. Fear struck Lirienne as she realized that the girl might be spiteful enough to ignore her plea and the boy might be too young to defy his sister.

The goats remained and the nanny nudged Lirienne in the side with her head. She was so warm. Lirienne reached out and patted the goat's soft head and it snuggled up to her side. She encouraged the goat to settle beside her, and it did for a moment. The kids pushed themselves in beside their mother. Lirienne patted their soft sides as well, enjoying the affection and heat they provided, though she knew it wouldn't be long before they became restless and left.

As she caressed the sweet animals, Lirienne reminisced on the day she had sheared them. If she could make them sleepy as she had that day, they might remain longer. It would only take the slightest amount of maru.

She sent them images of flowering fields on a hot summer day. The dam sighed and rested her head on Lirienne's shoulder, warming her whole side. It had been a while since she had felt this warm.

Another contraction squeezed her, and she tried to breathe with it, but the pain made her cry out instead. She remained there with her goats warming her as tears streamed down her cheeks. Another contraction wrung her, but this time she managed to breathe with it. She must try to get her control back now that she was warm again.

She lay back and closed her eyes, content to rest in between ever more frequent onslaughts. She mastered herself, gathering back her strength. She knew she would need it for the end.

Time slowed as Lirienne's world closed in around her. Nothing outside her cave, or even her bed, mattered at all. She mustered all of her will to survive. There was a baby boy who would need her help to be born this day, and after that to live and grow and learn. For him, she would not give up.

CHAPTER THIRTY-THREE

It was well past dark when Lirienne woke. The goats were gone, but she was warm. A fire burned nearby. Her lips were parched, but otherwise she felt well, if tired. Something tickled at her breast. She blinked as she investigated. A tiny baby with a head of curly black hair lay bundled up in swaddling by her side, rooting.

She tried to remember the rest of the evening but couldn't put the pieces together. She pulled the little babe closer to her and inspected him further. He blinked and opened his eyes. Like Lorenzo's, they were bright blue. At once, Lirienne was awed and grieved. The child would always be a reminder of the man she had loved.

Deducing that he was hungry, she helped him latch on and take his fill from her breast. He gulped and inhaled deeply by turns. She rocked him as he fed, keeping him calm, though she had yet to hear him cry.

"He's got spirit, I'll grant you that."

Lirienne turned to see Adina watching over her from the other side of the fire. She didn't know what to say. Her mouth opened, but she had no words to speak.

"You had us so worried, Nia. We had no idea where you had gone, and how you would manage in your condition."

Lirienne could hardly believe Adina was here with her. "How did you find me?"

"You can thank the goat herd boy. Although his sister saw you here, she is a spiteful child and wasn't planning to say anything. He had more sense, although he's very young, so he came to fetch me."

Lirienne was confused. "You delivered my baby after all?"

Adina shook her head. She came over and sat on the bedding beside Lirienne. She caressed the baby's dark hair. "When I arrived, you were already done. You had tied off the cord and cut it and the baby was all wrapped up. You were fast asleep with three snoring goats nestled in around you for warmth. It was quite a scene."

It was all a bit fuzzy to Lirienne, but it felt right. She had been determined, that had stayed with her.

"Ergin made the fire. He's gone back to the house to fetch some warm things. I didn't think you would have the strength to move for a little while." Adina paused and cleared her throat. "You have some explaining to do, I think. You have more than a basic knowledge of birthing, for one thing, and I can see that your baby, although healthy, appears to have unusual parentage."

It was a delicate way to put it. It surprised Lirienne that Adina didn't seem repulsed by her dark-haired baby.

She glanced at him again. He had fallen asleep. It amazed Lirienne that his face was entirely relaxed.

She looked back at Adina who waited patiently for an explanation. She owed her the truth. Adina and Ergin had been kind and generous to her.

"I was trained at the College of the Marukar. I am a fully certified healer, Prestige Class."

Adina grinned. "I suspected as much. There was no other reasonable explanation, though I wasn't expecting Prestige Class. I don't understand why you thought it was necessary to take such a huge risk to come here and have your baby alone."

Lirienne realized that Adina didn't seem to care about her baby's strange parentage, other than being curious. She had misjudged her friend, thinking her as bigoted as the people she knew back in the city.

"I thought you would be horrified that my baby's father was Trillas."

Adina gasped. "Horrified? He's adorable. I guess you didn't know us well enough to know that we wouldn't judge, and perhaps you worried we might reject you when you had nowhere else to go."

Lirienne didn't know what to say. She had never expected such an answer.

Adina patted her shoulder. It was an unusual gesture for the Hilliri, who typically avoided casual touch. "I'm just glad that you managed and that you're both okay. Things could have turned out a lot worse."

It had taken every ounce of Lirienne's determination to succeed. She was tired, but a newfound inner strength occupied her. She felt as if she could do anything, as soon as she had a nap.

"I knew I was strong enough to do this. I thought there were no other choices."

Adina lowered her head. "Are you going to tell me who his father is?" she whispered to Lirienne. "I'm dying to know."

It was past time that she told Adina the whole truth. "You should probably also know who I am as well. I'm afraid I've been hiding out in your village under an assumed name."

Adina's expression didn't change. "We knew you gave us a false name. Most people in Alterra do at first. We expected as much under the circumstances. You say you were a Prestige Healer, so I have to assume you're not from some border village in Kalad."

Lirienne shook her head. "No. I'm from Kaldene City. My name is Lirienne Godehera."

Adina's eyes widened. "The king's youngest daughter. No wonder the soldiers have been keeping a closer eye on our village the last few months."

"And my husband was Lorenzo Calimero."

Adina's mouth fell open. "Lord Carlosi's son. The heir to Castillon." She looked at the baby. "This is a very special baby to both sides."

Lirienne wished Lorenzo were alive to show him his baby. She imagined he liked children. He seemed like the sort who would.

"I'm just sorry that he'll never have the chance to see his child."

Adina furrowed her brow. "Why is that? Surely, he can be found if needed."

Lirienne shook her head. "I tried to find him, but it's been months. We were supposed to meet every Starbright, but he didn't show up, and then the house burned down in a thunderstorm."

Adina sat up straighter. "The soldiers guarding the village reported seeing him in the area last week. They came to warn us, but I don't believe he would have attacked us. His father agreed to let us settle there."

Lirienne's heart began to pound a loud rhythm. "Nearby? He's alive?"

She tried to get out of bed, but Adina held her arms. "You can't go to him now. You shouldn't try to move around for another day at least."

Lirienne pulled away. She must find him. She could hardly believe after all these months there was hope that he lived. She had given up.

"Wait, Lirienne," Adina insisted. "When you are strong enough, Ergin and I will help you find him."

Lirienne had to agree, for she was already dizzy from the sudden movement. She wouldn't get far in this condition, even if every bone in her body cried out to go find him immediately.

Adina tucked her in under the covers with her baby by her side. The baby smelled sweet and his skin was soft. Lirienne caressed him to settle him down for a rest. She smiled. Lorenzo was alive.

"As soon as I'm able, we're going to go meet your daddy," she promised her son.

A dimple appeared on Adina's cheek. No one was immune to the charms of a tiny newborn baby.

Lirienne would have to name him soon. She would ask his father.

CHAPTER THIRTY-FOUR

The next day, Ergin returned. He and Adina brought Lirienne and her baby back to their home. As they made their way slowly on foot, Ergin looked at the child often, but said nothing, his expression unreadable.

Back at the house, Lirienne found her room untouched, as if they had thought of her as a permanent member of their family who had only gone away for a while.

Ergin found a small wooden box, and Adina lined it with fluffy goat hair and supplied a soft blanket. They put it on the floor in the corner of her room. Once he was fed, Lirienne placed the sleepy baby inside and covered him, tucking the blanket up tight around him. He continued to purse his lips as he slept, as if still at her breast. Damp hair pasted the sides of his face.

His dark hair evoked the image of Lorenzo. Now that she knew he was alive, it was urgent she find him. He lived a dangerous life. He could be killed in the fighting or die in an ambush, never knowing that he had a son. She didn't know what the future held for the three of them, but she had to reunite with her beloved. There was still a war to halt.

She found Adina reviewing her supply of herbs in the kitchen. Ergin sketched beside her. While maru work comprised the bulk of a healer's skills, there was also a place for medicinals.

"I must find my husband soon. You said that you knew where he might be?"

Ergin looked up from his sketching. "I know where the Trillas fighters have camped. Even if your husband isn't there now, he is their leader, so he must certainly return there often."

Lirienne weighed the danger of walking into an enemy camp with her need to find Lorenzo. "I must not wait too long. He could be hurt or killed at any time. He has to know about his son."

Adina stowed her herbs in a box. "Lirienne, you just gave birth and you're nursing. You can't leave your baby behind, and the journey is too dangerous to bring him with you."

Lirienne heard her arguments. She should agree, but too much was at stake: lives, peace, and their happiness. "You've healed the birthing tear and restored my body's balance. I don't need any more rest. I can't rest. It's been months since I've heard any news of him. I need to find Lorenzo."

Ergin rose from his place and laid his work down. "If you must go, I'll take you there. I'm worried you might go alone if I don't help you."

Adina gazed at her husband. A line formed between her eyebrows.

Ergin turned to his wife and squeezed her hands. "Don't worry, love. The Castillonians will recognize me. We went to see their Lord before we settled here, in peacetime. They'll know we're not their enemies. The camp is a fair distance from the border where the fighting happens."

Adina straightened her shoulders. "Which is why I'm going with you."

Hearing this, Lirienne filled with warmth for her friends, who would go so far to help her. As Ergin said, he would be recognized, which would make the journey safer.

"Thank you both . . . for everything."

Ergin bowed his head. "I could do no less for the daughter of our late queen. I hope you will take her portrait with you when you leave us."

Lirienne clapped a hand to her mouth. The painting gave her a sense that her mother's presence had been watching over her during her stay in Alterra. It brought her so much comfort. "Thank you, Ergin. I will treasure it always. Let's hope this turns out well."

"We'll leave just after dusk, then. We want to be as close as possible to the camp before they see us," Ergin said.

"If we dress in our bright colors, the soldiers will see we're not coming from Kalad. We'll wear a dark cloak to keep from being seen until we reach their camp," Adina added.

Ergin agreed.

In winter, dusk rolled in quickly in Alterra. Once the sun had passed its zenith, the daylight dissipated in less than four hours. Ergin had wrapped his thin frame in a warm, dark cloak. The two women did the same. Then Adina helped Lirienne wrap a length of fabric around herself to make a carrier for her baby. Lirienne had seen women working in the fields with babes strapped to their back or front using this technique of knotting the cloth and wrapping it around themselves. So far, the baby was cooperative, sleeping much of the time and only waking long enough to feed. Adina filled her bag with travel rations: dried fruit, cheese, bread, and sausages. She looked at Ergin in his dark cloak. "Let's keep to the shadows and be careful."

Lirienne worried whether they really looked too short to be mistaken for Trillas. She thought of what Lorenzo had said, that there were Trillas as small as her, though it was unusual.

They departed, heading out into the dark as the stars began to light the sky. They walked slowly, Ergin setting a languid pace in deference to Lirienne's short legs. It would be at least two hours before they were in the area of the Castillonian camp, but lookouts were often posted along the routes. Alert to any danger, Ergin continuously scanned the woods all around them.

All at once Adina cleared her throat. "Why did you take a Trillas man as your husband? I wonder how you came to see him as someone you could love, especially when you knew he would not be accepted by your family."

A smile crept over Lirienne's face as she stepped slowly along. "The question should be: how could I not? He had all of the qualities I had always wanted but could never find among the many men considered appropriate for me. In Kalad they always talked about the Trillas like they were more beast than person, but when I healed Lorenzo of the terrible wounds my brother and his soldiers inflicted on him, I realized he was made exactly the same as we are. He has a heart that beats to the same rhythm and is located in the same place in his chest. His body works precisely the same as each of ours do. Our differences with the Trillas are minor and superficial. Coloring and height hardly matter at all. Would you believe you were better than I because your eyes are greener and mine are bluer?"

In the dark she couldn't see too much of Adina's expression, but she caught the sound of a sigh. Ergin shook his head. He paused for a moment, and she followed suit. He turned to face her. The spot where they rested was clear of branches and the starlight beamed down, lighting his pale features.

"I never thought of it that way. We're all a little bit different from one another, and the Trillas are just a bit more so." He hesitated for a moment, looking up into the sky. "How do you deal with the difference in lifespan, though? Aren't you concerned that you'll outlive him by many years?"

Lirienne felt tears coming on. She looked up in hope that the moisture would go back into her ducts. It was the one thing that hurt her to think on, and the one thing that she couldn't change. She would outlive Lorenzo. She could only hope they would have many years together. There is never really a guarantee no matter who one chooses. She thought of her brother and Talora.

"I love him. I wouldn't ever want anyone else. Before I met him, I was prepared to give up on marriage."

Ergin stepped forward and Lirienne followed. "You're braver than most, Lirienne Godehera. I've lived with Adina for so long that I don't even know if I could exist without her. She's so much a part of me now."

Adina leaned into his side and dropped her head onto his shoulder. It was a sweet picture. After a moment, they separated.

"I realize I may be alone in the end," Lirienne said. "Yet I will always hold Lorenzo's love with me . . . and his memory. I just hope it will be enough to help me carry on when he's gone."

They continued along a forest path for about an hour, speaking only occasionally. The second hour, the forest thinned out and joined up with a rough road, one that appeared to be little used and much overgrown. Ergin stopped now and then to check his bearings, but he seemed to know the way.

After the second hour had passed, the road began to look more used and less wild. The scrub in the ditch had almost disappeared. Finally, Ergin pointed ahead and they left the path, heading out into an open field.

"This is where it gets more dangerous," he said. "Try to keep to the shadows."

They marched through the field, lifting their knees as they went, for the grass grew taller here. Rocks and boulders dotted the landscape.

Ergin paused by a large boulder and bent to Lirienne's ear. Adina leaned in to hear as well. "Time for us to be very quiet. We're getting near. Be ready to reveal yourself the moment you see him. Otherwise, try to stay out of sight."

They crept along, pausing behind rocks and boulders as they went. As far as she could tell, they were heading northwest, toward the border where the bridge should be. Ergin had said that they would not get too close to the border, though.

Ergin stiffened and held out an arm to stop them from going farther. He placed a finger on his lips.

Lirienne waited, straining to see what was ahead. A shadow crossed the field in the distance. After a moment, another one passed, heading in the same direction.

They waited, watching as even more shadows went by. After the last one, Ergin continued to hold her back. Then his body relaxed, and he grabbed their sleeves and pulled them forward.

They scurried across the field, hunching over to avoid notice. When they reached the spot where the shadows had been, Ergin selected a boulder and tucked in behind it. Lirienne squinted to see if she could locate the Castillonians who were clearly in the area.

A snick of wood on wood caught Lirienne's attention. She turned to find a green-clad woman aiming an arrow right at her. She had focused all of her attention on the area before her; she forgot to check what was happening behind her.

Two other archers appeared in short order. Ergin turned and raised his hands, clutching a white linen cloth that fluttered in the breeze.

The faces of the Castillonians were grave. While they kept their bows aimed at them, the archers' posture seemed easier. The woman tossed back her curly auburn hair and signaled to the others to hold off.

"Explain your presence," she said.

CHAPTER THIRTY-FIVE

The woman spoke the common tongue with a heavy accent, rolling her Rs. It wasn't so different from the way Lorenzo spoke.

Ergin moved to face her. "We're from Alterra. We seek an audience with Lorenzo Calimero."

His own Common was smooth and crisp. It surprised Lirienne that he knew the language so well.

Lirienne stood up to her full height, slight as it was, and revealed the baby sleeping in his sling on her hip.

The woman took note. She turned to one of her companions. "Go to Lord Lorenzo, quickly. Tell him I said we have ghost visitors."

Immediate relief washed over Lirienne as she realized she would soon see her beloved, although the word the woman used puzzled her. It had never occurred to her that the Trillas might have derogatory names for the Hilliri as well.

The man saluted and left, fading into the shadows. The others snapped to attention and refocused their aim. Lirienne had expected they would be tense upon finding Hilliri wandering in their area. After all, it was their job to keep the Hilliri out of Castillon at all costs.

Another man approached from the dark. He was almost as tall as Lorenzo, but his hair, though following a similar fashion, was closer to dark brown than black. As she observed him, she realized there were similarities between the two, and wondered if he was a relative.

"What's going on here, Renata? Who are these people?"

"Ghosts, as you can see. The shorter woman has a baby too. They say they're from Alterra and have information for Lorenzo."

"How the blazes did ghosts get through our defense line? Someone must have been sleeping at their post." The man frowned, and again, Lirienne saw the resemblance to Lorenzo.

"We came from the east, not across the bridge." Ergin seemed anxious to allay their concerns. He lifted the white linen a little higher.

The man scowled even more. "I don't like this. And they speak Common. Surely they're spies."

Lirienne wondered why he didn't speak to them directly.

The man withdrew his sword from its sheath. The starlight reflected off the polished metal.

Renata stood firm. "They had a white flag and asked to speak to Lorenzo. I sent for him."

"That will take a while. He's gone back to the village again. Don't let them get away from here. If it were my decision, I'd execute them right now."

Renata pushed his sword aside. "The white flag should always be honored, Marcusi. If we don't respect it, we can't expect our enemies to either."

Marcusi rolled his eyes. Lirienne recognized the signs of an impatient personality. The man tossed his head and turned to stomp back several paces. Then he swiveled back again, as if he'd made a decision.

"I have to go," he said. "Let them wait and speak to him, but I'll have your hides if they escape. Once he's talked with them, I want a turn to question them before any decision is made."

With that, he spun on his heel and left.

Renata returned to Lirienne, assessing her, then Ergin. "You took a great risk in coming here. This is defended territory and it's full of soldiers hoping to kill some of your kind."

Lirienne decided she liked this woman. She lacked the sour suspiciousness of the man, and she wasn't afraid to speak to them.

She looked at Renata for a moment, trying to compose a sentence that had the right tone. "If it was up to me and I could make it happen, I would see an end to this war as soon as possible." Lirienne took a risk saying this; it was possible this woman liked battle and would be sad to see it end.

Renata kept her bow aimed at her charges. "Sometimes it's necessary to fight to keep your way of life and your freedom."

Lirienne bowed her head, appreciating the sentiment.

They waited there for some time. Lirienne thought the town Marcusi mentioned might be the one where Lorenzo's house had been located—the one where his brother had been killed. It was a fair distance from here, but if the soldier described her to him, she knew he would come in haste. She felt herself sway as fatigue set upon her. She was still somewhat weak from childbirth, even after several days of rest.

"May I sit?"

Renata gestured to the ground.

Lirienne slid down and propped herself up with her hands. The tufts of rough scrabble under her fingers reminded her that she could revive herself with maru. Feeling around behind her, she caught the branch of a weedy bush, sensing a greater store of maru there as it connected by its roots to a network of others. She dipped her consciousness into the rough vegetation and pulled, drawing its power to her. Her blood pulsed thickly, thrumming in her ears. She felt herself filling, to the top and over. She could hardly control it. Trembling with the strength that coursed through her, she summoned her last bit of will and cut off the flow. She wavered and nearly collapsed with the effort.

A burnt scent filled the air, but a lucky breeze sent the smell drifting away from their position and the darkness covered the damage she had done to the bush. She might need this boost before the night was over.

The stars moved across their paths in the sky until the night was almost gone. Finally, roughly an hour later, she heard hooves approaching, several sets, moving to a fast beat.

"Renata, I got your message."

The voice came from nearby in the dark. It warmed Lirienne upon the very first word.

"Lorenzo?" She called into the void.

She heard feet thump hard on the ground. Horse tack jingled then stilled.

"Lirienne?" His voice was rough with emotion.

Still brimming with power, Lirienne bolted upright. Lorenzo's strong arms wrapped around her. She leaned against his chest, listening for his heartbeat. He was alive. She had finally found him. "I'm so glad I found you."

He pulled back from her a little, the starlight illuminating his face. Lirienne noted his skin had faded to a lighter shade since last summer. His eyes darted about her face and body, before coming to rest on the sling and the baby wiggling inside.

His mouth dropped open. "Lirienne, you had a baby?"

He placed a hand on the dark head of the boy, struggling to understand. He looked into her eyes. She could have wept for gladness at the delight she saw on his face.

"A boy." He shook his head, unbelieving. "You've been alone all this time. I'm sorry, I had no idea."

Lirienne shook her head. "I've been with these people, Ergin and his wife Adina, in Alterra. I had to leave Kalad. I couldn't have the baby there. I tried to find you, but I kept failing."

Lorenzo caressed her cheek with his thumb. "I'm sorry, love. I kept missing our meetings, and when the house burned down, I didn't know what to do. Then I was under orders to organize an attack, and then I was in the middle of another battle. There was always something in the way. I couldn't get a message to you, and we hadn't planned for any contingencies."

Lorenzo turned to the others who still had their weapons ready and aimed. "Stand down, people. They are not enemies."

As ordered, they all lowered their bows, yet they remained where they stood, their bodies alert, appearing unconvinced of the status of their new guests. Lorenzo's eyes returned to the child and he smiled.

Renata moved a little closer. "My lord, is this woman one of your lovers?"

Lirienne's cheeks grew red. It surprised her that anyone would ask such a question. The thought of Lorenzo with another woman turned her blood hot.

Lorenzo looked up at Renata and spoke softly, as if he wished for her alone to hear. There was so much hope in his face. "No, Renata, not a lover. This is Lirienne. She is my wife."

CHAPTER THIRTY-SIX

Renata looked stunned. Her bow dropped to the ground as her mouth formed an "o." She looked at the others to see their reactions.

Lorenzo leaned down to her and spoke softly. "It's a long story. Right now, I want to get back to camp. I assume Marcusi is there looking after things in my absence."

She dug her fists into her hips and frowned. "I had to stop him from killing these people the moment we found them. He's always angry these days."

"We've lost a lot of good people these last few weeks. It takes a toll."

Renata tossed her head. "You don't see me hacking off the heads of all the strangers I meet. You have to talk to him."

By the manner of their interaction, Lirienne imagined they had known one another a long time. She bundled up her baby and rested his head on her shoulder. It was late in the night, but he was as bright-eyed as if it were midday. Lorenzo returned to her side to watch her as she rubbed the baby's back to make him sleep.

"We should go to the camp," he said. "I have business there. I'll introduce you to everyone so they give you a better welcome next time."

She beamed as she rocked her baby, though the idea of walking into a Trillas camp did not comfort her. Then she recalled what she had wanted to ask Lorenzo for a long while. "Our son needs a name, Lorenzo. I didn't want to choose one without you. I don't know your traditions."

Lorenzo looked pensive. "Among my people, the mother always chooses. What did you have in mind?"

Lirienne thought for a bit. "What was your mother's name?"

Lorenzo smiled. "Her name was Lira. She was kind, though I remember her always being sad. I'd like to think she would have welcomed you."

Lirienne's heart fluttered at hearing Lorenzo's pain. She went through the list of Hilliri names she had been considering and found one that drew her more than the others.

"I was thinking of a Hilliri name," she said, "but there is one that could honor her at the same time. The name is Liran. Do you like it?"

A bright flash of teeth indicated his approval, but he remained silent for a moment. "I think that sounds like a fine name. He will be Liran Calimero, then; one name from each of us."

Lirienne pressed her body against his. He was here. He was solid, real, and alive.

"I can't believe you're here now," she said. "I thought you had died."

He pulled her tighter to his chest. "And I can't believe you had a baby . . . we have a baby."

Savoring the moment, Lirienne could hardly speak. She remained wrapped in his arms, content to be there. All her worries about what to do and where to go vanished. Lorenzo would help her work it out.

"Where will we go, Lorenzo? Where can we live together with our son and be accepted?"

Lorenzo looked down at her and smiled, caressing the baby's dark head. He then turned to Renata, who stood a little distance from them, and then to Ergin and Adina. "We have to first stop this war. Until we have peace with Kalad, my father will bar all Hilliri from entering Castillon. He told me he was thinking of rescinding his permission to Alterra."

At hearing this, Lirienne looked over at Ergin and Adina. Their village would be dismantled, and they would be forced to return to Kalad. She knew it was the last thing they wanted.

Lorenzo looked back at Renata, standing a short distance away, then he took Lirienne by the hand. "Let's ride to my people's camp."

"Your camp is close to the front?"

"Yes, it is."

The unsolved issue of the war still lay between her, Lorenzo, and their happiness. How could they deal with it? If Lirienne and Lorenzo, children of the leaders of both countries, couldn't effect the change, Lirienne wondered who could.

She fingered his jacket of mottled green fabric pieces stitched together. It made him almost invisible in the dark. "I want to go back to speak to my brother. I want to try again to reason with him. Perhaps the baby and our union will change his mind. He should at least know what happened to me after all of these months."

Doubt spread across Lorenzo's face. "How do you plan to go?"

Lirienne thought about it for a moment. There was only one way that was safe.

"I will travel my usual way." She winked at Lorenzo and smiled.

CHAPTER THIRTY-SEVEN

Lirienne rode Lorenzo's horse with the baby in his sling tucked tightly against her chest. The starlight lifted the details from the forest. Ergin and Adina walked in silence beside the horse while Lorenzo held the reigns. It would take less than an hour with Renata guiding them. As a scout, she knew the safest routes and avoided the most likely places for an ambush.

The silence of their party made Lirienne a little uncomfortable. Breaking the stillness, Lorenzo, who had been musing to himself, turned to Ergin with a puzzled expression. "I noticed that you don't carry any weapons."

Ergin glanced back sagely and smiled. "I have no skill at arms. I'm afraid I would be as likely to hurt myself as to hurt an attacker. As such, it serves me better to be a man of peace."

Lorenzo appeared wistful. "I would like to be a man of peace, but circumstances have laid a sword firmly in my hand and commanded me to fight."

Ergin nodded. "Sometimes we have to fight now so we won't have to fight later, but it can be hard to make the transition away from violence once the cycle has started. I hope you find the chance to be that man, my lord. It would be a great gift for your son, to leave your land in peace for him."

Lorenzo did not respond, but he stared at Lirienne. She smiled. She too, would like to see those days of peace sometime soon.

They walked a while longer until Renata held up a hand to slow down. She had been glancing around, hoping to find some soldiers hiding out in the woods. She whistled a strange birdcall. Lirienne wondered if it was the call of some native species of this forest. Another call responded. Renata cocked her head to listen. She adjusted direction until they were heading toward the call.

Lirienne looked about for signs of hidden soldiers, but saw nothing but tall, straight pine trees for as far as the eye could see. Renata whistled again, a more complicated tune, and suddenly the forest filled with people.

It was the first time Lirienne had seen so many Trillas together.

They ranged in height and weight and coloring far more than her own people. Most were dark-haired. The odd person stood out with bright red hair. Their eyes were mostly dark, but occasionally gray, brilliant green, or blue. They walked toward Lorenzo, looking at her and her companions with suspicion.

The first to greet Lorenzo was Marcusi. He held his arms wide and smiled. "Cousin, you left in haste and without instructions. I'm glad you have returned. I see you've brought the captives." He jutted his chin in Lirienne's direction.

Lorenzo stepped into the man's embrace, thumping him roughly on the back. She had been correct about their relationship.

"Marcusi, I trust you managed well enough without me." He stepped back to survey the man. After hesitating for a moment, he waved his arm in her direction. "I made some new friends and caught up with an old one."

"Friends?" Marcusi crossed his arms.

Lorenzo returned to the horse, reached out for Lirienne's hand, and pulled her off, down into his arms. Marcusi wrinkled his nose in disapproval. Lorenzo placed her on the ground.

"This is Lirienne. She rescued me when I was a captive in Kalad. She's a healer. She used her skill to revive me from the terrible beating my captors inflicted on me. The others are Ergin and Adina, who live in Alterra."

The baby began to kick about and make noises. It was probably time to feed him again. It felt as if he was always hungry. Lirienne lifted him out of the sling and nestled him into the crook of her arm.

Marcusi seemed both fascinated and repulsed. "We can't have a baby making noise while we are hiding, Lorenzo. Why did you bring it?"

"We didn't have a choice. The baby is a newborn, and Lirienne couldn't leave him behind."

Marcusi's expression darkened. "I still don't understand why they have come."

Lorenzo leaned in to speak into his cousin's ear. "Lirienne's brother is a commander in the enemy camp. They're here to help me treat with him for peace."

Lirienne felt Marcusi's stare burn into her. She flushed as she realized he was working it out. He knew Lorenzo was the baby's father. He must know.

"Lorenzo, what have you done?" Marcusi's voice rose, his tone suspicious, angry.

In a moment the entire group crowded around them, everyone looking at her with threat in their eyes. Lirienne moved to stand behind Lorenzo. The baby whimpered.

"People, we've been fighting for a long time, and now we've come to hate the people we fight," Lorenzo said. "It's true, they have hurt us, but we have also hurt them. While these particular people here are Hilliri, they are unarmed. They're not soldiers, nor have they had any part in this war. They've come to stand with us, to demand peace with our enemy. I ask you to welcome them, though you may not love them. In time, I hope you will see them as I do."

Marcusi paced, peering into the faces of the others, looking for support. Lirienne could see his anger building and was afraid. Lorenzo left her side to go to him. He placed a hand on Marcusi's shoulder, but the man shrugged it off as if it burned. He glared back at Lirienne, then at Lorenzo. This wasn't going well.

"Cousin, please calm yourself," Lorenzo said. "Lirienne and I are married. She is the daughter of the king of Kalad. Do you not see the opportunity here for peace?"

Marcusi's eyes went wide as he stared at the baby. "That thing is yours!" His face was a hideous mask of revulsion. He ran his fingers through his thick curls and turned to the others. "Lorenzo's done it now," he announced. "The incorrigible Lorenzo can't keep his pants on for an hour!" He turned back to Lorenzo. "You had to . . . you had to do . . . that . . . with one of them." Marcusi's bright red face shone with sweat.

Lorenzo backed away, looking horrified.

Lirienne shrank back to stand by Ergin and Adina.

The woman, Renata, stepped forward. "Silly man, one might think you were afraid of a little baby."

Marcusi reddened even more and retreated.

Renata stepped closer to Lirienne and pulled back her thick auburn hair. Lirienne shifted the baby so the woman could have a better view.

Renata's eyes opened wide as the baby grabbed hold of her finger and squealed. "He's really sweet." She turned to look at Lorenzo in wonder. "He has your eyes." The woman withdrew her hand from Liran's firm grasp and spoke to Lirienne. "I'm Renata, I'm a scout. I'm sorry if we started out badly."

Lirienne appreciated the civility of good manners. "I am very pleased to make your acquaintance."

Renata waggled her fingers at the baby. "Men, they're always making a big deal about nothing."

A wide grin spread across Lirienne's face.

CHAPTER THIRTY-EIGHT

It took a while to settle the Castillonian soldiers down after Marcusi had riled them up. Lirienne received many suspicious stares, but she realized that it would take some time for them to become accustomed to her presence. Lorenzo, it seemed, still had the respect of his people, for he was able to rapidly shift their attention toward how to safely approach the Kaldene army's camp and gain access to Lirienne's brother.

They discussed their plans privately afterward. Lirienne would transport directly into her brother's tent and wait until he arrived to discuss her proposal. It was a dangerous endeavor, for no one knew what his attitude might be after so many months.

"I'll go to my brother alone. He'll be angry with me, but I'm not sure what he'll do if he sees the baby."

Lorenzo looked over at his cousin, Marcusi, who was off in the distance but keeping a watchful eye on their group as they stood around a fire gathering up its warmth. "I'm not sure it's safe here either, Lirienne."

Lirienne glanced at Ergin and Adina, who were speaking softly to one another. There were lines of worry on their faces from the news that Lorenzo had shared about his father rescinding permission for the settlement. If Alterra was at risk, they would need to return soon to discuss their options and prepare their people. Lirienne ached with concern for her new friends and the town that had taken her in. Returning to Kalad would break their spirits.

"Where should I leave Liran, then?" she asked. "Ergin and Adina will have to return to their home. The Alterrans need to know that there is a possibility they will be exiled from Castillon."

Lorenzo rubbed his beard a moment, his deep blue eyes unreadable. "Leave him with me."

Lirienne's gaze drifted to Marcusi and then back to Lorenzo. Many people in Lorenzo's camp had shown contempt for the child. It made her doubt that they could ever be together as a family.

"Are you sure?" she said. "You said it was dangerous here too."

"He's my son, Lirienne. I will protect him. It is dangerous here, but at least I'm in charge and I've earned the respect of these people. You won't be long, will you?"

After so many months apart, she felt unwilling to leave him so soon. Lirienne wondered where they could live that would be safe for her new family. Perhaps Lorenzo would be able to come with her back to Ergin and Adina's house for a while. There was a war to deal with, though, and if she could resolve this, then they might be able to remain together with their baby in safety in Castillon.

She pulled Lorenzo close and wrapped her arms around his waist. "I will return once I've talked with Valran and let you know the outcome."

Lorenzo held her against him as a long moment passed. Then he pushed her back a little, keeping his fingers entwined with hers. "You will be safe, my love?" His voice was a hoarse whisper.

"Of course, my love." She unwrapped the sling, handing it to Lorenzo while she held onto the baby. When he had wrapped the sling around his own broad torso, she passed him the child and kissed the baby's damp forehead. The baby glanced up at his father and smiled.

She would have to fill up with maru to make such a long trip. She searched around. There were many clusters of trees here, but she needed privacy to do this.

"Will you bring me somewhere nearby where we can be alone?" she asked Lorenzo. "I don't want the others to see what I'm about to do."

Lorenzo took her hand. He looked around the camp. People were busy going about their lives—cooking, sharpening swords, drinking and such. Walking down the path, away from the encampment, he came to a small side trail where he stopped and waited. Just when Lirienne was about to ask what he was doing, he pulled her off the trail, and they were quickly surrounded by a copse of trees.

Lirienne smiled at him. "Perfect."

He let go of her hand and cradled the baby.

It warmed Lirienne to see this tender gesture. She looked around for a moment. No one could see them here in the thick forest. She pulled off her gloves and approached one of the larger trees in the area, placing her hands on the rough bark of its trunk. She didn't relish the thought of taking maru. It seemed to require more than before to accomplish the same things and she never felt sated anymore. Still, she must go to see Valran and try again to make peace.

She smiled at Lorenzo as he looked up from attending to Liran. Then, turning her concentration to the tree, she closed her eyes and focused on the power within. As she drew in its energy, her mind filled with smokey yellowish light. The power filling her felt old and dank, but it would work. She smelled the odor of burning wood as she finished. Looking up at the charred husk of the tree, she exhaled. It was sad to have to do this to a tree that had taken decades to grow this tall and strong.

She dusted off her hands and turned to Lorenzo. He stood staring with his mouth open, blinking in shock.

"Travel requires a lot of maru. I must take some from other growing things to add to my own."

Lorenzo continued to stare at her, still a bit stunned.

"I'm ready to go," Lirienne said.

"That was quite a show!" he said, finally snapping out of it. Then he leaned over and kissed her. "May you bring us peace, my love."

She stepped back and waved at her husband and her son. She closed her eyes and brought up an image of Valran's tent, a place she remembered well, although many months had passed.

Lirienne held her breath until she arrived in the shelter of her brother's large tent. Upon realizing she had reached her destination, she located the nearest thing she could hold onto, a camp chair, and gripped it hard to keep herself steady as she caught her breath. It shocked her to note that the strength she had taken from the tree was all but gone with that single trip. In the past she could have gone there and back on the same amount of maru. She waited until the trembling subsided. Lirienne looked about the tent. She was alone, but there were voices just outside.

Suddenly, the tent's flap whipped open and Valran entered.

"Lirienne!" Valran rushed up to her and grabbed her by the arm. He dragged her into the back room, checking behind him to be certain no one had seen her. He let the curtain drop. They were in his private sleeping area, out of sight.

She didn't like the look on his face, but considering she had slipped away in the night almost half a year ago, he had a right to be shocked and upset. She needed him to be calm enough to listen, though. "Before you start, please hear me out."

He released her and paced the small chamber. His dark gray uniform was creased and dusty.

"Sit. You're not doing anything until you tell me where you've been for all these months. We searched everywhere for you."

Lirienne obeyed. Now was not the time for defiance. She must choose her words carefully. "The healing was draining me, and I had no one to talk to for support. So I left; I wandered away in the night."

"It wasn't supposed to be pleasant. We agreed that you wouldn't reveal your identity. This was to be a kind of punishment for your transgressions."

Lirienne looked down at her feet. She knew she had given him the most paltry of reasons, but it would be impossible to tell him what really had happened. "I know. I tried to endure it—really—I did my best, but there were other reasons as well for my leaving."

Valran examined her, assessing her in his military manner. He could dress down soldiers with a mere look.

"Val, don't look at me like that. I'm not one of the soldiers under your command."

He closed his eyes. His expression changed slightly. "Liri, you had me worried. Also, I was afraid to tell Father."

"You didn't tell him?" This surprised Lirienne.

He shook his head. "I covered for you. Besides, it would have made me look bad that I'd lost track of you, so I've managed to keep it from him, but when he learns of this, I guarantee his face will turn dark and he will rage on for hours."

"Thank you for keeping this between us. I hope he isn't too angry when he finally does learn the truth." She stared at the ground, trying to decide how to say what she needed to say. "You know, I've always felt a little out of place in Kalad. The College masters tolerated my questions, but only because of my Prestige status. I never seemed to see eye to eye with other people, so I've stopped caring about their disapproval. In a way, I am exactly the opposite of Selana."

Valran's eyes narrowed. "What are you trying to tell me?"

"I didn't do anything in order to make you displeased with me, Val, but I'm afraid that will likely be the end result." Lirienne looked away for a moment, gathering her courage. It would have been easier before, when they were still on good terms, but Val remained angry with her for not saving Talora and for rescuing Lorenzo. "All I want is for this war to stop. I have said so from the beginning. Healing the wounded here day after day was eating away at my spirit. I left for your sake, though. I didn't want you to have to deal with my situation."

Valran's brows furrowed. "Stop speaking in riddles, Lirienne.

What did you do?"

She moistened her lips. There was no easy way to say this. "I found myself with child."

Her brother's mouth fell open and remained like that. An unnatural silence filled the tent.

"I chose my husband, we made our vows, and I had a baby."

Now Valran just blinked. "Who is the father? Who did you marry?"

"You must first understand that I don't see your enemy the way you do, Val. He's just a man defending his home. It was our soldiers who marched into his lands."

Panic filled Valran's face. He shook his head. "Lirienne, I hope you aren't saying what I think . . ."

"The man I rescued from being beaten to death by your soldiers. The one you call the Slasher. His name is Lorenzo Calimero."

The look on Valran's face was both angry and horrified. Lirienne wondered why she had expected it might be different.

"You had a baby with that filthy Mundatar?"

Lirienne cringed at the slur. She hoped her son would never have to hear it.

"Shame on you for using that word. Lorenzo is the son of Lord Carlosi, a nobleman of the highest rank in Castillon. If he were Hilliri, you would have approved most heartily."

Val's expressions were becoming more and more unreadable. Lirienne wanted so much for him to understand how happy she was.

"We named the baby Liran. You should see him . . . he's just as sweet as any child."

Valran stepped back, covering his face with his hands, as if the very idea hurt him. "I don't understand it. How can the Hilliri even breed with the Trillas? The child will be sterile like a mule."

At least this time he used the correct word, but he brought up a point she did not think to consider. She would be sad if it were true. She had dreams for Liran, dreams that he might grow up to be a great man, like his father; a lord of his people.

"I can tell you for certain, as a healer, that there are no major differences between our two peoples. Other than the possession of less maru, I sensed nothing unusual when I healed Lorenzo's wounds."

Valran blinked again. Lirienne could see there were too many details to process, and his anger was getting in the way. "Lirienne, that man . . . we called him the Slasher for a reason. He's a vile brute. You have no idea the things he's done. He snuck into a tent one night and killed a dozen of my soldiers in their sleep. It was a bloodbath. And when we were up in the trees scouting in the forest, he had his men shoot us down. He has no mercy—no honor."

Lirienne could see that the losses affected him more than a military commander ought to allow. He was also still grieving for his wife.

"This is personal, Valran. I can see that. This is about Talora too. But you must understand . . . the Castillonians don't have a trained army of career soldiers as Kalad does. They resort to trickery and ambush because they lack the might to do otherwise. They're only trying to protect their land from invaders—from us."

Valran shook his head. "They are newcomers to these lands. They don't belong here. They should settle on the western side of the river where the other Trillas live. Castillon should be ours—at least the eastern part."

It was a common argument.

"But that doesn't change the fact that they are living there now. We didn't settle these lands with our people. We left it wild. Their claim is the stronger one. We need to let them have it and be done with all of the fighting and the death. Too many of our people have died already."

"All the more reason to honor their memory with a victory. The cost has been high, yes, but if we gain nothing it will all have been in vain."

"I'm worried for you, Val. Winning has too high a cost. In the end, even if you win this war, your hate will eat at you until you can no longer love anyone. You know, you could make peace to honor Talora and the others who died. Then you would begin healing from the hurt this conflict has wrought."

"I don't know how I can do that. Hate is all I know now."

"You know, Lorenzo has just as much reason to hate you. You killed his brother and his brother's pregnant lover as they lay sleeping in their bed. If each side holds on to its need for revenge, we will never be able to have peace with anyone. In spite of what you did to his brother, Lorenzo is still willing to talk of peace with you and leave his anger behind. If the man you call a brute can do this, can you not do the same?"

Valran stared at her. After a long moment, he hung his head down, his face collapsing from the strain of resisting the need to weep. Lirienne, touched by Valran's pain, swung an arm under his, pulling him toward her.

She reached up to caress his cheek, but he caught her by the wrist. "Don't, Liri, I can't bear that now. Leave me to my thoughts."

She pressed him close, imagining how, if Lorenzo died, she might easily turn bitter against his killer.

Pulling back a little, she looked at her brother with sympathy. "Val, this is a war. People die in wars on both sides. You can't tell me that your soldiers didn't do things that hurt the Castillonians just as much as they've hurt you. It has to stop."

"You're right, Lirienne."

Valran seemed more relaxed. She held him for a moment longer and then released him to look at his troubled face.

"If you want me to consider how to end this war, I will agree to have discussions with a Castillonian representative."

Lirienne was more than pleased to hear those words. Hatred would eat away and blacken her brother's heart if he didn't start to turn away from it.

"We can meet somewhere neutral," Lirienne proposed. "Would Alterra do? I can bring Lorenzo and meet you there at noon tomorrow."

"Alterra is a good choice. I will see you tomorrow. I assume you transported yourself here with your power."

Lirienne nodded, uncomfortable talking about her ability. He knew this much, but not about taking maru from trees. She would have to return without filling up if she wanted to keep her secret.

He looked tired.

She caressed his cheek. "You look like you need some rest, Val. Take care of yourself."

He went through the door flap into the tent's outer chamber, leaving her privacy for her trip.

CHAPTER THIRTY-NINE

Lirienne brought up the image in her mind of the spot where she had left Lorenzo. She hoped she had enough power to get herself back, wondering what would happen if she didn't. With Valran in the next room, there was no way to refill. She had to leave with whatever resources she currently possessed.

Then pain stabbed her in the side – she had arrived. All of her strength had vanished. Gasping for air and trying to stay upright, she grabbed hold of the nearest tree and began to absorb it's maru. Never before had she felt so weak. It took a long while. She ached for it to go faster, but finally she felt stronger as the tree grew dark and shriveled.

She walked back toward the Castillonian camp; each step had enough force to become a great leap if she didn't hold back. The sensation was queer and dizzying and most unpleasant.

Lorenzo was waiting alone for her by a fire set away from the tents on the perimeter, the baby sleeping contentedly at his hip. Lirienne warmed when she saw this. For someone who had only just learned of his new status as a father, he had adapted quickly. He stood cautiously, so as not to disturb the child, and took her hand. His eyebrows rose in question.

Lirienne smiled. "My brother agreed to talk to you. We will meet him in Alterra at noon tomorrow."

Lorenzo seemed calm, if tired. "Let us hope we can make some progress. Thank you for doing this, Lirienne, and for believing."

"Should we ride to Alterra, or should I take us there?"

Lorenzo considered. "No, we'd better ride. If we went your way, we would arrive too fast, and then you'd have to explain. Besides, you should rest. You look as if you haven't slept in a week. I'll gather a few trusted people to join us. I don't want us to be vulnerable. This might be a trap."

A shiver traveled along Lirienne's body. "I hope not."

She released his hand, and he passed the baby to her. She

slipped Liran back into his sling. He still slumbered, but he would need feeding soon.

Three hours later they were underway, with ten additional soldiers, dressed plainly while concealing weapons under their cloaks. Lirienne had napped for a little less than two hours. It wasn't enough but it helped. When this was all over, she would sleep for a very long while, if Liran would allow.

They followed almost the same route she had used with Ergin and Adina, only this time they all travelled on horseback. Lirienne rode with Lorenzo with her baby tucked into her sling. The journey took longer than expected since they had to send scouts ahead to check the route and only proceeded when the scouts had confirmed the safety of the path. When they arrived in Alterra, Lorenzo and Lirienne stopped at Ergin and Adina's house, which, to Lirienne now felt like coming home. After explaining the reason for their presence, their needs for the meeting on the morrow, and arranging for a spot for the ten companions to camp, Lorenzo, Lirienne, and their baby settled in the spare room that had been her home since she first came to Alterra.

***

In the morning, the baby awoke early and hungry. Lirienne fed him while Lorenzo watched in fascination. When he finished his meal, Liran settled down for a nap. Lirienne curled herself around his small body on the bed while Lorenzo caressed the child's chubby arms, helping him drift off.

"He's really a good baby," Lorenzo said. "Life is simple for him."

She chuckled at this. "It is, but he makes it complicated for the rest of us. We have to work around his schedule."

Lorenzo stretched out and let his head settle back on the pillow. He sighed and looked up at the ceiling for a bit. "This is a big risk, Lirienne. I'm not sure how much trust to put in your brother."

"I know, but we have this chance now; we have to take it. There's too much to lose if we don't try. There won't be anywhere we can be together to raise our son with a war going on between our two lands."

Turning and propping up his head with his elbow, Lorenzo looked directly at her. "You're right. We do this for him. I'm just not sure if I can win your brother over with my words, especially not when my actions have affected him so directly."

"You will do fine, Lorenzo."

***

Overnight, two camps had sprung up on the village green in town. Ergin had agreed to host these talks and mediate the discussion. Lirienne knew this was one of his talents. He was a talker, not a fighter.

When the sun stretched out to its zenith, both sides gathered by a circle of twenty-odd chairs that the villagers had placed at the center of the common earlier. There were three openings in the circle for people to come and go. Valran and five companions filed in from one side and stood in front of the chairs they selected. His other companions lingered outside the circle. Lorenzo and Lirienne had arrived earlier and chosen their places, along with a few of their companions, leaving half of their people on the outside as well.

Liran was at home with Adina. Lirienne had worried about the reaction her brother would have to the unusual-looking child. It was best that he not be present.

Glancing across at her brother, she saw that Valran appeared better. The darkness that encircled his eyes had lightened somewhat.

"I'm glad to see you again, Val. Thank you for agreeing to talk."

Valran looked away, as if he couldn't meet her gaze. "I'm here. I said I would listen."

Lorenzo stepped forward into the middle of the circle and stood beside Lirienne, facing Valran.

Lirienne peered from one to the other. "Prince Valran Godehera, I present to you my husband, Lord Lorenzo Calimero of Castillon." She gripped Lorenzo's hand, waiting to see how her brother would respond.

Lorenzo straightened to his full stature. Valran stepped back a pace as Lorenzo's height overshadowed him. Lirienne could sense Valran's companions stiffen in response.

Lorenzo reached out his hand. "Prince Valran, I wish to begin with an apology."

Valran nodded and returned his gaze to Lorenzo. His manner was clipped and stiff, his face bleached whiter than usual. Lirienne could hardly have expected warmth from him, but at least he was

187

listening.

"I understand that people you cared about died as a result of some of the raids we made; that one of those was your wife," Lorenzo continued. "I wish it had not happened. I am deeply sorry. We cannot change what has passed, but we can look toward the future."

Valran kept his expression still, though Lirienne thought she saw a twitch in his lower lip.

Lorenzo filled his lungs and carried on. "My older brother, Leonardo, was killed during a raid on one of the nearby towns; a raid executed by you and your soldiers. He was heir to Castillon; favored by our father. That duty now falls to me, but I am told I will never measure up."

Valran raised an eyebrow, but nothing more. Lirienne wondered at how he could be so icy. Silence echoed through the common as people waited to hear a response. None came.

Thankfully, Ergin stepped in and began his duties as host of this gathering. He handed each man a glass of wine and bade them to sit. "Gentlemen, I know these facts make this conversation difficult. Both of you have cause to hate one another. But we still have people we care about to consider and to protect."

Lorenzo raised his glass. "Yes, Ergin, I agree. I'm willing to put aside my own pain for them and for the sake of peace." He looked with soft eyes at Lirienne. Certainly, he was thinking of her as well as his people.

She turned to Valran for his reaction and found the simmering frustration in his demeanor troubling.

"That all sounds so lovely, Mr. Lotreah, but I am the most likely to be selected heir to Kalad, and with no wife, there will be no heirs after me. Castillon has caused this problem."

Lirienne tugged Lorenzo's sleeve. He leaned over so that she could speak softly into his ear. "Do not suggest he can remarry. Among the Hilliri this is taboo."

Lorenzo looked puzzled.

Ergin turned to Valran. "I am deeply sorry for your loss, Prince Valran. It is not my place to suggest, but does it sometimes happen that the children of a sibling may be selected in lieu?"

Valran's eyes widened in disgust. "You can't possibly suggest I accept my sister's child with a Trillas as my own heir!"

Lirienne cringed at the characterization of her beloved Liran. Lorenzo showed no reaction.

Ergin waited patiently for Valran to calm down. "I suspect

Lirienne's child will be required to serve as heir to Lord Lorenzo, but you have another sister."

Valran raised an eyebrow; he didn't look pleased.

Ergin cleared his throat. "But we digress. We are here to discuss a halt to hostilities between Kalad and Castillon, not the future of either land. After all, what future will either side have if we continue to have war? What do we risk losing if we don't treat for peace? Those are the questions I believe need answering most."

Lorenzo agreed. "I am willing to discuss such things. I have said I will lay aside my anger at the loss of my brother in order to seek a better future. Castillon did not start this conflict, but we are willing to end it. I do wonder, though, why you attacked us, if you were not prepared to risk the casualties."

Valran only glared at this. This discussion was not going well for him.

Lirienne wanted to shift the focus to something more positive. "Val, what would it take to come to a peace agreement between Castillon and Kalad?"

He leaned back in his chair to think. The surly expression shifted to a more considering one. "We would certainly want Alterra and the region surrounding it as reparations."

Ergin stiffened, and an audible gasp came out in unison from the other Alterrans in the area. Lorenzo set his jaw.

Lirienne wanted desperately to defend her current home. She leaped up. "Val, Kalad can't use those settlers to claim lands. Those people sheltered and looked after me this last half year. They left Kalad because they wished to live differently, and they have no desire to return to Kaldene society."

Valran remained unaffected. "Someone has to rule them."

Lorenzo sat upright in his chair, engaged. "They have agreed to Castillonian rule."

Valran's eyes widened. "And you can confirm this?"

"They have an agreement with Lord Carlosi," Lirienne explained. "However, I would like you to understand why they chose to leave. The people of Alterra never fit well into Kaldene society. They're people who developed unusual perspectives on life. For example, many of them don't wear gloves, and there are those among them who are married for a second time."

Valran looked as if he had an upset stomach. Perhaps mentioning that last part was not advisable, but Lirienne was desperate. She wished Valran could develop a more flexible attitude like the Alterrans. She imagined him remarrying. It would certainly have solved some problems if he did.

"I doubt Father would be pleased to have to deal with such attitudes among his people," she went on. "It is better for Kalad and for the Alterrans that they remain part of Castillon."

Unhappiness shadowed Valran's face. He stood. "What was the point of this war, then, if we cannot have those lands and the rule of those people? They're our people."

"I always said this war was pointless, but Father was eager for land, and there were few other places available for annexation. The problem is, Val, Castillon belongs to the Trillas, and they have fought to keep it that way. You would have done the same if someone attacked Kalad."

"Why do you care so much about stopping our conflict, Lirienne? You never involved yourself with politics before."

"I'm concerned for our son's future, and for Lorenzo and myself. We need a place we can be together and be accepted, despite our differences, but our options are limited as long as there is a war between the Hilliri and the Trillas. We hope to settle in Madrezza and raise our son. With our union we can forge blood ties with Kalad, so there will never have to be another war."

Her brother mused, saying nothing. He looked at each of them.

Lorenzo held out a hand toward Valran. "I would prefer to trade and prosper with Kalad, rather than to fight. If you will go to your father, I can speak with mine. I hope we can put the fighting and the cruelty behind us. Will you make peace with me and with Castillon?"

Valran remained stubbornly silent.

Lirienne held her breath. She closed her eyes and released the air slowly. She waited for her brother's answer. When she opened her eyes again, Valran looked completely different. His face had turned crimson. He looked up to his men with a nod. Before she had a chance to cry out, they were all surrounded by gray-clad Hilliri soldiers. There must have been thirty or forty of them, appearing from nowhere. They forced Lorenzo to the ground and pinned him there. They blocked Lirienne from going to him. The unarmed Alterrans were also blocked. The Castillonians were outnumbered three to one.

"Val, what are you doing?"

Her brother had betrayed her, and she hadn't foreseen his deception.

"Lirienne, I hardly know you anymore. You've completely

changed. I blame him." He pointed to Lorenzo, positioned with his face pressed into the grass.

"Release him, Val! You promised you wouldn't harm him."

"I'm sorry, sister, but it was necessary to have this meeting to assess the extent of your complicity. I can see that you have been manipulated by these people and by this man into joining their cause. Who knows what purposes he has for you? You were always a little bit odd, but now you've broken completely with reality." He stared up at the sky. "Did it ever occur to you that you've started a hybrid race? Have you even considered that your child couldn't possibly fit in anywhere—neither among the Hilliri nor the Trillas? Who will want to play with him? What woman will want him for a husband when he is grown? Will he live a short or long life? Lirienne, sister, I hate to sound unkind, but . . . your child is a freak."

Stunned, Lirienne could find no voice to rebuke her brother. He was right, in a way. It would be hard for her son to grow up so different. Yet, this was no way to resolve anything. She looked down at Lorenzo with apprehension. What they were going to do with him now?

"You haven't even seen our son, Val, yet you judge him and us as his parents. If you don't want to treat with us, then please, just let us go."

She watched Lorenzo struggle with the soldiers who held him down. A soldier handed Valran a spear. Lirienne's gut churned when she realized what he was about to do.

Valran looked at her and shook his head. "Lirienne, this man has killed my wife, and butchered countless soldiers in ambushes and in their sleep. He has defiled you, a princess of Kalad. You can never recover your reputation from that. There's a price to pay for this."

Lirienne dropped to her knees as her legs gave out. "No! Please!"

Valran lifted the spear and thrust it hard into Lorenzo's back. Lirienne attempted to shout, but no sound came from her tightening throat. She watched as a dark red stain spread out from the center of the wound. She crawled forward and grasped Lorenzo by the shoulders. Valran's men stepped back to give her space.

"Lorenzo!"

He still lay face down. "Marcusi . . . will . . . come."

Lirienne puzzled over these words for a moment. His cousin

wasn't with them when they rode to Alterra. She needed to deal with his injury quickly. He was too heavy to turn over, so she pulled back his shirt and found exposed skin at his neck. She wrapped her fingers around the spot. Her consciousness slipped into his body, working at lightning speed, searching for the wounds inside. She grasped the end of the spear and pulled it out with her free hand. Then she found the place where ribs were cracked and blood vessels spilled out their contents. All the while, she could hear fighting around her, but she blocked it out. She must concentrate on healing.

Lirienne staunched the wound by cauterizing the blood vessels. She knit the muscles and bones back to whole. Her hands began to tremble, not for lack of maru, for she had filled up during the previous night. It was the fury and panic pumping blood through her own veins that fueled her tremor. She could not allow Lorenzo to die, not now when she had just found him again.

The commons and its inhabitants spun about her. She shook her head to clear it, but that only made things worse. The puddle on the ground had spread, but finally, she knew she had repaired the damage. Lorenzo would live.

With the healing done, Lirienne finally had a moment to look around. Fights had broken out between Valran's men and the Castillonians. There were more Castillonians now than before. She realized this was what Lorenzo meant. Marcusi must have brought other fighters and emerged when the skirmish started. The unarmed Alterrans kept their distance, looking fearful.

Lirienne glared at her brother. Valran stood nearby, watching his soldiers fight, occasionally fending off an attacker with his blade. He said that she had changed, yet he was different as well. The war had warped him, grief and death had maimed him as surely as a blade might have. She rose and stared into her brother's eyes. At least he wasn't much taller than she was. Anger heated her, radiating from her face.

He reached out and grasped her by the wrist. She twisted to free herself, hissing at the pain. Before she could get loose, two of his soldiers gathered in close and held her by the shoulders. She tried to shake herself free but was unsuccessful.

"Valran Godehera, you have changed more than I." A fury was building in her that brought her strength. "I demand you allow us all to leave now."

Valran didn't budge. Neither did the other men holding her.

"I finally have the prize you denied me when you swept him away," he said. "I will make sure that this time he gets the death he deserves." His grip on Lirienne's arm tightened, increasing the pain. He grinned. "Thank you for healing him, sister. I will enjoy killing him again."

Lirienne eyed her brother in horror.

His smile widened. "And you, sister, will find yourself in one of those nice prison cells you're so familiar with."

"Please stop hurting me, Val."

"And your little half-breed baby will be taken from you. You've dishonored your family. There will be consequences."

If Lirienne didn't do something right now, Lorenzo would die, and the baby . . . who knew what they would do? She assessed her reserves of maru; she didn't have much left after healing a nearly mortal wound. With Val's iron grip on her wrist, she couldn't reach a tree to tap for more.

Caged in, Lirienne saw no good choices. Valran would leave her with nothing, and lives hung in the balance. There was one choice, a terrible choice, but she could do something. She reached out with her free hand to one of the two soldiers holding her and touched him on the wrist where his skin peeked out from between his sleeve and the edge of his glove. He held onto her shoulder, surprised but unconcerned by the contact. She hated what she was doing. She tried to think of something else, some alternative that would bring them out of this free and whole, but she could see no other option.

She inhaled, drawing in the man's maru as she drew air into her lungs. It made her sick to think of it. She felt his strength fill her, like too much strong wine, making her dizzy. The world spun about her and she gloried in it. She felt taller, larger, and stronger. Maru throbbed through her, making her pulse with pleasure. She turned to Valran who stood staring, uncomprehending.

The soldier collapsed.

In one swift movement, Lirienne twisted herself free of her brother's grip and that of the soldier still holding her other shoulder. She reached down to grab Lorenzo's hand and thought of home—Ergin and Adina's house—and in a blink they were there.

CHAPTER FORTY

The moment she opened her eyes to check her surroundings, Lirienne saw Adina. Her shocked friend stood nearby with the baby crying in her arms. Lorenzo, still unconscious, lay on the ground. It was a relief to be home.

"He should be okay. I healed him just before we left," Lirienne explained.

Adina stared at her. "You appeared—out of thin air. That's quite a skill. I've never seen anyone transport."

Lirienne reached over and took the crying baby from her friend. "It takes a tremendous amount of maru."

Lirienne lifted baby Liran up to her shoulder and rubbed his back and whispered sweet noises into his ear until he settled; her own heart still pounding like thunder. Holding him comforted her.

Adina knelt by Lorenzo's side.

He stirred. "I'm . . . all right." He sounded surprised.

Adina inclined her head in agreement. She turned to Lirienne. "You just healed him and transported. How did you manage that?"

Lirienne looked blankly at her friend. How could she explain what she had done? Remembering the face of the soldier whose life she had taken—the cost had been too high. But she knew she would do it again if she had to.

***

That afternoon, Lirienne could hear fighting all around them. She remained in the house, worried that her brother's soldiers might break in at any time and drag her and Lorenzo away. Finally, Ergin arrived as the sounds of battle were subsiding.

"The Castillonians have driven the Kaldene army back. Lorenzo's cousin Marcusi had more men in hiding than Valran did. We're lucky that the casualties were so few. My people stayed back, as most were unarmed. Lirienne, your brother has retreated to his camp."

Lorenzo went outside to find his cousin. He returned a while later, his aspect quiet and thoughtful.

At dinner that night, both Ergin and Adina spoke little as they considered the events of the day.

Ergin speared a morsel of pickled cabbage from his plate. "Will you go back to the front to fight, Lorenzo? You seem well enough."

Lorenzo swallowed his mouthful. They had talked a long while about what to do next. He covered Lirienne's hand with his larger one, giving it a squeeze. "Lirienne and I will go to Madrezza to speak with my father. I think he needs to communicate directly with the king in order to achieve peace. We've seen where Valran's heart lies."

Ergin shook his head. "That is an understatement. He tried to kill you and double-crossed his own sister."

Later on, after Lorenzo and Lirienne settled the baby to sleep in her small room, Lirienne found she couldn't shake from her mind the surprised look on the soldier's face as she drained his life force. How could she live with what she had done?

Lorenzo watched her as she absent-mindedly rocked Liran in his little bed. "You're upset. I can see that. Today has been very eventful. What worries you the most?"

"I took a life today. I may have had a good reason, but I'm a healer. I'm supposed to save lives, not take them."

"Valran didn't give you any choice. Taking a life is a terrible thing. I know. I've taken so many." He chewed his lower lip.

Given the way she felt right now, Lirienne doubted she would ever be normal again. She looked forward to meeting Lorenzo's father, but her stomach churned at the thought of the reaction he might have to her.

"I hope your father will be more welcoming to me than my brother was to you."

Lorenzo drew in a breath. "He won't be warm at first, I'll wager, he never has been, but I'm his only living son, and he needs me to carry on. I can't see him disowning me and sending me away, not even for marrying you. He's going to have to be practical now."

The thought of his father disowning him gave Lirienne a shiver. People could be stubborn beyond reason and sense. Certainly Valran had been.

***

Ergin lent them the use of his horse. Lorenzo rode behind Lirienne with the baby tucked away in his sling strapped to her chest. It was time for the child to meet his grandfather.

They rode south for a while. When they reached the shore, Lorenzo called for a break. He swung down from the saddle. Lirienne noted his movements were unrestricted by pain. She had done her job well. He held out his arms to assist her. She swung a leg over and let him carry her to the ground.

"You're as light as a feather."

Lirienne peeked into the sling to find Liran sleeping peacefully.

Lorenzo smiled as he watched. "He's a good traveler."

Lirienne looked up and grinned.

He took her by the hand, leading her along a dry beaten path through a scraggly pine stand. "Come see the ocean."

Lirienne had never been to the ocean. The air turned fresher and cooler where the trees ended, and a vast expanse of azure stretched out as far as she could see. She held her breath as she took in the view from left to right, seeing water all around. The sound was deafening too, as frothy white waves pounded the rock cliffs beneath where they stood. Over and over, the water beat a rhythm like blood pounding in her ears. Lirienne exhaled. She tasted salt on her tongue.

"It's beautiful!"

She shook her head. She had never seen water so huge that it filled her vision. The immensity scared her a little. It made her feel especially small, but the wind rallied her courage and she stood there, silent and impressed.

Lorenzo enjoyed her reaction. "Welcome to Castillon-by-the-Sea, my dear."

"It's a fitting name." She could say no more.

They continued riding west for another hour, watching the ocean on their left as they passed. The land was mostly dry and rocky, sparsely covered with shrubs and stunted pines. Below the cliffs on which they rode, she could see leagues of empty sand beach, as golden bright as her own hair in the midday sun.

They rode up to the mouth of the river Eraldis, the same river that passed by her own city. The torrent of icy water fed by mountain streams became a wide, lazy waterway at this point, which drained out into the ocean, stirring up mountains of brown silt as it mixed salt water with fresh.

Across the river, the cliffs became grassy hills instead of a stony wall. Ramshackle huts huddled by the water's edge. Larger, better-appointed houses perched on the tops of the sandy hills above them. On the highest rise, with the forest closed in around it, stood one large, sprawling villa encircled by stone walls.

"Wrap your hair in a scarf. I don't want people to notice that you're Hilliri until I've had a chance to explain."

Lirienne could sense Lorenzo's tension through their bodies touching.

Lorenzo leaned over to her ear. "Don't worry. You know, not all Trillas are as tall as I am. Many are shorter, and although Castillonians are darker, northerners, like those from Estallium, are paler, and sometimes fair-haired like you. Here, though, your coloring will give you away at once as being a foreigner."

"How do we cross the river?"

Lorenzo pointed upstream. "Over there."

There was a bridge made of bundled timbers that crossed the river before it became too broad to span. A road led up to the bridge on each end. Lorenzo turned the horse inland in that direction. Crossing the bridge was disconcerting. The planks of its surface were spaced so a small gap remained between each board. Lirienne could see the water underneath her as it flowed past. Lorenzo explained that this was to allow the rain to drain out so the wood didn't rot.

When they finally reached the wooden gates of the stone-walled villa, they dismounted. The butterflies in Lirienne's stomach flipped about with renewed energy. Lorenzo took her hand as they waited for a young man to unlatch the gate and swing it open. When he saw Lorenzo, he quickened his pace. As they led the horse through the opening, the servant bowed several times, then took the reins.

Lorenzo led Lirienne into the large house. It was built on a grand scale impressive even to her, who had lived in a great palace all her life.

"It's bigger than I had expected."

Lorenzo leaned over to reply. "The high ceilings are to accommodate the tall occupants."

They chuckled. The comment eased Lirienne. What would happen here next mattered.

Another servant, this one better dressed and groomed, approached. His hair was iron gray and his face lined and weathered. Lirienne stared at him. The Hilliri aged so slowly; few of them had many lines on their faces. She had never seen an old Trillas, and this one was obviously ancient.

"Pagolo, I'm back, and hoping to see my father. Where can I find him?"

The old man bowed slightly. "Welcome Master Lorenzo. Lord Carlosi is in the main hall. It's the time for reviewing disputes."

Lorenzo was thoughtful. "Is he almost finished?"

"I believe he is seeing the last supplicant now. It should only be a matter of minutes. Why don't you and your companion wait in the drawing room. I'll tell him you're here as soon as he's done."

Lorenzo leaned over conspiratorially. "How is his mood?"

The old man lifted his bushy brows and let them settle again.

Lorenzo smiled. "I see."

They waited over an hour for Lorenzo's father. The stiff chairs provided for them made Lirienne uncomfortable. She shifted frequently but never found an ideal position. There were carpets on the floor and tapestries on the walls that muffled sound, but the effect stifled rather than soothed. Liran fussed, so Lirienne fed him, but she was so anxious about the meeting, her worry transferred to the baby, and he drank restlessly. She kept him soothed with much bouncing and rocking. The last thing she wanted was to meet her new father-in-law with a screaming baby in her arms.

Finally, Lirienne heard the sound of footsteps coming down the hall, and the door opened.

An old man, not quite as lined as the ancient Pagolo, walked in. From his fine clothing and the pinched look of importance on his face, Lirienne assumed this must be Lord Carlosi. He frowned, making the lines around his mouth appear even deeper. Lorenzo rose to approach him, and Lirienne moved back several paces.

"Lorenzo, boy, what are you doing here? I sent you to lead the soldiers in battle."

Lirienne kept her hair and face wrapped as she moved into the far corner of the room. She wanted Lord Carlosi to notice his son first, allowing Lorenzo time to tell their story before he detected her. Lorenzo appeared to struggle for words.

"Well, boy. Answer me. What are you doing here?"

CHAPTER FORTY-ONE

"I'm here because there are some things I need to discuss with you, Father."

Carlosi looked impatient. "Well, I'm here. Discuss."

Lirienne was surprised his patience was so short, especially with his own son.

"How long are we going to continue this war? Is there anything we can do to make peace? We need to get on with life, to build Castillon into the land we have dreamed of."

Hearing his plea, Lirienne loved Lorenzo even more.

"You surprise me with such simple questions," Lord Carlosi said. "You know what has to happen. The Hilliri have to withdraw." He looked around. His gaze landed on Lirienne.

She held her breath.

"Why have you brought a woman here? You know it's not appropriate to entertain women in this house."

Lorenzo looked uncomfortable. If his father was anything like hers, whatever he had been rehearsing in his head had probably abandoned him under the man's intense stare.

Moments passed in uncomfortable silence. It would be up to Lirienne to speak. She stood and approached this old and irritable man.

"I am Lirienne, my lord, Lirienne Godehera."

She gave the man time to think as she unwrapped her scarf. When he saw her pale locks, his eyes narrowed.

"You are my nemesis's offspring, I suppose. What are you doing here in my house? Has my son taken you as a hostage? If so, then I applaud him for his ingenuity."

Lirienne held back a sharp retort. "No, I'm not his hostage. I'm his wife."

She let the idea sink in. The next message would be even harder to tell. Carlosi turned to his son and stared up into his face. Lorenzo waited, without guilt in his expression. Lirienne was proud of him.

"Are you joking? Trillas don't marry Hilliri."

Lorenzo ran his fingers through his hair. "I know it won't please you but my marrying Lirienne might offer a solution to help find peace."

Carlosi spat. "Please me? It would have pleased me if you had agreed to marry the daughter of the lord of Gildahest when I asked."

"Please, Father, hear me out. It would have accomplished nothing to marry that girl. We are not at war with Gildahest. If you would talk to Lirienne's father, the king of Kalad, you might be able to create a treaty with the marriage to bind it."

Carlosi turned an odd shade of red. Lirienne feared he might have a brain bleed in front of them.

"I doubt the mighty king of Kalad would be any happier than I am with this."

He was probably right. Her father would likely have a similar reaction. These two powerful men had a lot in common.

Lorenzo bent to his knees and looked up at the man. "Father, will you try? I can't bear to watch our people dying every day while we fight. Fighting has cost me my brother, my friends, and so many others."

"What would please me, foolish son, is if you would set this woman aside."

A chill ran through Lirienne as the man spoke. Lorenzo looked shocked as well. They had expected resistance, but this was too harsh. She wondered if Lorenzo was tempted to do what his father asked. She had to trust him.

Carlosi glared at her. "Did you even go through the proper ceremonies?"

Perhaps, Lirienne thought, when he knew the whole story, Carlosi would shift his opinion. It was time to show him the rest.

She lifted Liran out of his carry sling and held him up for the old man to see. He was just awakening.

"We have neglected to introduce you to another guest. This is our son, Liran."

She watched as Carlosi simmered. He stared at the baby. Liran wriggled and smacked his lips. She willed Carlosi to see the child for what he was: sweet, innocent, harmless, and lovable.

"Your grandson."

Carlosi began to shake. He stared at his son, then lifted his arm and pointed to the door. "Get out," he murmured through his teeth. "Get out and don't come back." His voice rose as his face turned from red to almost purple. "I can see that I will have to take over your duties and command my soldiers myself." He straightened, lifting his nose into the air. "I disown you, Lorenzo. You are no longer my heir or my son."

Lorenzo looked lost. He stood, stooped, staring at his father as the man fumed. "You would rather have no one? No family? No heir at all?"

Carlosi's eyes bulged. "I would."

"You can't mean that. What will you do?"

Carlosi rolled his eyes. "I will manage somehow. Perhaps your cousin Marcusi will oblige me. He would never do a stunt like this."

Lorenzo wilted.

Lirienne tucked the baby back into his carrier and took him by the arm. "Come, my love," said Lirienne softly, avoiding Carlosi's blazing eyes. "We're not wanted here."

Lorenzo pulled away from Lirienne's grasp and faced his father. At first, it looked like he was simply going to stare him down, but after a long moment, Lorenzo took a deep breath.

"I thought you were better than this. I've brought you my son, your own flesh and blood, and you disown both me and your grandson in a single moment." He rose to his full, most impressive height, a full head taller than his father. "You never approved of me when Leonardo was alive, but since his death, you've lost all of your heart. I've brought you a peace offering, a blood bond between you and your enemy. You could have put aside your fighting, but you don't want to stop fighting. You want to fight until you die so you can join Leonardo."

The moment he spoke the words, Lorenzo looked terrified. Lirienne wondered if he had gone too far, but really, there was nothing left for him to lose.

For a moment, Carlosi was so taken aback that he remained speechless. He blinked as he absorbed Lorenzo's words. The hardness of his expression never changed.

Lorenzo shook his head. He took Lirienne by the hand and pulled her toward the door. "Come, love. We have nothing left to talk about here."

As they turned their backs to Carlosi, Lirienne heard the man draw in a deep breath. "Guards!"

There was no time to run. She didn't have enough maru to transport back to Ergin's house, but Lirienne thought of the horse. She had seen the outside of the stables on her way into the grand house. She clasped Lorenzo's hand tightly as she recalled an image of the stables. In a blink, they were out in the clear air, with the stables right in front of them. Lorenzo wobbled as he adjusted to his new location but steadied as he reached the stable door.

Guards were running across the open yard this way and that. They would soon realize where she and Lorenzo were and come after them.

The groom emerged from the stables to investigate the commotion.

Lorenzo rushed up to him. "Saddle the horse. Lord Carlosi is in ill humor. I don't want to stay around while he yells at me for several hours. We're leaving."

Half brushed, the horse waited, tied off in the open area of the stable. His saddle rested on a stand nearby. The boy grabbed the saddle and threw it over the horse's back, tightening the girth strap in a single smooth movement. Lirienne was thankful for the boy's skill and experience. They mounted while the boy opened the back gate and with a click of Lorenzo's heels, they were gone.

CHAPTER FORTY-TWO

They looked back often, thinking that Carlosi might have sent guards in pursuit. With two of them riding one horse, they would be easy to catch. As they reached the top of the cliff, Lorenzo turned down an overgrown path. It was little used and appeared to lead nowhere in particular. It wasn't long before they were alone in the middle of the forest. If guards had pursued them, they wouldn't know the tiny path. Soon it merged with another small path that headed north.

Lorenzo kept silent. Lirienne knew he hurt. She could have helped if he was injured, but she couldn't draw this kind of pain from him.

The baby, safely tucked away, fussed noisily as they rode. Finally, they had to stop so she could nurse him.

Lirienne fumed quietly in a tiny clearing just off from the path while the baby gasped and sucked at her breast. She wondered how a man could turn away his only living child. Lorenzo hadn't betrayed his father as she had defied hers, although he had done something Carlosi would have difficulty accepting. Still, there were worse things he could have done.

When the baby had finally had his fill, Lirienne tucked him into his sling and mounted the horse once more. "Where do we go? We have to hide from your people or they will bring you back to your father. I'm not even sure that Alterra is safe."

She worried that their actions might have goaded Carlosi into expelling the Alterrans.

A deep crease rippled across Lorenzo's forehead. He rubbed the dust from his face. "You're right, and we can't go to Kalad. We need to hide."

Lirienne realized she knew exactly where they should head. It brightened her at first to have somewhere familiar to go, but then the idea of never returning to civilization darkened her humor. "I know a cave where we can hide. It's just along the southern edge of the ravine near Alterra."

Lorenzo's shoulders seemed to sag.

Lirienne hugged him for a long time. "It's only for a while. Your father will change his mind, he has to."

Lorenzo shook his head. "I doubt my father will change his mind. He never does. He was angry when my brother died. I was angry too. He said that all he had left was the useless son and it was better to have no son at all. He has his way now."

The words stung Lirienne. "Let's just find shelter and regroup. We'll have time to figure out a new strategy."

Lorenzo didn't reply, but he gave her a squeeze as they rode quietly through the trees, heading northward whenever there was a choice of direction on the meandering path. The weather was warmer now, as spring was well underway. The sun brightened patches of the forest with the occasional flash of brilliance as they went, but nothing could illuminate the gloom of their spirits.

They made a wide circle around Alterra to the east, in an effort to avoid the Kaldene soldiers on watch in the area, as well as the Alterrans themselves. Lirienne was sure that Ergin and Adina would have been willing to help them, but she was uncertain what the cost might be. They had given enough already. She wouldn't ask more of them.

After a few hours of slow riding through the trees, they arrived at the ravine's edge. The wind blew wildly through the deep-carved rock trough, increasing the chill in the air. Lirienne wrapped her cloak tighter around her shoulders. Lorenzo leaned in to press against her, sharing his warmth.

Finally, she spotted the gouges in the forest floor that demarcated the string of caves. She pointed to the far end of these, and Lorenzo urged the horse onward. When they arrived, he tied the horse up near a thick bank of bushes. He would return it later.

Her cave was as she had left it. She found the trunk in the back corner, dusty, but still locked. Opening it, she was delighted to find some dried meats and fruits, as well as a few warm blankets.

As they tidied up the space, brushing out the dried leaves and collecting firewood, Lirienne smiled. It was almost as if they were settling down in their own home. She stared out the large opening that faced the ravine. It was a majestic view but would be dangerous once Liran learned to crawl.

Lorenzo cleared his throat but didn't speak. He hadn't said much all day.

***

They settled in for a couple of days, trapping animals and

foraging for their needs. At night they bunked down in their small bed, with the baby asleep nearby, rediscovering their love in the dark with the starry skies just beyond the cave opening. It was as domestic a scene as Lirienne could ever have desired.

One evening, while Lorenzo tidied the cave, he cleared his throat often, as if he had something he didn't want to say. "I'm going to bring the horse back to Ergin."

Lirienne stood bolt upright. "Are you sure? With the patrols around, won't it be dangerous?" She sidled up to him and wrapped her arms around his neck. "I just found you. I don't want to lose you again."

He grinned. "It's almost dark. I may be tall, but I know how to keep hidden." He kissed the top of her head. "Besides, I know you're waiting here for me with my son. I won't be long."

He released her and wrapped his cloak around his body. With one quick movement he turned, leaped up the stone stairs, and was gone.

Lirienne busied herself about the cave and even ventured out for a while in the dusky light, with Liran in his sling, to check a few traps.

The night dragged on, with Lirienne tossing in her bed, trying to sleep, but waking every hour to check if Lorenzo had returned. By dawn, Lorenzo still had not come back and she became increasingly worried.

The baby dozed at the back of the cave on some blankets while Lirienne paced, going over their options, pausing occasionally to feed the small fire. She peeked over at him and saw that he was making sucking motions with his lips as if feeding in his sleep. He was so small and helpless, but one day he would be grown and perhaps as tall as his father. Lirienne wondered what kind of man he would be then.

It was well after sundown when Lirienne heard scuffling sounds near the cave entrance. She rose and walked to the stone stairway and looked up at the opening to the ground above. Her heart pounded. It had to be Lorenzo.

She let out a breath as his long legs appeared by the entrance. He descended quickly and clasped her in his arms.

She squeezed him tightly as her breath returned to normal. "You had me worried. It's less than an hour by foot to Ergin's house from here, and you had a horse for half the trip."

"Ergin had news." His somber expression made it clear it was not good news.

Lirienne guided him to the hearth and sat down. He joined her, reaching over to the bundle of blankets to pick up the baby one-handed. He tucked Liran into the crook of his arm and toyed with him, touching the tip of his nose until Liran wrinkled it and sneezed. Lirienne wanted to laugh, but her chest was tight.

"Tell me."

Lorenzo shook his head. "Ergin's been sending villagers out to see what's happening with the fighting. He says he needs to know if the conflict moves nearer to the village, so they can evacuate."

"What did they find?"

"It was quiet until today. They saw a new group of Castillonians on the march toward the front."

Lirienne grasped his sleeve. "What were they doing?"

"The scout said it looked like everyone in the whole country was on the march. All the men were armed. Some even had armor, and there were banners flying."

Lirienne rolled her eyes in frustration. Everything was getting worse instead of better. "How many were there?"

"I'm not sure, perhaps a thousand or so. It's difficult to estimate when they're stretched out and moving. Apparently, my father rode in the lead. He had threatened to do that. I wasn't sure he would, or rather I didn't think he still could. He's much too old to be on a campaign."

"What could he be hoping to accomplish, then?"

The baby began to squirm. Lorenzo handed him back to Lirienne.

"He's trying to end the conflict by forcing a single decisive battle. He must have dedicated every last resource to mount such an offense." He looked at Lirienne. "It's a very risky move. He's either going to win very soon or be utterly defeated. I led the defense in his stead because he was ailing, but now that he has disowned me and taken over, he's making rash decisions. I would never have advised such a course." Lorenzo hung his head. "Whatever the outcome of the battle, he, and many others, are likely to die."

Lirienne gripped her baby to her chest. The war was only getting worse. Many people on both sides were going to get hurt and die and everything she tried to do to stop it had failed. What else could she do? She must find a solution or their deaths would be her responsibility and the guilt would crush her.

That night she curled up beside Lorenzo after scrubbing the

baby's soiled clouts in a nearby stream, where she nearly fell in, and feeding him what seemed like every hour. It was rough living, but lying on a blanket with Lorenzo curved around her while she curved around Liran, a spark of joy glowed within her that refused to be extinguished.

CHAPTER FORTY-THREE

The next day Lirienne woke suddenly with a sense that something wasn't right. She blinked to clear the stickiness from her eyes. The fire had burned down to embers and extinguished. The cave was dark and cold, but the first glimmerings of sunrise cast a pink glow on the back wall. The baby began to stir.

Lorenzo had gone out again early that morning in search of information, scouting near the front lines to see how the battles were going. After he heard about his father's troops marching toward the front, he had grown increasingly concerned about his soldiers and the way the war was being fought. His father's sanity and health worried him as well, but he no longer had any influence with Lord Carlosi, if indeed he had ever had any to begin with.

He needed good information, unfiltered by others, so he went himself. Lirienne understood this but she couldn't help but worry about him. He promised her that he would keep hidden.

She had waited late into the night for Lorenzo to return, trying to stay awake, but she eventually fell asleep and slept through the rest of the night. Now, at the first light of day, Lorenzo still had not come back.

She changed the baby's clout and put him to her breast. The routine helped her remain calm. She leaned against the cave wall, her jaws clenching until she noticed and forced herself to relax. Waiting was the worst.

The day passed without incident, but Lorenzo never appeared. At dusk she heard a noise above, and then Ergin and Adina entered her cave. She rushed forward to greet them, hoping they might have news.

Adina folded Lirienne and the baby into her embrace. "We thought you might need an update."

Lirienne pulled her tangled hair out of her eyes. "Yes! Please tell me what you know!"

Adina smiled. She took the baby and played with him while Ergin settled in by the fire.

"Your husband went out to scout last night," Ergin said. "He stopped by to collect information from me before heading to the front to observe."

Lirienne sat down beside Ergin on a large rock that served as a bench. "I don't understand why he hasn't returned. Do you have more information?"

Ergin appeared calm, but when he saw her confidence waver, he placed a hand on her shoulder. "I told him that according to the latest reports from the villagers watching the conflict, Lord Carlosi had been killed. He had rushed forward too far in front of his own line in a battle. Ever since, the Castillonian army has been in disarray."

Lirienne leaped up and started to pace. At least Lorenzo wasn't dead. "He's gone to take his father's place."

"He said he had to talk with his people," Ergin explained. "He asked me to keep you informed, and then he rushed off. We haven't heard anything since then."

Lirienne's fingers began to tremble. Either his people would capture him as a traitor for marrying her — and because his father had disowned him — or they would welcome him as their new leader because they loved him. She didn't yet understand the Trillas well enough to know which it might be. She shook her head. Either way, he was right in the middle of the war.

"He's going to get himself killed. I have to do something."

A line appeared on Adina's forehead. "You're not going to the front on your own?"

Ergin and Adina exchanged glances. Adina grabbed Ergin's sleeve. "You can't go either. It won't help, and you're going to get hurt or worse. Please, Ergin."

Realizing that Ergin was going to volunteer to help her, Lirienne interrupted. "She's right. It won't help to have you with me, and you'll only put yourself at risk too. I'm going alone. I can always transport away if there's danger." She turned to Adina. "Can I leave my baby with you? I won't be long. Either I can talk Lorenzo out of this, or I'll leave, but I have to try something. I just found him again."

"Of course," she said.

"I'll feed him now," Lirienne said, "then he'll be okay for a few hours. I'll come back as soon as I find Lorenzo and talk to him."

She took the baby back into her arms and sat down to nurse him. Having to sit calmly while he drank did nothing to settle her. Afterward, she kissed his forehead and passed him back to Adina.

The woman wrapped her free arm around Lirienne and

hugged her. "I'll take care of him, but you had better come back. He needs you."

Lirienne drew herself up and set her shoulders back. "It seems a lot of people need me."

She grabbed her silver robes and veil and tucked them into her carry bag, and then climbed out of the cave. She didn't know where she might need to go and what she might need to do, so she walked into the forest, selected a huge tree, and drew as much maru as she dared, turning the tree to a charred husk in a minute. She thought she might be sick but held it back. She trembled with the weight of the added power.

The Castillonians camped near the front. She chose her location carefully and with only a breath missed in between, she was there. The maru she had taken filled her with a heady brightness. It swirled through her, bringing her mind into sharp focus, and she smiled. Nothing would stop her from reaching her goal.

It had been the right choice to leave Liran with Adina. Without his added weight she felt light. Where she was going was no place for a baby.

Peeking out from behind a big boulder, she caught a glimpse of the Castillonian camp. Shouts, clanging metal, and cries of pain revealed that the fighting was not far away.

Thinking on the death of Carlosi saddened Lirienne. She would never have the chance to get to know her father-in-law in better times. The man had been a fool and had paid for it with his life. She knew Lorenzo had more sense.

She listened to the sounds of the conflict, waiting until the direction of the sounds changed and grew fainter.

Within the hour, the battle seemed to dissipate. She relaxed a little. Finally she heard a horn signaling retreat as both sides withdrew to their camps. The nearby noise increased, indicating the Castillonians had returned. She waited, peering out anxiously, not seeing Lorenzo in their midst. She did see the surly Marcusi conferring with the woman, Renata, and others from her first visit here.

She wanted to speak with them, but hesitated. They had made it clear that they didn't recognize her marriage. Would they welcome her or capture her? She reminded herself that for them she represented the enemy.

Finally, she saw a taller man join the group. The shape was so familiar. From a distance, she couldn't see enough detail to know for certain, but her heart told her it was Lorenzo.

She came out quietly from hiding and walked as directly as she could toward him.

Lorenzo didn't see her immediately, but Renata turned in her direction and waved. "Look who's here, my lord."

The rest of the group of Castillonians turned as one. All of them were of a height that made her seem as small as a child. Lirienne walked forward, trying to keep herself steady.

Marcusi sported a frown. "It's your latest woman, Lorenzo."

Lirienne saw Lorenzo's surprise and joy, mixed in with a hint of fear. He stepped a few strides toward her and pressed her to his chest. "How did you get here?"

"You know how I travel." She would say no more, not in this company.

Lorenzo nodded. "Where's the baby?"

Lirienne's heart skipped a beat. "I left him with Adina. I'm not planning to be long."

Lorenzo looked relieved. "A good choice."

Lirienne turned to Lorenzo's cousin and pulled herself up as tall as she could manage. "Greetings to my husband's cousin. You saved the day in Alterra when my brother's soldiers attacked. Thank you."

Marcusi scowled down at her. He turned his head to Lorenzo and lifted his brows in mock appreciation. "I had hoped this would end the way all of your other liaisons have."

Lorenzo's expression flattened. "Marcusi, please show Lirienne some respect, if not as my wife, then as the daughter of King Tarkhan. Show her we know how to behave among other nobles."

Lirienne could almost detect Marcusi's thoughts churning just under the surface of his blank aspect. The man moved his gaze away from her. "As you command, my lord."

During this exchange, Renata had been speaking with another fighter. When the man left, she rejoined the conversation. "Lorenzo, there are many wounded. The fighting has been difficult since your father joined with reinforcements."

Lorenzo puzzled over her words. "But there were more people fighting on our side than ever."

"True, but when Lord Carlosi came with so many, the Hilliri called for reinforcements, and they arrived with surprising speed. The fight merely escalated. We have more than twice as many injured as in past battles."

Lorenzo hung his head. "I should have been here. Father was hoping for a quick end to the fighting. Instead, he received a quick end to his life."

Marcusi stared at the ground for a moment. "You came in time to help stop the worst of it. You couldn't have stopped your father, though. He was afire with fury. I've never seen him like that."

Lorenzo gave a sad smile to his cousin then moved away, pulling Lirienne along, just out of earshot.

"I'm so sorry about your father," she said, once they were clear of the crowd. "I wish we had met under better circumstances."

Lorenzo nodded. "He was always so quick to anger. I wish I could have made him prouder of me, but he just couldn't see my merits. Leonardo always overshadowed me in every way."

A thought tickled Lirienne's mind. "What's happened since your father was killed? Who will be Castillon's new lord?"

Lorenzo drew a hand through his hair. "No one here knew that my father had disowned me. Everyone is looking for me to make decisions as they always have."

Lirienne felt a weight lift. At least, their plan was back on track now. But there was still more to do.

He leaned closer to her ear. "I was thinking . . . can you heal some of the fighters? If you show them you care, I believe they will warm up to you."

"I can only work on a few before I tire, so only the most grievously wounded. I'm sorry your father wasn't simply injured or I could have healed him too."

"I doubt he would have let you. He thought he was invincible, and his hatred of Kalad would never have allowed him to agree."

"He might have surprised you."

Lorenzo stared at his feet. "Perhaps you're right. Now we'll never know."

Lirienne cupped a hand to his cheek. "I regret that your father was killed in battle. I believe my actions played a part in this."

"No, you didn't know him. Since my brother's death he had become careless, as if he no longer cherished his own life." Lorenzo hugged her to him. "Now I must take my father's place. At least I will have you by my side. We still have so much to undo."

They returned to the circle of people discussing their plans. Lorenzo looked at Marcusi. "Cousin, you know the Hilliri have special talents. Lirienne is a gifted healer. She saved my life after I was beaten and near death. She can only heal a few people at a time, but is there someone important who is seriously hurt?"

Marcusi eyed her with suspicion. "I wouldn't let a ghost touch me if I were dying."

Lorenzo moved to object, but Renata stepped in. "Luckily, you're not. Lorenzo, I'll go see who is most in need and bring your lady to them."

CHAPTER FORTY-FOUR

Renata led Lirienne to the tent where the wounded were kept. Along their way, fighters cleaning their weapons stood and stared in undisguised shock at her presence, but the woman commanded some authority. A sharp glance at the offenders drove them back to their tasks. Lirienne felt their eyes on her back, though, as she continued. She wondered if these people would ever be willing to accept a Hilliri among them.

As she followed Renata toward the tent that housed the wounded, she spotted many injured soldiers scattered about outside as well. Clearly there were too many to give them all shelter. Inside, the Trillas healers worked on their patients. Crudely stitched wounds lay open and crusted over. Bandages appeared soiled and unchanged. She shivered at the basic level of skill on display. No wonder their people were dying in large numbers.

Inside the tent lay a dozen more wounded, likely the most damaged of the lot, and those with the highest rank. A woman in a blood-soaked apron with a saw in her hands turned from her ministrations to stare wide-eyed at Lirienne.

Renata approached and looked the woman directly in the eye. "This woman is a healer from Alterra. She is a friend, not an enemy. She is willing to try to help a few of the most injured here. Who is in the most need?"

The woman looked Lirienne over, scowled, and barked a laugh. "Miss Renata, are you playing a joke on me? You brought me a ghost and say she will work on my patients. She's one of them that's killing our people! Besides, she's the size of my wee granddaughter."

Renata stared at the woman. "This is an order from Lord Lorenzo. The lady is his wife."

Lirienne wondered if sharing that bit was wise.

The woman stared at Renata, eyes blinking in shock. She shook her head and resumed her regular stance. "I don't care if Lord Carlosi came back from his grave and ordered me. I'm not having a healer I don't know working on my patients. As for wives, I know nothing of this, and I'll keep my opinions to myself."

Renata clenched her fists and pressed her lips together. After a moment, she relaxed and brightened. "She healed Lord Lorenzo when he was captured and near death. Surely, that's as good a reference as one can get?"

The woman shook her head. After a pause, she pointed over to a bloody body in the corner on the floor. "Well, if you're so eager to have her work on my patients, you can start with your own father. I've done all I can for him. It's up to the Guardians now."

At the mention of the gods, Lirienne realized the Trillas prayed to the Guardians as well. Something in common that she could share if the opportunity came up.

Renata's expression had turned to one of horror. She rushed forward and dropped to her knees before the ailing man. "Papa?"

Lirienne gave her credit for remaining calm. The man was far from young, nearly as old as Carlosi, but more vigorous, even with his injuries. If all of the blood that soaked his clothing belonged to him, then his injuries must be very serious. She couldn't tell without touching him.

"Will you permit me to help him?" she asked Renata, crouching low to be nearer to her and her father.

Renata looked up at her with a pleading expression, eyes shimmering with unshed tears. "Please, Lirienne, you must save him."

The weight of her plea troubled Lirienne. What if her father died even in the face of her healing efforts? Would she be blamed, as Valran had blamed her when Talora died? Still, she must try. Not trying would simply result in a different set of problems. And if she succeeded, she would win a small victory in her efforts to be accepted.

Lirienne knelt to begin, peeling back the man's crusted coat; the dried blood stuck to his flesh. She had to take care not to rip his wounds open. Bloody slashes punctured his dark skin. Fortune had not been kind, placing him in the path of a volley of arrows, which unfortunately, some overzealous Trillas healer had pulled out, resulting in the excess of blood soaking his clothing. She looked up for a moment to see the Trillas healer watching her with guarded interest.

Cataloging the many injuries and ranking them for severity, Lirienne focused on her work. It was a long healing. The maru she had taken in kept her going past when her own stores might have failed. It felt odd to be continuing past the limit where her training had taught her to stop. With the transport and this healing, there might not be enough for any more patients. She would also have to refill again before she could return to Alterra.

Satisfied after a quick scan of her work, she withdrew her mind and exhaled. She stood and looked toward Renata, who waited, wringing her hands as she paced. "He is better. I have closed his wounds. He lost a lot of blood, and he needs rest, but I believe he will live."

Renata rushed back to her father on hearing those words. "That was the most amazing thing I've ever seen. You hardly touched him!" Renata jumped up and engulfed Lirienne with a hug. "Thank you for this."

Lirienne looked over at the healer as she wiped her hands.

The woman had her mouth open, but for a long moment, no words came out. "How did you do that?"

Lirienne struggled with how to respond. Simple was best. "The Hilliri have a gift of power. I've spent many years training to use it for healing."

The woman nodded, though her blank gaze demonstrated her inability to comprehend.

Lirienne covered Renata's father with a blanket to guard against shock. Her hands trembled. She swayed and nearly lost her balance. Her maru had depleted more quickly than she had anticipated. "That took most of my energy. I'm afraid I won't be able to do more for a little while."

A visit to a lonely tree tempted her, but something made her stop. She felt odd and out of sorts. Taking more power, she knew, would only increase this feeling.

The healer bobbed her head automatically.

"One more thing," Lirienne touched the woman's sleeve. "If your healers can cleanse the wounds with clean, warm water, and change out the soiled bandages for clean ones every day, it will improve the success of their ministrations."

The woman still looked dazed.

Lirienne grinned, suspecting she might need reminding later.

In order to stay with Lorenzo in Castillon, she needed the approval of his people. She hoped she gained a little ground this day in terms of acceptance.

Renata guided Lirienne back to Lorenzo. The sour-faced Marcusi was still with him. Renata announced that Lirienne had saved her father from certain death. Marcusi seemed to tighten his scowl. He would be difficult to win over, but Renata made certain that everyone knew how Lirienne had helped.

Overall, the tone of the Castillonians' chatter was lighter, which reassured her. Even Lorenzo seemed happier, though she sensed an edge. She thought it might be grief. His father had died while they were in conflict, and now he would never have the chance to resolve things with the man. Heartache like that could eat away at a person.

CHAPTER FORTY-FIVE

Less than an hour later, an alarm sounded. Shouts echoed throughout the camp. Lirienne jumped at the noise. The sharp metallic sounds of people gathering their weapons filled the air.

Lorenzo ran here and there calling people to arms, organizing his fighters.

When he came to check on her, she looked up at him with a furrowed brow. "What's happening?"

"Scouts have spotted the Kaldene army on the march. They're heading this way."

Lirienne's heart began to pound.

Lorenzo placed his hands on her shoulders and looked into her eyes. "I want you to go back to Alterra. That way you'll be away from the fighting. I need you to be safe."

The thought of separation troubled her. "I could be more useful here. People will be injured." She realized as she said this that she couldn't remain for too long. Liran would need feeding soon.

"You won't be able to heal them all, and you'll be in danger. I can't be distracted worrying about you. Please, Lirienne. At least go to the village where we used to meet for a while. You can return to help the wounded when the battle is over."

Lirienne clutched his arm. "You mean when you're dead? No, we've been parted for too long."

He waved someone over. It was Renata. "I need my wife to be somewhere safe. Can you take her to the village?"

If Renata was unhappy she would be missing a fight, she didn't show it. She grabbed Lirienne's hand, pulling her away.

Lirienne resisted. "Wait!"

Lirienne wanted to say goodbye, but Lorenzo, thanks to his long legs, was already elsewhere, giving orders. She took a moment to will him to be safe, then she turned to follow Renata away.

They ran for a little while, putting some distance between them and the camp, before slowing their pace. When they finally took a break on a distant hill to catch their breath, they looked back to see the camp small and far away. They could hear the sounds of the Kaldene army cresting the hill beyond, coming into range of the Castillonians. The first blush of dawn cast its glow over the world, but it was hard for Lirienne to find beauty when a war was within her sight.

"Come, Lirienne, we need to get further away. The battle will begin in moments!"

Lirienne couldn't move. It had happened too fast. She stood within the shelter of a stand of trees on a rise, watching as the banners of Kalad rippled in the breeze. She gazed in fascination as the Castillonians lined up to face the Kaldene army, who had paused, waiting for their opponents to assemble.

In the distance, Lirienne spotted a man on horseback, a brindled bay with one white sock. Her heart sank as she realized that her father was in command. He always rode a horse with that rare and unusual coat. Lirienne hugged the tree for support. No matter what, she would lose someone she loved on this day.

"We have to leave," Renata said.

She forced herself to form words. "My father is in command."

Renata paused. She watched the scene unfold beside Lirienne. Neither could leave now.

Tears began to stream down Lirienne's cheeks. "I wanted to stop this war so much."

There was no way to stop it now. Many lives would be lost today.

"There are more Hilliri coming from the east." Renata pointed to a group of people, all on foot, who were heading toward the other parties.

Lirienne watched them creep slowly forward, flanking the others. As the sun rose and the light improved, she strained to determine who they were. She noted their civilian dress. These were not soldiers. Their clothing was brighter in color and more varied than the dress of the people in Kalad, though. It struck her that the only people who dressed like that were the villagers of Alterra.

"Those people aren't armed."

Renata frowned. "What are they doing here, then?"

"Trying to stop a war, I think. Renata, we need to go to them."

"Wait, no. I have orders to take you to the village."

"I'm afraid I can't do that. Come with me or go where you will.

I'm sorry I have to force you to choose."

If she stayed, Lirienne reasoned that she would likely need to do some healing soon. As she held onto a tree already, she simply tapped into it, gathering a small portion of maru. She moved on to the next tree and did the same, and then did three more after that. Renata wouldn't realize what she was doing as long as she didn't go too far and she stayed behind the woman.

Lirienne wondered how much was enough, and when would it become too much. She clasped a sixth tree, absently almost draining it before she released her grip. She had miscalculated, and overfilled herself. In addition to feeling over-strong, she shook and swayed a little, and her stomach churned. An unpleasant taste filled her mouth. This was not a good sign, but she had to go on.

They headed back down the hill toward the Alterrans on the plain. The armies held their places, no doubt waiting to see who these newcomers were. She strode boldly, not trying to hide. There was little point. The maru simmered inside her. It brimmed over, drifting out, but she was certain no one could see. She felt as if she could fly. Nothing could touch her. She practically floated down to greet Ergin, who led this group. She looked at their number. There were so many unfamiliar faces, too many to be just from Alterra alone, though they were mostly ungloved and dressed in similar fashion.

"Ergin, where did you find all of these people? What are you doing here?"

She followed him as he continued walking. He looked a bit wild. He was taking a huge risk. Just being here was terribly dangerous.

"You shouldn't be here, Lirienne. You have too many ties to the other side. You will be conflicted."

Lirienne shook her head. "No, Ergin. This is where I must be. We have a war to stop. I presume that's why you're all here too, and unarmed."

"Not only have we brought the Alterrans, but four other villages as well," Ergin said.

"Other villages?" This information struck Lirienne. How many Hilliri lived in Castillon? Did her father know about the other villages?

"Alterra wasn't the only place in Castillon the Hilliri have established."

Ergin focused on Renata, who was still walking near Lirienne but looking less sure of why she was there.

Lirienne realized the woman likely wouldn't understand

their conversation. She turned to explain to her in the common language of the Trillas. "You remember Ergin from Alterra. He's brought the people from four other villages to join him in this intervention."

Renata's eyes widened.

Lirienne continued. "The king of Kalad, my father, wants to claim the village and the lands around it for his kingdom. He is using these people as the excuse for his invasion; however, these villagers have come here to be beyond the reach of Kalad and its ways. They would prefer Castillon's rule over a return to their old country."

"I see." It was a lot to take in at one time.

Lirienne turned back to Ergin and spoke in the common Trillas language now. "What are you planning?"

He was still heading straight toward the two sides who were readying to fight. "We plan to stand in the way, Lirienne. We have awoken to our true natures here in Castillon. If we can't stay here, or if Kalad overruns Castillon or takes our villages back under its rule, our way of life is forfeit."

Lirienne understood. She respected their right to choose to defend their ways. She decided she liked this plan and would stand with them, walking right into the battle in order to stop the war. Lorenzo would be upset, angry even, but she could no longer be someone who stood by and waited for others to fix problems. This year she had changed so much. She belonged with these people now.

"I'm coming with you, Ergin. Renata, you can either stay with us or return to your people and fight."

The woman began to protest, but she looked around and saw determination on every person's face. "I'll stay with you and protect you if I can. I think that's what Lorenzo would want."

Lirienne continued to walk on with the others. "Thank you."

CHAPTER FORTY-SIX

When they reached the space between the two parallel lines of troops stretching out across the hills and plains, Ergin's people filed out to stand between them, all the way along, a third line sandwiched between the others. Lirienne walked on until she could see her father nearly straight in front of her. He didn't appear to notice her yet. The borrowed power simmered in her, changing in quality from invincibility to nausea. She swallowed and continued.

She saw panic in the Hilliri soldiers' eyes as she passed. No doubt they hoped not to have to attack unarmed people, and certainly not Hilliri people. They stared at their ruler, checking to see if his resolve had changed.

Lirienne came to a stop before him. She breathed in. "My lord and father. Do you not recognize your own daughter?"

The man on the brindled bay urged his horse forward, squinting at her. As he neared, Lirienne could see he looked tired, unhappy, and unsure. It was a new experience for her to see such things on her father's face. His long white hair under his helmet blew out behind him in the wind. His eyes were almost clear, his skin paler than watered milk.

"You've changed, child."

"I am no longer a child. Lorenzo Calimero, son of Carlosi, is now lord of Castillon. He is also my husband."

The king pulled his head back and his expression revealed his confusion. "How is it that you've chosen a Trillas, Lirienne? It's not right or natural."

Lirienne steeled herself. This wasn't going to be an easy discussion, and less so with thousands listening in. "It was my choice, Father. He was right for me. We want to live in peace, here in Castillon. Your presence with an army is an impediment. I beg you to make peace with my husband for the sake of his people and yours. They did not start this, nor do they give you any cause for concern."

"That may be, Daughter, or it may not. I have lost many in

battle here over the last while, and there is still the matter of the Hilliri who live in these parts. I intend to keep them under the wing of Kalad. I cannot afford an exodus."

Lirienne couldn't help but think he'd brought this on himself. "The people of whom you speak are here. I think you'll find they are an unusual lot. There are not many like them in Kalad. Your fears of an exodus are unfounded." Lirienne opened her arms wide to indicate the people who had walked with her. "They stand in between your army and the people of Castillon. They are not many, and they are not armed."

She motioned for Ergin to come forward.

Ergin bowed just enough. "Greetings, my lord, welcome to Castillon. The people here represent the four villages we have established in secret as well as Alterra. We left Kalad because we were unhappy there. Our dreams led us to establish a new way of life here. We ask you to leave us here in peace."

The king sat stiffly on his mount. "But to whom will you pledge allegiance? Surely Castillon will object to the Hilliri living within their borders?"

Lorenzo, who had been standing on the opposite side, near enough to hear the exchange, sheathed his sword and stepped forward to join Ergin and the village people standing by Lirienne.

Lirienne's father stared at him, running his eyes up and down Lorenzo's impressive height. She could imagine him wondering what she saw in this man. She looked at Lorenzo too and felt only love. While the future was uncertain, standing here between two armies, facing possible death, she had no regrets for the choice she had made.

Lirienne turned to face her father. It was time to end this war—past time.

Slowly she approached the brindled horse that stamped its hoofs in impatience. Once she came alongside the bay, she looked up at her father, perched in his saddle. "Father, I have a son. His name is Liran. His hair may be dark and his eyes over-bright, but he is my flesh and blood, and therefore yours."

Her father sat in silence.

She waited for him to respond, watching his face as his expressions changed repeatedly. She saw revulsion, distrust, and fear, but she thought she could also discern love, pride, and compassion. She waited a long moment, wondering which emotions would prevail.

Lorenzo moved up to where she stood. She looked up at her

husband, glad for having chosen him. A sharp pain stabbed her in the chest. How odd that love felt like such a painful thing. She watched his face as his expression turned to horror, wondering why. Her legs buckled under her. He reached forward and caught her, placing her gently on the ground. She reached out and touched his face. There were tears streaming down his cheeks. The pain in her chest spread as a numbness flowing outward from her heart.

She looked down and saw red on her silver robes.

Struggling to understand, she looked back at Lorenzo. He was staring across at the Hilliri ranks—at a bowman without an arrow.

She felt cold working its way into her bones. Her father dismounted and rushed to her side, across from Lorenzo. His face was pained. Lirienne wondered why he should be sad when she felt such joy. Her breath became ragged as the world tipped and turned and a sharp pain began to throb in her chest.

She heard Lorenzo cry. "No!"

CHAPTER FORTY-SEVEN

Lirienne began to understand. The pieces fit together. Someone had released an arrow without orders. They had aimed at her, hitting her in the chest. Once an arrow had been released, there was no going back. Skirmishes broke out between the two armies.

She felt a throbbing sting through a filter of joy—a strange, intoxicating blend. A wall erected in her mind to hold back the pain. She looked again at the wound, the arrow protruding, the fine fletching skillfully crafted.

"Pull it out, Lorenzo. Please." Her voice sounded so small and sharp against the battle cries all around them.

"Are you sure? Won't it hasten . . .?"

The grief etched on his face shocked her. She had never doubted his love, but here it was so clearly drawn. She had connected mind to mind often enough to know he had never wavered in his choice either. A small truth came to her. Love meant pain. There would be a parting, she had always known that, but this was never how she had imagined it. She had simply thought of Lorenzo growing old long before her.

She tugged on his shirt to pull him closer. "I'm sure."

Her father shook his head and grasped Lorenzo's wrists, pulling them aside. "No, you mustn't. We will be robbed of her soon enough." Her father's voice cracked.

Lorenzo shed many tears. She touched his face. Little remained of Lirienne's strength. She looked at her father, longing to tell him it was all right, but not having the breath to speak.

He released his grasp on Lorenzo and Lorenzo withdrew his hands. Lirienne smiled weakly. Her father pulled up his sleeves and tugged off his gloves. He reached out to her again and touched her ungloved hand as he closed his eyes.

Lirienne's eyes fluttered as she connected with her father's mind. He never allowed this, although most parents did, but she had accepted his restrictions. He was a king, after all. In one touch, all of his pain and grief washed over her. His wife, taken from him too soon, his fault; the guilt pressing down on him even now, after so long. His daughter, lying here, dying. The strong, independent daughter who made him so proud. He would stop this. He knew how.

Lirienne opened her eyes wide. How did he know? A flow of maru filled Lirienne, familiar, yet odd, being the recipient rather than the giver. A great itch deep inside pulled at her waning consciousness.

Her father looked up at Lorenzo. "When I give the signal, will you pull it out?" He had to shout over the noise of combat closing in all around them.

Lorenzo nodded and swallowed. He clasped the shaft close to the entry wound, his other hand ready to press down to stop the bleeding. Lirienne gripped his arm when he pulled, easing the arrow out in one steady movement. Pain flowed in where the arrow had been and Lirienne cried out. Lorenzo pressed hard on the wound, making it difficult for her to breathe.

She followed her father's mind with her inner senses toward where the damage lay. The arrow had missed her heart by a finger's width. The head had nicked an artery, allowing blood to drain quickly once the pressure of the arrow's presence was removed. She sensed her father gathering his maru, focusing his mind on the damage done. She followed as he concentrated on the torn edges of the artery, forcing them back together, knitting the material of their substance to itself. Once he stemmed the blood loss, he reviewed the other damage and began to work from most severe to less grave. The noise of fighting muffled as she focused on her inner workings. The power she had filled herself with eddied and sloshed about inside her. Pressure built up, bringing a discomfort with it. She had taken too much.

After a few minutes, she felt her father's hand tremble and a shower of droplets fell on her face—sweat from his efforts. His maru was ebbing. He would not be able to finish what was needed, and there was still torn flesh and broken bone to deal with. She felt him pull away. Lirienne clutched his hand to keep it in place. It wasn't possible to heal herself, but she could give him some of the additional maru she had drawn before coming here. She released a flood through their connection, easing the pressure within her. The pain eased with it.

The king's eyes widened in surprise as he took in what she gave him. His strength renewed. She wondered how he knew all of this. Had he been trained like she had at the College of the Marukar? Why had he never told her? Healing must have been one of his skills, but she had only known of his abilities as a gardener.

Once he finished, Lirienne's eyes flickered open. She looked up at her father and saw tears dampening his cheeks, a surprising display of emotion from a man who usually showed little warmth.

Lorenzo arched over her, weeping great wracking sobs without reserve.

She wanted to shout, but her voice was mute, and the world was already too full of sound. Screams filled the air as the fighting drew nearer. She wanted to say, "Stop crying, my love, I am alive and well," but her voice only produced more silence.

She gripped Lorenzo's shoulder to get his attention and once he realized that Lirienne was healed, he calmed enough to help her sit up. A Castillonian soldier deflected a blow aimed in their general direction, but Lorenzo continued to stare at her in wonder. He looked at her chest, searching for the wound. There was a hole in her dress, but underneath it, she was unblemished.

The king was still crouched on her other side. She turned to look at her father. It had been a while since she felt affection for him, but right now, she wanted his arms to be around her as much as she did Lorenzo's. She felt too much love. A trivial problem, she thought, and laughed.

The two men looked at each other with puzzled expressions, then back at her.

Finally, she found her voice. "I'm fine. Will you help me up?"

For a minute, her father and her husband stared dumbly at her. "I said I'm fine."

Lorenzo still appeared dazed. "My love, I thought you were dying."

"My father healed me."

Her father shook his head. "It's been a while since I've done that. I didn't think I had enough maru for it, or the skill, but I could see in your mind some of what you would have done if it were you doing the healing. I'm just baffled that I had enough power to complete the task."

If he was looking for an explanation, Lirienne wasn't about to give him one. No one should know about the drawing of maru from other living things. She had come upon it by accident. While she was glad she survived, a part of her felt empty and craved to be filled. She had a terrible urge to find a tree and tap it to ruin. It frightened her how strong the desire was. She shook as if frozen. Lorenzo held her to his chest.

The king stood, glancing around at the two armies engaged in battle. He steadied his expression and cleared his voice. "Lorenzo of Castillon, I will acknowledge you are a kinsman by marriage to my daughter. What will you do if I withdraw my army back to our original borders?"

Lorenzo pulled Lirienne back up to her feet and held her against him. He took a moment to gather his words. "I accept your claim to kinship. I will withdraw my people to a defensive position and take my place in Madrezza as lord of this land. I ask no reparations for the death of my father or my brother if you will do the same for your kin. We have both seen enough bloodshed and lost too many we love." He looked around at Ergin's people standing by, watching. "I will accept the allegiance of the people of Alterra and the other villages of Hilliri people living within Castillon's borders. If they chose to remain here, it will be by our laws they shall abide."

The king winked at Lorenzo. "Then let's stop this battle, shall we?" He held up a hand. "Cease fire! Fall back!" he cried in a booming voice in the direction of his army. Slowly his people spread the order down their line and complied.

Lorenzo lifted his own arm and waved to the Castillonian side. "Hold!" he called. "Cease fire!" and slowly the sounds of battle subsided. Both sides looked to where the three of them stood for explanation.

Lirienne finally felt she had the strength to stand on her own and pulled away from Lorenzo. She hugged her father, something she hadn't done in many years. At first he stood stiff, but eventually he allowed himself to put his arms around her in return.

He looked down into her eyes and shook his head. "You were always a wonder. Different, talented, but unruly. I never understood you, but I'm proud of you nonetheless." He kissed her forehead. "I think I understand you better now."

Lirienne exhaled. She closed her eyes, allowing relief to spread over her like a mist. She drew another long breath. It felt good to know things were turning out right. As she warmed, she felt love for everyone—for Marcusi, in spite of his suspicious nature; for Renata who welcomed her so readily; and for all the people of Alterra who looked after her during her flight from Kalad. She felt love for Ergin and Adina, who wanted a life free from social oppression and conformity, and for Valran, who needed her love and care more than he knew. Most of all, she felt love for her father, who showed pride in his daughter, his people, and respect for the Castillonians. Lirienne's face was damp with tears.

At last, she had found the peace she had sought for so long. Peace for Castillon and Kalad, and peace for herself. But she recognized that the cost to herself might be higher than she had accounted for, as the urge to draw some maru remained, tempting her, tainted though it might be.

CHAPTER FORTY-EIGHT

They returned to the manor house of Lorenzo's childhood, now devoid of family. Settling in a pleasant room, not the one that Lord Carlosi had used, they made themselves comfortable. They talked about their future, about how they would raise Liran, and about building another home across the river by the beach. Lorenzo dreamed of a castle of sorts, a grander place, but also easier to protect.

Bleary-eyed, Lirienne fed Liran and changed his clout in a stupor when he woke three times that night. Each time, Lorenzo rose to keep her company. He watched them as if he could gather them in with his gaze and hold on to them.

Her fatigue dragged on for days. In between feedings, she slept poorly. Operating on little sleep was never easy, but Lirienne could sense the effects of her maru use dragging her down as well. A deep exhaustion took hold, refusing to be released. Bouts of shivering followed by profuse sweating overwhelmed her. Lorenzo held her quietly then until it passed. In those moments, all she wanted was to go outside to find a tree and suck it dry. Now she fully understood the cost of drawing maru from other things. Fearing the damage it had done to her, she swore she wouldn't do it ever again unless the circumstances were dire.

During these times they spoke little, though Lorenzo's eyes asked many questions. She was thankful for his silence. She needed the quiet and his support to heal.

***

One morning Lirienne finally awoke feeling brighter, despite a harried night. Lorenzo had his arms wrapped around her more tightly than ever, as if he feared someone would rip her from him. The baby started to whimper, so she brought him back to bed with her while Lorenzo shook off his slumber. Again, he watched as she fed their child.

Feeding drained her more than she expected, tempting her to break her resolve, but she had to resist for her family's sake.

Lorenzo rose and dressed. She watched as he slipped into worn leather breeches and put on a clean linen shirt. He was beautiful. His toned muscles and bronzed skin gleamed in the early light.

He reached over and kissed her, pulling back her hair from her face. "You look tired. You should stay here and rest today."

She grabbed his forearm and pulled him toward her. "Only if you do the same."

He smiled. "I wish I could, but there's too much to do. We have to finish drawing up the treaty to ensure that your father is satisfied. He's sending your brother to work out the details today." He tucked his shirttails into his waist. "Then I must meet with Ergin and his council. The hidden villages are offering to pledge their allegiance to Castillon in a public ceremony this afternoon."

It had been a big surprise to learn that so many of her people had moved to Castillon. Her father had some work to do if he wanted to stop the exodus, but as she had said to him that day, they were an unusual group, not representative of most Kaldene citizens. She missed Alterra and her people, as she now thought of them.

"That's important. I should be there too."

"It would be nice, but you've been through so much." He held her gaze for a long moment, assessing her.

The baby had fallen asleep, his stomach filled. She thought he might be getting plumper. She placed him in the cradle they had found. Finally, they had a real home that was properly equipped.

She breathed deeply as she rose from the crib. "I need something to take my mind off my fatigue."

Lorenzo dropped down to the floor on his knees and pressed his forehead against hers. "You were very bold, my lady savior. You took a huge risk walking unarmed in between two armies. I still can't believe it worked." He cupped her face in his hands and pressed his lips to hers. A long moment passed before he released her. "You're quite something." He smiled, shaking his head.

"My father will have questions. I can't tell anyone about how I tapped those trees. I realize now it's too dangerous. I had taken in so much maru, I don't know what would have happened had I not been injured. I couldn't have contained it much longer. And now,

I am so depleted it's as if I need more, but I know I mustn't. It's a terrible cycle of temptation."

Lorenzo's brow shaded his eyes, but she was certain she saw concern in them. "Please don't take any more risks, Lirienne. You're needed here. I need you."

He nudged her so that she tumbled back against the pillows, and she pulled him down with her.

Concern bloomed in his expression. "Are you sure you have enough energy?"

Lirienne could only laugh as she pulled Lorenzo's shirt off again.

***

After breakfast, Valran arrived on horseback with a small contingent of soldiers. He wore a crisp steel-gray uniform and looked well rested, though there was still the shadow of grief in his eyes. Lirienne thought that at least he looked resigned to the pain of it. When he passed the reins of his horse over to the page and accepted her kiss of greeting, she noted he looked at her with a new respect.

"I heard about what happened on the battlefield. How you stepped between two armies—and how our father healed you of a mortal wound. Either you're brilliant or you're mad. I'm not quite sure which."

"I assure you, Val, I'm quite mad. You know, I didn't realize that Father had attended the College of the Marukar before apprenticing for the Gardeners Guild. I see him in a totally different light now."

He shook his head. "Yes, that was a surprise, but it does explain much. Funny, he seems different since he returned—gentler." Valran's clear blue eyes seemed deeper than before.

Lirienne lifted an eyebrow at the comment. "Well, we were all somewhat changed by the experience that day—hopefully for the better."

Valran reached out to touch her arm. "I think I owe you an apology, sister. Looking back on it, I can't believe I tried to kill your husband."

"Our relationship has been strained for a long time, Val. I would like to see it set right again. If we are all in the mood for forgiveness, I see no reason for me to hold a grudge."

"I realize now that you tried to do what you could for Talora. I shouldn't have blamed you. I just didn't want to accept her death."

Hearing this warmed Lirienne. She hated being at odds with Valran.

He wrapped her in a hug and squeezed her a little harder than was comfortable. When he released her, she caught the shine in his eyes. "You have changed most of all, I think. You look tired, sister."

Lirienne struggled with what to say. She wouldn't tell him about the trees. "It's hard to get enough rest with a small baby. They don't sleep through the night." She hoped he could leave it at that. "Come inside. Lorenzo is eager to talk to you." She tugged his sleeve to get him to move.

He seemed reluctant. "If I were he, I would not be so eager. I tried to kill him."

Lirienne laughed. "He's fine. Now you'll understand why I married him. Besides, I made sure he would be in a really good mood." She punctuated her sentence with a bright smile, making her brother blush.

Valran headed into the study while Lirienne scooped Liran from his crib where he fussed for food. What a bottomless pit! She settled in a nearby lounging room to feed him. From where she sat, she could hear the whole conversation in the study. She wanted to be sure her brother was indeed on the path to forgiveness. He'd tried to fool her before.

"As you can imagine, we are concerned that the presence of the Hilliri villages in Castillon might encourage an exodus of citizens from Kalad. How are we going to prevent that?"

So far, Valran sounded reasonable. It was a legitimate concern.

"From what I've seen, the people leaving are a fringe group— people who didn't fit in well in your society. While we welcome them here, there is a limit to how much space we are willing to give away. For the next ten years, I'm going to suggest that we don't offer any more land for additional villages. That will put some pressure on the existing communities to make the best use of their location and to limit the number coming without actually putting an upper limit to their population."

Lorenzo also sounded reasonable and considered. She liked that he didn't want to have a lot of detailed rules.

"That might work. Let them decide who they will take in."

"In the meantime, you will have some time to review your policies and decide what you will do to encourage your people to stay."

Lirienne stifled a giggle. Lorenzo wasn't pulling his punches.

"Are you suggesting we aren't doing a good job?"

"Look, I'm not trying to tell you what to do. The fact is—there are a number of people who are more comfortable in Castillon. I suppose they find the Trillas more similar in outlook. If I were you, I'd be worried if others were going simply because they could. I'd be making sure they weren't tempted. I also wouldn't prevent anyone from returning either."

"I'm glad to hear that."

CHAPTER FORTY-NINE

In the late afternoon, Lorenzo and Lirienne took some fine horses from the stable and rode with a large contingent of Castillonian soldiers to Alterra. With the baby tucked into his sling at her side, Lorenzo riding beside her, and the wind running through her hair, Lirienne felt refreshed and invigorated.

Valran returned to the Hilliri camp at the border to review with their father the details of their treaty. They would meet in Alterra at dusk to sign it with witnesses from both sides. Lirienne wondered where all those people were going to fit in the small village.

When they arrived, she had her answer. The townspeople had erected awnings and tents all over the commons. Waving pennants filled the field. The villagers had brought out soft chairs and sturdy tables and placed them in amphitheater fashion. They had also constructed benches out of wooden planks set atop whole logs and placed them further back for additional seating.

"You've been busy, Ergin." Lirienne wondered how they had managed it all.

"We occasionally have meetings with the other villages. Some of this is brought out for those occasions."

The place was full of people, Trillas and Hilliri, villagers and soldiers. The tranquility of Alterra was gone for the moment.

Everyone was obliged to lay down their weapons before entering the area. Alterrans took charge of supervising this. Many on both sides were reluctant to relinquish the assurance such possessions gave them. Adina was there to soften them, kindly reminding them that peace required different tools.

Lirienne smiled at seeing her friend in such a role. She decided healers were suited for peacekeeping.

At length, Lirienne settled herself in a comfortable chair, meant more for indoor use with its padded seat and back, but excellent for weary mothers with hungry babies. She swayed a little to settle Liran as he fussed at the noise of the gathering. As she nursed, she watched the villagers offering the Kaldene soldiers seating. The soldiers reacted uncomfortably, dealing stiffly with the Alterrans and also the Castillonian Trillas who sat among them. It was going to take a long time for everyone to get used to the new order of things.

"Daughter, may I join you?"

Lirienne looked up to see her father, looking worn but resolute. She smiled at him, and he picked up a nearby chair of similar design and brought it over beside hers.

"Lirienne, is this the boy, my grandson?"

The question stopped Lirienne. There was acceptance in his words and how he spoke them. She examined her father's face. Tarkhan Godehera was developing that weathered look that Ergin and Adina had. She didn't remember how old he was, but he might very well be nearly their age.

"I didn't have much chance to talk with you about what you did on the battlefield," Lirienne said.

He waved dismissively. "You're surprised that I have the healer's gift, especially when I objected to your choice of training. There's a story to tell, I'm afraid, which involves your mother as well. Some time when we are not talking about peace, I will share it with you." The king patted her arm with his gloved hand. It had been so long since Lirienne had bothered with gloves, she had almost forgotten how common they were in Kalad. "I'm glad you live, Lirienne. You have always been unusual, and I admit I have never been good at understanding you . . . I guess I just want to say . . . I'm proud of the woman you've grown into."

A lump formed in Lirienne's throat, making speech difficult for a moment. Those were words she had always hoped to hear, but never expected. "I will never forget that you healed me, and that you made peace for my sake."

He patted her arm again and withdrew his hand. There was a commotion building in the center of the common.

The king stood, looking down on her. "I believe it's time for things to start. Are you staying here or going to the center?"

"I should be beside my husband."

She tucked Liran back into his carrier now that he had gorged himself thoroughly at her breast.

Her father watched in fascination. He was seeing his daughter as a mother now. He held out his hand to help her rise and led her over to the center table. All the other benches and chairs circled it. There were chairs there for her father, her brother, for her and Lorenzo, and for Ergin and Adina and the other village leaders.

Lorenzo smiled as she slipped into her place beside him. He

touched her hand.

As people settled, he stood and addressed the crowd. "I wish to welcome everyone, Hilliri and Trillas, Castillonian and Kaldene, to this gathering. I will propose the first toast."

He paused as villagers went around the group giving out cups and filling them with wine. Lirienne wondered if it was the dry, crisp white that they loved in Kalad, or if it was the smoky sweet Xeres of Castillon. She accepted a cup and sniffed. Someone had thoughtfully selected an Estallese red. She smiled at the neutral choice.

"To old friends and new friends." Lorenzo raised his cup and swallowed the contents in one gulp.

Lirienne sipped slowly.

The king rose as Lorenzo sat back in his chair. "I toast to include new family as well."

Lirienne was pleased with this acknowledgment.

He took a long draft and set his cup down.

Finally, Ergin stood. "To a new existence filled with possibilities." He also took a long drink and finished his cup. How like him to talk about existential things.

Ergin read the entire treaty in full before the crowd. Lirienne watched the faces of the attendees, looking for those troubled by the direction events had taken. Many held reserve in their expressions, which was acceptable, but more than a few brazenly displayed contempt. She noted these were from all parties and made note of their faces for future reference.

Marcusi was among those who caused her concern. The man was loyal to her husband, but she worried he might do something wrong out of a misplaced sense of duty. She watched him carefully as the proceedings continued. Whenever their eyes met, he turned away quickly.

After the reading of the treaty came the signing. Her father signed, and then Lorenzo, and Ergin signed as a witness, as well as Adina, Valran, and finally Lirienne. All appeared to be going smoothly.

Lorenzo went to shake hands with the king. Lirienne smiled to see them together, cooperating. When she turned to look at Marcusi again, she was troubled to find that he wasn't sitting in his place anymore. Her eyes darted around the village green, frantically trying to locate the man.

She didn't have to look far. He was right behind Lorenzo,

though her husband appeared not to realize it yet.

She caught the glint of steel flashing in the late afternoon sun as he drew a small knife from his sleeve. She cried out as he moved forward, approaching her father. The sound of her shout alerted Valran, who pushed himself into Marcusi, toppling him.

In the subsequent commotion Lorenzo moved in and stepped on Marcusi's wrist as he lay in the grass. The knife fell from Marcusi's hand. There was fury in his eyes, and she feared she had made a real enemy this time.

The king kicked the knife away from Marcusi, and Ergin scurried over to pick it up and take it back to the weapons pile.

Lorenzo reached out his hand to help Marcusi stand.

The man looked at the ground, refusing to meet Lorenzo's eyes.

Lorenzo grasped his cousin by the front of his shirt, lifting him up and shaking him. "Why did you do that, cousin? You could have spoiled the day."

Marcusi stood mute as Lorenzo shook him again.

Lirienne thought this wasn't helping. She interceded, placing a light hand on Lorenzo's muscular forearm. "My love, your cousin resists the changes being effected here. I believe he is unsure of his place in the new order we are creating with this treaty. Indeed, we are all apprehensive. Can you reassure him that you will still need his aid in the future?"

Marcusi appeared surprised by her words.

"I understand what you're saying," Lorenzo said. "But how am I supposed to trust him now?"

She acknowledged it was a problem. She took a moment to consider options. The only way she knew to ensure loyalty was to search the mind of the suspect. It wasn't an acceptable practice among the Hilliri, for it was a huge invasion of privacy, but if she was right about Marcusi, he would be desperate to prove himself to Lorenzo, and he might be willing to do something drastic.

"I believe I have a solution."

CHAPTER FIFTY

Tension echoed throughout the glade. Everyone was staring at Lirienne.

Marcusi was restrained in a chair, flanked by two large Castillonians.

Lirienne approached him, meeting Marcusi's eyes with her most gentle glance. "My lord Marcusi, I know you love Lorenzo. I know you believe what you do is right, but you have gone against his will and now you must prove your loyalty and obedience to him in an irrefutable way."

He tossed his hair back with a jerk of his head. "What would you have me do? Cut off my own hand?"

Lirienne winced at the barbaric suggestion. "If you speak your pledge, I can verify your sincerity with a simple touch."

The Hilliri contingent among the gathering murmured in surprise.

Marcusi scanned the whisperers with concern and the furrow in his brow deepened. "Even your people gasp at this suggestion."

Lirienne nodded. "They know of this practice. It was once called hand-swearing and was used to assure the loyalty, sometimes without their permission, of those who served closest to the Royal family. The practice is now considered an invasion of privacy, but it still has its uses. It is only acceptable now if the oath-speaker volunteers."

Marcusi quivered. "You would bewitch me to say what you wished. Lorenzo would have me executed for treason, so I would not be able to trouble you any further."

Lirienne struggled with her impatience. Why did this man think she had such odious motives? It was best to ignore the accusation. "I understand your suspicion, but the method I propose cannot force you to say things against your will. You see, the Hilliri are able to connect minds using touch. We can hear each other's thoughts and sense the sincerity, or lack thereof. That is all. If someone were to exert influence on you, you would be well aware of it. At the very least, you could choose not to speak rather than to speak words that were not your own."

The Hilliri in the gathering appeared to concur. Displeased, Marcusi struggled against his captors.

Lirienne wasn't pleased either. She didn't want to know this man's thoughts and his hatred. He couldn't recognize that this was a sacrifice for her as well. Perhaps someone else should be doing this, but many would refuse.

"What I propose can be done by any Hilliri. Perhaps someone from Alterra could do this—someone already sworn to Castillon?"

She noted the Hilliri watching her. The Alterrans were more likely to see the practicality of her suggestion, and less likely to be repelled by the thought of it.

Marcusi struggled to make a decision. It was clear that he was the kind of man who resisted change at all cost. He met eyes with Lorenzo, who held his gaze for a long moment.

Marcusi returned to look at Lirienne with resignation. "I always wondered what the gloves were about. I guess they protect you from accidental mind reading. What do I have to do, then?"

"Just tell Lorenzo your promise. When I put my hands on yours, through this contact, I will be able to sense if your words are true or conflicted—unless you want someone else to do this?"

"No, I think Lorenzo trusts you the most, or at least, he trusts your abilities. I have one condition, though: allow me to see what you are thinking as well. If I am to accept you as my lord's wife and lady, I want to know what's in your heart too. I think it's only fair."

Gasps followed from the Hilliri. What he asked was audacious, especially from a princess.

Yet, she agreed. He was correct. It was only fair. "I give my consent."

Lorenzo approached Marcusi. He indicated to his captors to release him.

Marcusi dropped to his knees.

"Cousin, will you reaffirm your fealty and promise me you won't do such a thing again. I need you, but I have to be able to trust you." Lorenzo looked at Lirienne. Marcusi began to sweat. "She won't hurt you, cousin. I swear it."

Marcusi looked at each of the men of Castillon who were assembled in the circle as he prepared himself. Lirienne followed his gaze. "Very well, but I declare I will not say anything against Lorenzo, so if I do, you know this woman is lying."

Lorenzo stood beside her as she sat facing Marcusi, her arms outstretched. Marcusi placed his hands on top of hers. As usual, there was a moment where the world seemed to turn, as her thoughts linked with his and she caught a glimpse of what he saw. She tuned her focus into Marcusi's brown eyes and nodded her head to indicate he should speak.

He turned to Lorenzo. She could sense turmoil in his thoughts. He was not wholly at peace with his situation. Fair enough. "I pledge my oath of fealty to you, Lorenzo Calimero, Lord of Castillon. I accept you as my liege. Should I break this oath, death shall be my reward."

The oath was strongly worded and the consequence of breaking it equally harsh. As it should be. She had to give Marcusi credit. He didn't balk. His voice remained steady and his thoughts firm while speaking. She picked up his anger directed at her. She had come between them in some way, but the attestation was altogether honest. He would live or die by Lorenzo's word. She couldn't ask for more, nor should Lorenzo.

Marcusi glared at her. The request he made came to mind. Reluctantly, she lowered her barriers and allowed him to hear her thoughts. *I am not your enemy, Lord Marcusi. As you are my husband's kin, I wish to know you better, and hope to come to love you as he does.* She kept her gaze steady on his face. He glowered in return, but as the moments passed, he blinked and his stare softened slightly. It was enough. She stood, smoothing her gown.

The whole gathering watched as she took a moment to report. "He's being forthright."

A ripple of sighs passed through the audience. It was done. Marcusi moved to loosen the tension in his shoulders and stepped aside as his guards released him. Lorenzo bowed to him as he filtered past the others to take a place farther back.

Ergin motioned for the Alterrans and those from the other villages to come forward. Lorenzo remained at the front, Lirienne at his side, as they lined up to speak to him. Lirienne watched as the people she had come to know from Alterra brought him gifts: beautiful handmade things of the finest quality. Lorenzo bowed to each as he accepted their gifts and their oaths. Lirienne took the gifts from him and thanked them as well, then placed the items on the table with the rest. It took a long while, as there were a surprising number of villagers, but Lorenzo made no effort to hurry them. This was a solemn occasion to be remembered for many years.

At the end, Adina came to them and kissed them both, then kneeled. "I accept you as my liege, Lorenzo Calimero, Lord of Castillon." She held out a small package wrapped in colorful fabric.

"I accept your pledge, Adina Istamine, healer of Alterra. You have already given me a great gift in caring for my wife and son. I can accept no more from you. In fact, I believe I am still in your debt."

"Nonetheless, my lord, you may have need of the healing herbs and salves that I have prepared, especially if I am not around to attend your hurts. Or perhaps there is a healer in Madrezza who could put them to good use? I leave it to your discretion. As for any further debt, I will accept a voucher on future aid should we have need of it." She smiled and winked at Lorenzo, then stepped aside for Ergin to approach.

He knelt and waited.

Lorenzo indicated for him to begin.

"I give my oath of fealty to you, Lorenzo Calimero, Lord of Castillon." He paused a moment, clearly not finished speaking. "I also have a request, my lord. Will you promise all of the Hilliri living in Castillon that you will always allow them to live as they choose?"

"Ergamin Lotreah, I accept your oath and agree to preserve your people's way of life. All those here, witness my pledge: the people of these Hilliri villages intend to live in a manner of their own choosing, and I will not ask them to change, nor will I allow others to do so." He turned back to Ergin. "Is that good enough for you?"

Ergin smiled. "Thank you, my lord."

They shook hands and Ergin bowed to Lirienne. "I have a gift for you, my lady."

Ergin turned to look back as a group of villagers approached with a large flat package covered with a sheet. They stood, waiting.

Lirienne reached out and pulled the sheet off. As the fabric fluttered in the breeze, she saw the image revealed on the canvas underneath. It was a painting, done with a rough, loose brush, of the battle scene of only a few days before. He must have rushed to do this work, perhaps been greatly inspired by the events. All the elements were there: the two armies, poised to fight; the villagers, passive, carrying no weapons; and she and Lorenzo, facing the king.

Taking in the whole scene, she realized how well conceived it was. The roughness lent immediacy to the emotions it evoked. As she examined it, she was transported back to that very moment, as painful and poignant as it was the first time.

She hugged Ergin. "It's remarkable. What an absolutely incredible depiction."

Lorenzo examined the work as well. "Thank you for this exquisite gift, Ergin, though I would have applied what I said to Adina to you as well. You owe me nothing. I owe you much. Thank you all the same."

"I was inspired to record the events while they were still fresh in my mind."

Lirienne flushed and Lorenzo gave Ergin a squeeze as well. Ergin stiffened for a moment, then relaxed. As Lorenzo released him, Lirienne noted that Ergin smiled.

As the gifts were gathered and put aside, Lorenzo held up a hand for quiet. "I have one more thing to add to this proceeding. It has been pointed out to me by my cousin and others—" he paused to get everyone's attention "—that Lirienne and I have chosen one another and made our vows in private, according to Hilliri custom."

He looked over at Lirienne, and there was no mistaking his expression of affection. He held out a hand for her to join him. She handed the baby over to the king, who, surprisingly, appeared nearby with open arms, and stood by Lorenzo, wondering what he was planning.

"My dear, I hope you will forgive me for surprising you like this."

Lirienne smiled.

"But we haven't spoken public vows in the manner of the Trillas. While we are all here making our various pledges, I would like to make wedding vows in the manner of my people."

The gathered people murmured in low tones.

The small formality didn't trouble her. Still, it was different. Looking around at the hundreds of people gathered there, Lirienne felt a big contrast between a public vow and their private words. She realized how different their cultures were, but this promised new experiences and opportunities for learning in the future.

She stepped forward. "If it pleases you, my lord, I am willing."

Lorenzo turned her to face him, a crooked smile broadening on his face. "Oh, it pleases me, very much."

He waved for someone to come over to them.

A young blind woman was led over and placed before them, her back to the crowd. Lirienne had heard of the religious leaders of the Trillas, their Sibyls, who had lost their sight but had gained an internal sight instead. The Sibyl faced Lorenzo and Lirienne, radiant with the inner peace of knowing her gods. She wore long braids of hair twined with bits of bright ribbon, like the other Castillonians, and a simple, plain gown of crimson fabric.

She waited only a moment for everyone to be still. "People of Castillon, guests, lords and ladies of the realm of Kalad, we are here at this important time to celebrate the union of two special children of two special families." Her voice rang out clear and loud over the hushed observers. "Bring the families to the front, please."

People shuffled a bit to allow Lirienne's father and brother to come forward, and Marcusi stepped in close, looking resigned.

"I speak to you, families of these two. The fate of both your people lies with Lirienne Godehera, daughter of King Tarkhan of Kalad, and Lorenzo Calimero, Lord of Castillon, son of Carlosi. It is your task to respect and support them as they attempt to join two disparate cultures. The fate of both of your countries is intertwined in this marriage."

Someone handed the Sibyl a bowl of water. She dipped her fingers and reached out to place a drop on Lirienne's head with surprising accuracy and repeated the gesture with Lorenzo.

"May the Guardians bless both of you and keep you until the end of your days together. Lorenzo, do you pledge yourself—body and soul—to Lirienne, until your last breath?"

"Until my last breath, and beyond," Lorenzo replied.

Lirienne gave him a questioning look. He nodded assurance.

"Lirienne, do you pledge yourself—body and soul—to Lorenzo, until your last breath?"

"Until my last breath, and beyond," Lirienne responded.

"These words are spoken before the Guardians of Estallium, as I bear witness in their name. Your union shall be acknowledged and accepted henceforth by the people of Castillon."

The Sibyl emptied the rest of the water on the ground before their feet and the Trillas, understanding the significance, cheered.

This encouraged the Hilliri to cheer as well, not to miss the celebrations.

Lirienne filled with joy at the acknowledgement. At last, she had found her place and acceptance for herself, her husband, and her son. Together they had achieved peace between their peoples. She also realized that this was only the beginning. Bridges needed building, both real ones and figurative ones.

Servants brought out trays of food and pitchers of wine.

Lorenzo watched baby Liran, still buried against his grandfather's chest, staring at all of the people and the activity with glassy eyes. Even the king had shed a tear or two. "I would like my son back, if you don't mind. I've not had much time with him thus far."

The king looked down at the small package he carried as if he had forgotten. He took the baby with care and handed him to Lorenzo. "So, this little one is going to be heir to Castillon. He's an odd little creature. I don't know what kind of life is in store for him. He will be different and find acceptance hard to come by, I think." The king looked thoughtful. "Which reminds me, I have to figure out my own succession, but there is time."

Lorenzo bounced Liran on his hip. "As heir to Castillon, he will need his people's acceptance and support."

Adina approached to stand by Lorenzo and Lirienne and caressed Liran's nearly bald head. "I wouldn't worry about that. He will be loved by many, both Hilliri and Trillas."

Lirienne stared at Adina. She wondered if the healer had received some kind of premonition. Adina smiled knowingly, as if she possessed a secret she wouldn't share. Perhaps it was just Lirienne's own belief that she mapped onto her friend, bound by hope. One day Lirienne would know the truth, but for now, she believed hope was good enough.

For free stories and publishing news please join

Rebecca's newsletter @ www.rebeccasimkin.com

ABOUT THE AUTHOR

Photo credit: Kelly Borgers

Rebecca Simkin brings a lifelong passion for fantasy to her writing. Her love for the genre runs deep and began at an early age when she named her first cats Pippin and Merry. After spending her career in fundraising for non-profit organizations, she now writes epic fantasy novels and volunteers with the Sunburst Awards for Canadian Literature of the Fantastic, and is a regional leader for Soaring Spirits International supporting local widowed people.

Outside of writing and volunteering, Rebecca likes to keep active, enjoying cycling, hiking, and cross-country skiing. A student of culture, she also finds inspiration in traveling, exploring cities, museums, and visiting national parks around the world.

A York University graduate with a BFA in Visual Arts, Rebecca furthered her writing skills at Humber College School of Creative Writing and gained theatrical training at the Banff Centre for the Arts. More recently, she was recognized for her literary promise by being awarded a scholarship from the Writer's Circle of Durham Region.

Rebecca's diverse experiences infuse her work with themes of compassion and understanding, heroism and care for others.

www.ingramcontent.com/pod-product-compliance
Lightning Source LLC
Chambersburg PA
CBHW061802190726
48289CB00007B/2034